Comes the Dark

Comes the Dark

David Stuart Davies

ROBERT HALE · LONDON

ISBN-10: 0-7090-7971-0
ISBN-13: 978-0-7090-7971-2

Robert Hale Limited
Clerkenwell House
Clerkenwell Green
London EC1R 0HT

2 4 6 8 10 9 7 5 3 1

Typeset in 10½/13½pt Sabon.
Printed in Great Britain by St Edmundsbury Press,
Bury St Edmunds, Suffolk.
Bound by Woolnough Bookbinding Ltd.

The sun's rim dips; the stars rush out:
At one stride comes the dark.

The Ancient Mariner
Samuel Taylor Coleridge

This book is dedicated to
dear Freda Howlett,
with love.

prologue

They walked down the empty street like lovers, holding hands and pausing occasionally to steal a kiss. She leaned against him, happy to be with such a good-looking man. Tonight love-making might even be enjoyable, for a change.

It was late and only a sliver of a moon provided a meagre illumination. He gazed down at her face. It was a young face but somewhat careworn and far too heavily made up. He felt a strong desire to scrub all the muck off and see the real face beneath.

She giggled again. The silly bitch. But it was pleasing to him that she irritated him so much. It made the killing easier.

'Where are you taking me, you naughty man?' she said, her voice light and playful. She wriggled with pleasure. He could not tell whether it was genuine or not, but assumed that it was part of a routine she used regularly. You get what you pay for.

He did not reply to her question. He said nothing. It was not necessary to say anything any more. He had baited his hook and she was caught on it. Now it was time for him to take control, to complete the task. Words were no longer important.

Affecting a smile he squeezed her hand and then gently pulled her into the darkened doorway. She came – eagerly – like a lamb to the slaughter. Leaning against the wall in the darkness she unbuttoned her coat and pressed her warm body against his, swivelling her hips against his groin. For a fleeting moment, instinctively, his body responded to her seductive movements before he squeezed such thoughts from his mind.

Her lips reached up to his, but before she could kiss him, he had his bare hands around her throat. Suddenly, for the first time since they had met earlier that evening, she felt uncertain. What was he playing at? She didn't like it rough. She tried to pull away, but it was too late. He held her fast.

Her body stiffened with fear. With an awful clarity she realized what was happening to her.

The touch of her smooth throat beneath his firm grasp
aroused him far more than her writhing body had done. Now she
began to struggle against him in a desperate attempt to break
free. This pleased him further. His eyes glittered with amusement.

This was fun. Now he was having a good time. The tedious
preamble being over, he could enjoy himself. He watched her
face contort with terror, the silent mouthing lips, the frantic,
rapid eye movements.

For some moments he delayed the inevitable, revelling in the
power and inhaling the stench of fear. She wriggled in his grasp
like a crazy marionette but there was no escape.

His fingers squeezed tighter. An obscene croaking noise
emanated from the girl's overly painted face as he crushed her
windpipe.

Saliva drooled down her chin.

Tighter and ... tighter.

Slowly, her body began to sag and slip away from him. Her
eyelids flickered like the wings of a damaged butterfly and then
closed for ever. He smiled and relaxed his grip, allowing the girl's
head to loll sideways, her tongue protruding like some grotesque
appendage.

Now it was his turn to giggle.

He stood back, gently releasing his hold and allowing the
girl's lifeless body to slide to the floor. In the gloom he could just
make out her rag-doll posture, limbs all askew, as though she
had been cast aside by a careless owner.

Perfect.

He bent down and kissed her cheek lightly. 'Good night,
darling,' he whispered in her ear, then he pulled a tube of
lipstick from his pocket and inscribed a bright number 2 on the
dead girl's forehead.

After checking that the street was still deserted he stepped out
on to the damp pavement and went on his way, wondering how
long it would be before the constable on the beat would discover
the tart.

one

Spring came hesitantly to the city this year. After the bombing and destruction London had suffered during the winter months there were limited places where the season could erect its green flags of renewal. Reluctant weeds sprouted amongst the debris that had once been houses, factories and shops. Daffodils bloomed warily in the remaining city gardens and in the parks trees slowly began unfurling their leaves despite the dusty atmosphere that now seemed to pervade the metropolis permanently. While occasionally the weak infant sun bathed London in a pale yellow light, very few of the inhabitants of the capital noticed. Their minds were elsewhere. Spring no longer heralded the warm lazy days of summer, holidays by the sea, the hop-picking season, the odd glass of ale on a bench outside the local, sunbathing on the lawn. All that belonged to the past now.

Before the war.

Now there was a new set of concerns and values.

For a one-eyed private detective operating in London business had been sprightly in the early part of the year. It was true that there had been no Maltese Falcon for me to chase after or any other dramatic/romantic investigation to raise the tempo of my heartbeat, but these dark days had certainly stimulated the infidelity rate. London appeared to be the adultery capital of the world. It was as though the uncertainty that the war had brought to all our lives had caused moral codes to be cast aside like an empty fag-packet. Grab some love today, who knows what will happen tomorrow, seemed to be the creed. As a result there had been a stream of irate husbands, distressed wives and suspicious mothers-in-law calling at the office of Hawke Investigations, Priory Court, just off Tottenham Court Road. It was up to me, they said, to find out the truth: to nail the cheating bastards. And for a fee, I did their bidding. Well, it was a job, I told myself in my gloomy moments. It put bread and Spam on the table, whisky in my belly and a full packet of Craven A in my inside pocket. What more could a man ask? A lot more, if the truth be known.

And yet it was a living. Not the kind of living I'd hoped for, though. I would have been much happier dressed in khaki on some battleground, fighting for my king and country instead of checking cheap hotels, peering through windows and trailing sad middle-aged men as they kept an assignation with some tart. But as an ex-copper with an eyepatch I had been deemed worthy only of office work. I couldn't be trusted to shoot the enemy. Being a cyclops, not only might I miss, but I'd most likely hit one of our own men instead. That was the official line anyway. I determined that I wasn't going to spend the duration shuffling paper around, so Johnny One Eye became a private detective instead.

I soon found out that the glamorous image of my new profession as presented by the flicks was a purely fictional one. Certainly, in my experience, no beautiful blondes in low-cut gowns came seeking my help to get them off a murder rap and, similarly, I'd never been involved in a case of international intrigue where the stakes and the fees were high. Instead, I spent most of my time, when working, dealing with domestic disharmony.

As I lay in bed one morning in May, contemplating my lot, while fine splinters of fierce early morning sunlight struggled into the room around the rough edges of my blackout curtain, I wondered what my brother Paul was doing this fine day. The last I'd heard of him had been around Christmas. A brief letter which told me little apart from the fact that he was fighting somewhere overseas. Since then no message, nothing. I supposed that was a good sign really. If he'd been killed I would have received one of those dreaded 'We regret to inform you' telegrams.

I missed him. He had been my rock during our youth when we had been shunted from one orphanage to another. He is three years older than me and took on the role of mother and father. I'm not sure I would have survived without his strength and guidance. Then, as we hit adolescence and so-called maturity came our way, we had drifted apart somehow. I joined the police force and he moved south to Dover to work in a munitions factory. When war was declared, unknown to each other we both joined up in the same month. He sailed through training and was assigned to a regiment and was soon in the thick of it, but a jammed rifle going off in my face quickly put an end to my military career and my twenty-twenty vision.

I scrabbled on my bedside table and snatched up a packet of cigarettes and a box of matches. I lit a fag, inhaled deeply and immediately felt better. I was not going to get maudlin today. As there was no case on hand and I had some cash to call my own, I would treat myself to one of Benny's breakfasts, what he called his 'Air-Raid Breakfasts', served from 7a.m. until 10. One rasher, an egg, bread and butter and a large mug of tea for 1/8d. A real bargain. At the thought of this I hastily stubbed out the fag, leapt from the bed and headed for my tiny communal bathroom along the corridor.

Half an hour later, washed, shaved and suited in my second-best blue pinstripe, I was on my way to Benny's in Greek Street, Soho. Somehow the sunshine made London look worse. The smoky streets and the crippled buildings appeared more pathetic when bathed in bright light. There was something incongruous about the canopy of a clear, pale-blue sky above the shored-up damaged edifices and gaping rubble-filled spaces where houses and business had once stood. Where some buildings had been hit, leaving a gap, next to the lucky one next door that still remained standing one could see surreal signs of habitation on the once interior walls now exposed to the harsh daylight: mirrors, calendars, family pictures still hanging there. It was as though the city was being unmade, house by house, courtesy of the *Luftwaffe*.

It was just after nine when I turned the corner into Greek Street. It was busy with people hurrying past, mouths tightened and heads down as though they didn't want to acknowledge the passage of strangers or really take note of their surroundings. Trying, I suppose, to keep reality at bay.

Benny greeted me like a long lost son. 'So the prodigal returns,' he grinned, patting me on the back. 'I thought you had deserted me, Johnny.'

'How could I do that, the man who makes the best salt-beef sandwiches in the West End?'

Benny's grin widened and he gave a little shrug. 'That I can't deny. You want one now?'

'Not this early,' I grinned. 'I've set my mind on one your Air-Raid Specials.'

'A wise choice. Take your usual table by the window and I'll see to it.'

I did as I was told, and he scuttled off into the small back kitchen. Benny's was quiet this morning. There was a young couple, holding hands and whispering to each other across the table, ignoring their food. Lovers, immune to the outside world, held in their little bubble. Towards the back there was a grey-haired fellow eating voraciously, his ARP helmet sitting on the table by his plate. He looked tired and had obviously been on watch in the night and was getting some grub before heading home for a well-earned snooze. Near the door there sat a stern young man in a belted raincoat who stared ahead of himself as though lost in thought, while he stirred his tea mechanically. His hair was plastered back in a severe fashion and there was a strange ferocity about his expression.

While I waited for my breakfast to appear, I pulled out a copy of the *Daily Mirror* to catch up with the latest unpleasantness. The war was not going well for us. The Nazis had consolidated their control of Europe. That spring the Nazis had invaded Denmark and Belgium and had made advances into France. It was as though Adolf was breathing down our necks. The paper told of more bad news: the German battleship *Bismark* had been at it again. This time it had sunk one of our best ships, *HMS Hood*. At home, criminal violence was still rife. There were reports about looting and black-market scams and another murder in the West End. 'The Blackout Strangler Strikes Again' announced the lurid headline. Another young girl, a prostitute, had been found strangled in a doorway. A PC Benson had found her in the early hours of the previous day. It was the second such murder in a month.

It was a relief to discard the newspaper when Benny arrived with my breakfast. I saw that he had slipped me an extra rasher. To be honest, this was a mixed blessing. I loved going to Benny's and I was fond of the man himself, but his food was another matter. A cobbler could have found a fine use for these rashers. Still, with a hearty dollop of OK sauce and a vivid imagination, not to mention a firm set of teeth, eating them could be quite an experience.

As Benny returned to the counter the young man rose stiffly from the table and went to pay his bill. I took little notice until, seconds later, I heard his voice raised in anger.

'Don't come that with me. I gave you a pound note. Now give me my change.'

Benny looked astonished at this outburst. 'I'm sorry, mister, but you're mistaken. Look, look in the till, there ain't no pound notes, just your ten-shilling one. Pound notes are rare. I'd know if you'd given me one.'

'You cheating bastard,' snapped the young man.

With a swift determined movement he leaned over the counter and grabbed Benny by the lapels of his white jacket. 'I want my proper change,' he growled.

Benny was too shocked to reply. His eyes widened in fear and his mouth worked silently like a goldfish out of water.

I dropped my knife and fork and went over to them. 'What seems to be the trouble?' I said easily.

The young man turned in surprise, his face shiny with perspiration and his eyes blazing with anger. 'This dirty little Yid is trying to cheat me out of my change.'

'It's not true, Johnny,' cried Benny. 'He gave me a ten-shilling note. He says it was—'

The young man tightened his grip on Benny's lapel, pulling him even closer to his face. 'Don't lie, you bastard Jew.'

'I think you'd better let him go,' I said quietly, curbing the anger that was swelling within me.

The young man looked astonished. 'So you're on the Yid's side, eh?'

'I said let him go.' My words were slow and deliberate.

The young man frowned and slowly released his grip of Benny's lapels.

'That's all we need in this country,' he sneered. 'Bloody Yid sympathizers.'

Now it was my turn to grab lapels. I yanked hold of the young man's jacket and with some force pulled him towards me. 'I think you'd better leave now,' I said placing my face as close to his as I could.

His eyes registered uncertain emotions. He was not sure how to react to me. He was fine bullying small aging café owners but someone his own size and age was a different matter. Suddenly his body stiffened and he began to push against me, resisting my grip. His mistake. With a quick, sharp movement I kneed him in the groin. He let out a yelp of pain and crumpled before me.

'That's all we need in this country – bastards like you who pick on innocent fellows,' I said. Still maintaining my even tones. 'Now beat it and don't come back or I won't be so gentle next time.'

The young man glared at me but I could tell from his demeanour that he had no intention of taking this encounter any further. Awkwardly he moved towards the door.

'You'll be sorry about this, I can tell you,' he snarled in my direction, then he pointed an accusative finger at Benny. 'We don't want your sort in our country. You've been warned.'

He slammed the door shut with such force that the glass rattled.

'And we don't want your sort in our country either,' I said quietly to myself.

Benny slumped against the counter, the colour drained from his face. 'There was no pound note, Johnny. Honest.'

I nodded. 'I know that. It was just an excuse. He just wanted to have a go at you. He was a member of the Britannia Club, the fascist mob. Jew-haters. He was wearing their small red-white-and-blue badge.'

Benny shook his head in disbelief. 'I thought they'd shut the fascists down. They've put Mosley away in prison. I thought that was all over.'

'They put away the figureheads, including Ramsay, but you can't stop this sort of thing by a few arrests. The Britannia Club is a private organization. They're still legal – no public meetings or demonstrations....'

'But they attack little café owners, eh?'

'If they're Jewish.'

'That's me,' he flashed me a feeble grin. 'Well, thank you for coming to my rescue, You're a regular Tom Mix, riding to my rescue.'

'Just let me know if you have any further trouble. I must admit it would give me great pleasure to have a reason to smack that chap hard in the face.'

'You bet. But ... oh your breakfast, it'll be cold by now.'

'It'll be fine. Don't worry.'

I returned to my table. The other customers avoided my gaze. They didn't want to be tainted with the rather nasty scene they had just witnessed. To be honest, I couldn't blame them. The incident had rattled me somewhat. I knew about the fascists and their perverted hatred of the Jews but this was the first time I had encountered it at first hand and it left an unpleasant taste in the mouth that Benny's breakfast could not dispel.

t w o

He curled himself up on the bed into a foetal ball and screwed his eyes shut, hoping the pain would go away soon. It was particularly bad today, eating away inside of him. He knew he would just have to ride it out with some of the pills and whisky. Each day was different and sometimes he almost felt normal, but these spasms were growing more frequent now. He'd been told that would happen, but he'd fostered the hope that they'd go away.

He clutched his genitals and squeezed gently as though this action would expunge the fierce gnawing feeling there. It didn't; it only made him more acutely aware of his distress.

He'd tried praying and then cursing but neither had supplied any respite.

He began rocking to and fro like a traumatized child. He knew he was doomed, but it was too soon to go just yet. He needed more time. He had so much more to do. More urgently, he needed to be better by the evening when he was due in to work. He couldn't afford to have any unexplained absences now. That would be far too dangerous.

Beyond the open window, where the black-out curtain rustled in the spring breeze, were the sounds of the city, a city filled with people going about their daily business untainted by the ache and degradation he felt. He was a leper in their midst.

three

I n the upper reaches of Scotland Yard, in a tiny, cramped office, Detective Inspector David Llewellyn gazed at the picture of a young girl lying in a doorway, her legs spread-eagled in an obscene fashion and a look of terror etched upon her dead face. Her name was Molly Yates. She was just twenty-five at the time of her death, two days previously. An unmarried mother and a prostitute. Probably, he reasoned, a prostitute because she was an unmarried mother. It was not an uncommon situation. Sadly, the city was full of such women.

Llewellyn gave a weary sigh and ran a hand through his thinning blond locks. Wasn't it bad enough that Hitler was hell-bent on destroying London and its inhabitants, without some maniac joining in the mayhem, going around strangling young prostitutes? It was the second such killing within a month and there was no doubt that the two murders had been carried out by the same pair of hands. This was clearly revealed by the number branded on Molly's forehead in crimson lipstick. The number was 2. The previous victim, nineteen-year-old Eva Bracewell, who'd only just started on the game, had been found two weeks earlier in similar circumstances, with the number 1 on her forehead. 'I wonder how many he wants to make a match set,' Llewellyn muttered to himself.

'They put people away for talking to themselves,' observed Sergeant Stuart Sunderland, plonking down a mug of hot tea at Llewellyn's elbow.

'Good. The sooner they take me away the better. Then you'll be in charge of all this.' Llewellyn indicated the pictures of the dead girl on his desk.

'In that case I think I'll go with you.'

The two men exchanged cynical smiles.

Llewellyn sipped his tea, making a slurping noise as he did so. He was a well-made, beefy man, running a little to fat now that he had slipped over into his thirties, but with his square jaw and light-blue eyes he was still regarded as good-looking by women on the force. He peered at his sergeant over the lip of the mug.

'Tell me, boyo, how do you solve a murder where there are no bloody clues? Two young prossers murdered with only the *modus operandi* to link them.'

The sergeant raised his eyebrows in an amused quizzical fashion. It was not like his down-to-earth boss to use such posh terms.

'The method of working. In this case the means of murder,' explained Llewellyn, too weary to smile at his assistant's feigned ignorance. 'It's random killing, isn't it? Therefore there's no motive. So we're in the bloody dark.'

'They were both found within a mile of each other.'

Llewlleyn nodded. 'I've noted that, Sergeant. Number One was found in a doorway on Eagle Street off High Holborn, and Number Two about half a mile due south on Portugal Street. Perhaps he's working his way down to the river. Whatever …'

'There must be some pubs in the vicinity well known to the trade.'

'Maybe. I've got young O'Connell sussing that out now. Let's hope he's up to the job and doesn't come back drunk as a lord or with a nasty dose of the clap.'

Both men permitted themselves a brief smile.

'The trouble is,' Llewellyn continued, 'since the war began, London has been overrun by the ladies of the night. In fact they're not just ladies of the night any more. Now they're ladies of breakfast, lunch, and evening meal – and moments in-between. "Hello ducky, I can fit you in anytime." With soldiers milling around the city on leave they offer a bloody twenty-four-hour conveyor-belt service. So, boyo, you show me a pub in London that *isn't* be harbouring some painted whore in the corner touting for business.'

'Point taken.'

Llewellyn looked at the pictures again and shook his head

sadly. 'They're not bad girls really. Just trying to get along. Whatever happened they just don't deserve this.'

Sergeant Sunderland made no response. In truth, he didn't know what to say. He'd been working with Inspector Llewellyn for six months now and had always found him chirpy, cocky and immune to the nastiness they often had to deal with. But this case had really got to him, got under his skin, partly, Sunderland supposed, because of the unpleasant waste of young life but mainly because there was bugger all to work on. Frustration was etched deep on his guv'nor's brow.

Llewellyn took another noisy slurp of tea. 'The awful thing, Sunderland, is that I don't think we're going to move on this case until the bastard strikes again. We have to wait until our man makes a mistake, gives us a clue. And how many women is he going to throttle before that happens? Christ!'

'Let's hope O'Connell comes up with something, eh?'

Llewellyn nodded. 'Yeah. In the meantime you see if you can trace this poor girl's parents, or any of her family. Just ... just occupy yourself, there's a good fellow.'

Sergeant Sunderland drained his mug. 'Sure thing, guv.' He gave a mock salute and left.

David Llewellyn stared at the ceiling and swore. Just then the telephone rang.

As was his practice, he lifted the receiver without a word and listened.

'Hello, boyo,' came the tinny voice on the line.

Despite himself, the Scotland Yard man chuckled. 'You son of a bitch, Hawke, what the hell do you want now? How many times have I told you not to ring me at work? What if the wife finds out?'

'We'll just have to elope.'

'Just take a running jump, eh?'

'That's a fine greeting.'

'It's as fine as you're likely to get at the moment.'

'Ah, suffering from work overload are we?'

'And what would a cock-eyed bastard like you know about work overload, you dilettante dick.'

Johnny laughed. 'Never been called dilettante before.'

'That's just for starters.'

Both men, old friends, laughed.

'I thought you might fancy downing a pint at The Guardsman this lunch-time.'

'And I repeat, what the hell do you want now?'

'Just a chat.'

'I've heard that one before. All right, boyo, see you there at one – and it's your round,' said David, dropping the receiver.

He sat back and beamed. Some beer and conversation with old Johnny One Eye might just help to lift him from his depression.

four

The incident in Benny's café affected me more than I realized at first. In essence it was just a little fracas, a disagreement about change, but the man's calculated ploy to threaten and abuse Benny and his naked hatred had made it more upsetting, more sinister.

It was still preying on my mind after I'd returned to the office and checked the morning's mail for anything of interest. There was just one small cheque from a satisfied client. Usually this would have given me a lift, but the image of the young man's grim face with those manic eyes kept flashing into my mind and souring my mood.

I knew I couldn't just let the matter rest. I had to do something about it. What, I wasn't certain. I needed some help and information, so I rang up my old friend at Scotland Yard, Detective-Inspector David Llewellyn, and arranged to meet him for a drink at lunch-time. I wanted to find out more about the Britannia Club and its members and how dangerous they were. I recalled the young man's parting threat, 'You've been warned.' I got the impression they were not idle words. I reckoned David was the man to fill me in with the details.

I had worked with him briefly before the war when I'd been on the force and we had got on well. A lad from the valleys, as he often referred to himself, David was a shrewd detective with no pretensions or arrogant airs, unlike many of his colleagues. We shared the same tastes in music – jazz mainly – and humour – we were pro Will Hay and anti silly George Formby – and we have been known to sink a few pints also. Just the thought of that chubby Welshman brought a smile to my lips.

As expected The Guardsman, situated just around the corner from Scotland Yard, was very busy. More than ever, these days pubs were little havens where, with the help of a few pints and the company of a crowd of happy strangers and isolation from the world outside beyond the frosted windows, one could forget the harsh realities of the blackout, the blitz, and the various deprivations heaped on us since autumn of 1939.

A thick curtain of cigarette smoke hung in the air which was filled with the rowdy chatter of animated conversations. Although I was twenty minutes early for our one o'clock appointment, David was already there. I spotted him through the fug at the far end of the saloon bar where he had managed to commandeer a couple of stools. He sat hunched up, leaning on the bar looking thoroughly miserable. If he'd been a cartoon figure he would have had a little grey cloud hovering over his head labelled 'Worried'. On seeing me he raised his half-empty pint-glass in greeting and tapped it lightly with his forefinger. It was a signal for me to get him another. I obeyed instructions.

I popped the fresh pint on the bar beside him and climbed on to the neighbouring stool. Like polite public schoolboys we shook hands.

'Smart suit,' David said after he'd drained his glass. 'Looks like you're going to a wedding. Things must be pretty buoyant at the moment'.

'They were. It's a little slow at present.'

'Lucky bastard.'

'Oh.'

'Oh, indeed. I'm in the shit and sinking fast.'

I frowned. 'What's the problem?'

'You read the papers, I suppose, apart from the funny pages?'

'Don't tell me you're involved with the sinking of the *Hood*?'

'Try again.'

'Ah, the blackout strangler.'

David rolled his eyes. 'A turgid bit of journalese; they've got to find some convenient label, I suppose. But that's the case.'

'It's landed in your lap, I take it?'

David nodded. 'Certainly has, right on my bollocks. Two random killings with no clues and the probability that there'll be more.'

'You're certain they're the work of the same man?'

He nodded again. 'What we kept out of the papers is that the bastard marked the forehead of each girl with a number in lipstick – number one and number two.'

'Numbering his victims?' I shuddered.

'It's as though he's taunting the police.'

'And there's no connection between the victims? Did they know each other or—'

'No, no. Simply two young tarts picked off the tree at random and strangled. He just takes them into a doorway, throttles the life out of them and leaves 'em. Girls he's only known for an hour. No sex, no funny business, just ...' He put his pint on the counter and mimed a strangling action.

'That is a tough one.'

David took a large gulp of beer. 'You can say that again. I really have no idea what we can do. We've had coppers out warning the girls to be more vigilant. A water-off-a-duck's-back exercise, of course. I've got one of my men checking pubs in the area where the bodies were found to see if anyone saw anything that might help – but it's pissing in the wind stuff. In the mean-time—'

'You wait for number three.'

David groaned. 'For Christ's sake, don't say that. You can think it. *I* do think it, but for God's sake don't say it aloud; it's more than tempting fate, it's bloody encouraging it.'

I had never seen David so downhearted before. Of course, I knew his misery was brought on by frustration. He was a good, dedicated copper but in this case he couldn't formulate a plan of action. If you had nothing to go on, you couldn't go. It was the cruellest of situations: he was at the mercy of the murderer.

'If there's anything I can do ...'

'Apart from buying me another pint, d'you mean?' He grinned and for a brief moment the old David emerged from underneath that cartoon cloud. 'No, I'm only joking. Two pints is enough for me at lunch-time or I'll be asleep across my desk by three. And besides, the brain is addled enough without pick-ling it in booze as well. Look boyo, I appreciate the offer. I know it was genuinely meant and if I think of anything, I'll get you on the blower. Anyway, what's new with you?'

I shrugged easily, but my casual response didn't fool Detective-Inspector David Llewellyn.

'If I know my old one-eyed friend, he didn't just lure me here just to ply me with alcohol for the fun of it. There was some other reason. A favour or some information, perchance?'

'I'm that transparent eh?'

'Like a window.'

'Thanks. I'll pull the curtains in future'

'So ...' David raised a bushy eyebrow.

'I wondered what you knew of the Britannia Club.'

'Scum.'

'Succinct, but a little more factual gen would be helpful.'

'There's not a lot to say. As you know, the government have pulled the plug on the big fascist boys, outlawing the British Union of Fascists and throwing Oswald Mosley into clink for the duration, but there are still little cliques of the bastards, parading as private organizations. They're secretive, underground and keep their heads well down. The Britannia Club's one of them. They've got their so-called headquarters in Manchester Square. As long as they don't pass out literature or demonstrate in public they keep within the law. Just. We can't stop people holding their own opinions, or we'd be as bad as the Third Reich. The problem is that a fair number of the aristocracy, those chaps we used to think of as the bloody ruling classes, including some members of Parliament, support the fascist view. Basically, it's England for the English and get rid of the rest. The Jews are their main target. They have some cock-eyed notion that the Jews are responsible for all the ills that ever beset this country. The figure-head of the Britannia Club is Sir Howard McLean, member of Parliament from some god-forsaken place in Scotland. We can't work out whether he's just a misguided fool or an out and out villain. His basic stance is that we should stop fighting and nego-tiate with Hitler. Don't worry, Johnny, we've got our eye on them. It wouldn't surprise me if Intelligence hadn't squirrelled a man into their midst to keep an eye on things. Can't say for certain of course, I'm only a lowly copper and not important enough to be told things like that. Anyway, what's your interest?'

I told him about my encounter with one of the Britannia Club's roughs at Benny's Café.

David nodded sternly. 'Yeah, that's about their style. They can't march and shout anti-Semitism from the rooftops, but they can indulge in individual acts of violence.'

'One wonders if they will be more dangerous now that they've been forced underground.'

'Probably. It's the way of the world'. Suddenly he grinned broadly. 'Well, we are a couple of cheerful chappies this lunchtime. Shall we just slit our wrists and have done with it.'

I laughed. 'I'll give it some thought.'

While we were enjoying this brief moment of humour, we were joined by a young woman in a pretty black-spotted dress. She leaned against my companion and put her hand on his knee.

'You two gentleman seem to be having a good time,' she said sweetly in a voice borrowed from a Hollywood movie, as though she were addressing two ten-year-old children. 'I like to see men being happy. Perhaps I could help you … help you prolong your fun. I'm very experienced at coping with two gentlemen at a time'.

David rolled his eyes. 'Would you believe it? You've come to the wrong blokes this time, dearie.' He reached inside his jacket and pulled out his badge. 'Police.'

Beneath her heavy make-up, the girl paled. 'I didn't mean anything by what I said. I was just being friendly. Just … just making conversation.'

'Of course. And very nice it was too. But conversation like that can get you a night in the cells. Now on yer way, my gel, and back to the convent with you.'

Without another word the young girl turned on her heel and virtually ran from the bar.

David couldn't help chuckling. 'What chance have you got when silly little girls like that approach total strangers offering them sex on a plate. For all she knew I could have been an axe murderer and you could have been Doctor Crippen.'

'I'm not happy with the casting, but I get your point.'

David eyed his empty glass. 'Ah, it's a wicked world, my friend. And if I stay here any longer, I'll be tempted fill this up again, so I'll love you and leave you.'

He slapped his trilby carelessly on his head, cast a friendly nod in my direction and left. I sat for some moments in deep in thought before noticing that our lady-friend in the spotted dress had returned to the bar and was chatting to a young soldier. She was laughing and he was nodding. He drained his glass, took her arm and they headed for the door.

I gazed through the smoky haze at the frosted windows through which one could see the blue of the sky and the bright beams of sunlight outside. Sadly, I thought, despite the comforting arrival of spring it was, as David had observed, a wicked world.

five

On leaving The Guardsman I decided to take a detour via Manchester Square on my way back to the office. I wanted to take a look at the HQ of the Britannia Club. Manchester Square is a pleasant location almost tucked out of sight behind the upper reaches of Oxford Street. It boasts fine buildings and a small leafy park. As I entered the square I felt as though I were stepping back in time. There were no visible signs here that there was a war on. Remarkably the buildings had been untouched by the blitz. Only half a mile away many shops and stores along Oxford Street had been battered and shattered and crippled by the bombing. One could not walk a hundred yards along that street without encountering boarded-up windows and damaged edifices; but here in serene Manchester Square all was magically pristine and smart. There were few people about, but those who strolled casually along the pavement seemed from another age also: smartly dressed, heads held high with confident expressions. I felt like Ronald Colman in *Lost Horizon*: I had found Shangri-la. Perhaps I should move my office here, I thought. It would be very pleasant to wake up in such surroundings, to pull back the blinds each morning and gaze out on the little park and pretend that Hitler was just a dream. Only one snag, I hadn't even enough money to rent one of the nice green benches in the park, let alone an office in this gilded place. Indeed, money whispered at me from every elegant window, every neatly cultivated window-box and every shiny motor-car so carefully parked by the kerb, probably by a liveried chauffeur. For Shangri-la read Richville.

I had to circumnavigate the square twice before I found what I was looking for. Then, on the corner, I spotted the doorway of a tall, distinguished town house which bore a discreet brass plaque: The Britannia Club.

I stared at the entrance for some moments, then I mounted the short flight of stone steps and rang the bell. I heard it echoing inside the building, as in one of those haunted-house movies where the unsuspecting guests have just arrived, their car having broken down outside. No doubt Bela Lugosi or Boris Karloff would answer the door carrying a six-branched candelabra decorated with cobwebs.

I couldn't have been more wrong.

Eventually, when the door opened – without a creak, standing before me was a tall, graceful woman with bright blue eyes and a benign expression. I guessed that she must have been in her mid to late sixties, but she was wonderfully groomed, wearing an expensive blue dress, set off by a diamond brooch, while her carefully coiffured white hair framed her handsome features. At one time she would have been a real beauty, and even now there was something alluring about her face. Her composure and serenity were quite sexy.

She looked at me kindly. 'Can I help you, young man?'

The voice was cultured, upper class, but not condescending. I felt as though I was about to be invited to the vicar's tea-party.

I raised my hat. 'I was wondering if I could find out about the Britannia Club.'

Her eyes registered suspicion but her smile remained intact. 'You are interesting in joining?'

'I ... I ... er ... think so. I wanted to find out more about the aims and objectives.'

'Of course.' She pulled back the door and bade me enter. I found myself in a large dimly lighted hallway which, like the lady, was smart and elegant. The floor was richly carpeted and the panelled walls were adorned at regular intervals with portraits. I didn't recognize any of the mugs staring back at me in the gloom, except one, which I suspected was Oliver Cromwell but I could have been wrong. Certainly there were no pictures of Hitler and his cronies as might have been expected.

'Are you an ex-service man?' my elegant hostess asked. 'Your eye?'

Instinctively, I touched my black patch. 'Yes. I was invalided out.' Well, it wasn't a lie – not really.

'You poor man,' she purred in a practised way. 'Tell me, how did you hear of the Britannia Club?'

'It was something in the papers ... a while ago.'

'Well, if was in the papers it was no doubt inaccurate and derogatory. I am afraid we are pilloried and persecuted for our beliefs.'

'Which are...?'

'Our basic stance is Britain for the British and a condemnation of this foolish war. It is a noble stance, wouldn't you agree?'

I nodded with as much enthusiasm as I could muster.

She moved to the large hall table which was covered with various leaflets and pamphlets. Carefully, she chose several of these, scooping them up in her hands.

'Take some of our literature, Mr...?'

'Hawke, John Hawke.' I never gave an alias unless it was absolutely necessary. It's a practice that can cause a lot of trouble.

'Well, Mr Hawke, as I say, take some of our literature with you and study it. If then you feel you'd like to become one of our number, you would be very welcome.'

Solemnly, I took the leaflets, folded them carefully, and slipped them inside my jacket pocket.

'That's very kind,' I said. 'I'm very keen to do something to stop the war.'

She scrutinized me carefully with her penetrating blue eyes and nodded slowly.

'I think you'll do very well with us, Mr Hawke.' She retrieved a purple card from the table and offered it to me. It just bore the word **ADMITTANCE** in bold type. 'Come along to a lunchtime meeting we're holding tomorrow. Our deputy chairman, Guy Cooper, will be giving an address. I'm sure you will find that stimulating and it may well answer all your questions and any doubts. Half past twelve in our meeting-room here.'

'Thank you. That sounds grand,' I said, taking the card. 'I really appreciate your help, Miss...?'

She chuckled. 'It's been long time ago since I was a miss, Mr Hawke. But thank you for your gentlemanly flattery. I am Lady McLean. My husband Howard is the president of the Britannia Club.'

It was good to get back out on the street again and breathe in the fresh air. I'm not fond of charades but in my line of work they are an occupational hazard. I had felt very uncomfortable pulling the wool over the eyes of the woman I now knew was Lady McLean. She seemed so kind, rational, elegant and normal! Certainly she was not at all the sort I had expected to encounter at the Britannia Club: a ranting, bigoted, violent anti-semite. Instead, here was a woman who could have stepped out of the pages of Jane Austen or a Noel Coward play.

I grinned at myself, as I opened up the door of Hawke Towers. You are a naïve bastard at times, I told myself, and I found myself agreeing with the sentiment.

After creating a steaming cup of Camp coffee, I settled down with my homework. It made unsettling reading. One leaflet in particular stuck in my craw called *The Pollution of Britain*, it stated that British Fascism represented a return to the glorious ideals of the past. What glorious ideals were these I wondered? The serfdom of the Middle Ages maybe. Its main thrust however was an attack on the Jews:

We do not oppose the Jew on racial or religious grounds. We oppose them because they have become an organized interest within the state, pursuing a policy which threatens British lives and homes. Organized Jewry is as much a threat to the traditional way of life in this country as the forces of Adolf Hitler. Indeed, it can be seen by careful examination that in fact the organized power of the Jewry was responsible for dragging Britain into war with Germany.

We must band together as true British brothers and sisters to fight, to expunge this menace, the parasites of humanity – this enemy within.

There was more of the same.

I threw the filth down on the floor, my stomach churning violently. Coming into contact with such blind, perverted hatred made me feel sick. I thought about the stately and elegant Lady McLean who was peddling this nasty garbage. It was hard to equate her kind and civilized treatment of me with the viciousness and vehemence of the sentiments expressed in the leaflets. Did she really believe these lies? Had she read this stuff? Foolish question again, Johnny. Of course she did and she had.

A phrase from the foul spiel returned to my mind: *The enemy within*. Never mind the Jews, I thought, the bastard members of the Britannia Club were the *real* enemies within. I felt unclean just handling this material.

I pulled out the bottle of Johnny Walker which was nestling in the bottom drawer of my desk and poured myself a decent slug. I wanted to wash the nasty taste from my mouth. Out of my mouth, out of my system, out of my mind. I just wanted to forget what I'd read. Oh, David boyo, you were so right: it is a wicked world.

By eight that evening I was in my regular night-time haunt, the Velvet Cage, a bar-cum-jazz club-cum-eaterie in the heart of Soho. It was warm, dark and smoky and comfortingly claustrophobic. It was my second womb.

I was sitting at the bar nursing yet another whisky, enjoying the strains of the Tommy Parker sextet having fun with Gershwin's *Rhapsody in Blue*. I'm fairly sure that the late, great George would have approved of the extravagant rhythms and brave improvisations in the group's version. Tommy on trumpet excelled himself, which I have to admit was not a difficult task. Not to everyone's taste, I suppose, but I liked it.

However, it appeared that most of the other customers had better things to do than appreciate the jazz. They talked, their voices adding an irritating background soundtrack to the music. But the guys in the band were used to it: they were playing for themselves anyway and for those few odd characters out there in the dark, like me, who cared about the music. To be fair, some of the men in uniform shuffled around the floor with a girl they hardly knew in an approximation of dancing. Who knows, I thought, letting my mind wander along whatever tributaries it wanted, the blackout strangler could be one of those men and one of those girls could be his next victim.

'Well, hello Johnny, who's stolen your smile?'

My thoughts were interrupted by Blanche, one of the club hostesses. We knew each other well and were close companions in 'The Lending An Ear Club'. We held mutual moan sessions on a regular basis. She climbed on the bar-stool and dug me in the ribs. 'You can cheer yourself up by buying me a drink, Mr One Eye.'

'And why should I do that?'

'Because I's thirsty,' she replied, adopting her squeaky little-girl voice.

'OK, you temptress. Tell you what, I'll buy a drink for myself and then give it to you. I'm not paying Cazmartis's extortionate prices for "the hostess's drink".'

'You don't have to go through that charade with me, Johnny. I'll tell Ray to charge you regular.'

Ray, the barman, did that thing without batting an eyelid, but even at regular prices champagne doesn't come cheap. What the hell, I bit the bullet and dipped into my wallet. The cash in there was gradually doing a disappearing act.

Blanche took a sip of the fizzy stuff and giggled. 'Don't worry, I'll buy you a drink back one day … when my ship comes in?'

'Which ship is that? The *Titanic*?'

She giggled again. 'So how's the detective game?'

'Slow at moment. Too slow for another glass of champers, I can assure you.'

She held her glass aloft. Already it was half-empty. 'One will do me fine,' she said. 'And thanks, Johnny. You're a sweetie. I really needed this'. She leaned forward and kissed me on the cheek. 'Things are slow for me, too. Nobody wants to be just nice any more. At least not for the sake of being nice. They all want something in return. A little dance and some female company isn't enough. They want more.'

'Bed *and* breakfast, eh?'

'You got it.'

'Do you get any of these fellers who are unpleasantly insistent?'

'Oh, I know how to handle myself, Mr One Eye.' She gave me a knowing nod. Blanche was a tough little bird and, indeed, I believed that she well knew how to handle herself within the confines of the Velvet Cage, but I reckoned she wouldn't be so confident if she found herself in a darkened doorway with someone's hands around her throat.

'Oh, oh,' she said, 'here comes Fat George. I'd better get working the floor. More drinks at hostess prices or I might be coming around your place looking for a job as your secretary or something'. She drained her glass and drifted away into the gloom.

Fat George, or Mr Cazmartis to the likes of you, was the obese Greek who owned the joint. If there is such a thing, and I believe there is, he was Soho royalty. Cazmartis wandered by, his cockatrice eye observing everything carefully. I was sure that he'd had part of his brain removed and a miniature adding machine placed there instead. I'd helped solve a little pilfering problem for him in the early days and so now I was a privileged member of the club. As such, he gave me an oily smile and a gracious nod of the head and passed on.

I got up to leave and noticed Blanche skittering around the floor with an eager little corporal whose head only came up to her ample bosom. He seemed to be in heaven. Blanche gave me a smile and a conspiratorial wink as I passed by.

Outside, the night was quiet. No bombing. No ack-ack and little traffic. And the air was filled with the rich scent of spring, seducing one into forgetting the hardships of winter. Suddenly I felt the best I'd done all day. I didn't know why but I was sensible enough not to question it. These moments are rare. They may be illusory – so what! Accept them for what they are. I decided I would stroll home casually, having a couple of cigarettes along the way and taking a cuppa at a tea-bar if I found one open. I hummed snatches of *Rhapsody in Blue* as I sauntered along.

As it happened there was no tea-bar open so I treated myself to a third smoke instead. As I turned into Maple Street, not far from the Hawke residence, I heard what sounded like a muffled scream. It was a woman's voice in distress, which pierced the comparative silence of the night.

I tensed with apprehension. The sun had slid behind the bloody clouds once more. I flung my cigarette into the gutter and hurried up the street in the direction of the strange cry. I heard it once more: a stifled exclamation of pain and surprise. It seemed to be coming from a shop doorway across the road from me. My heart started racing, I pulled out my pocket-torch and crossed the street as quietly as I could.

It had now gone very quiet, but I could still hear movement and heavy breathing and I was certain I could detect a presence in the doorway. I clicked on the torch and shone it into the darkness.

six

Despite feeling like death warmed up, as his mother used to say when she had one of her turns, he managed to make it into work. Dosed with an excess of aspirin, he reckoned that being active and having his mind occupied might help to ease the discomfort.

He arrived on time at the changing-room, which was empty except for one of his colleagues, a garrulous Irishman who was known as Paddy, although that wasn't his name. Paddy looked up as he entered and gave him a cheery wave, then frowned.

'Saints preserve us, here comes the walking dead. You look rough, old boy. Been on the booze again?'

'You could say that,' he replied evenly, affecting a grin.

'You look as though you should be home in bed, my son.'

'I'll be all right.'

'I'm not so sure,' responded Paddy, lacing up his boots. 'If I were you ...'

'You are not me. I said I'll be all right.'

The vehemence of the response shut Paddy up in mid flow. 'Suit yourself,' he muttered to himself.

Oh, I will, he mused. I will most certainly suit myself. And with this thought, he suddenly began to feel better. He grinned to himself. Anger will carry me through. That is my strength. It fuels my revenge. I've still quite a bit of work to do and I must begin again ... soon.

seven

The beam of my torch illuminated the interior of the doorway and a woman screamed.

She was up against the door of the shop, her dress hitched up to her waist and knickers down around her knees. The man who was pressing himself against her turned his head furiously into the full beam of the torch.

''Ere, what's your bleedin' game?' he cried, his eyes ablaze with anger.

'It's the police, 'Arry,' cried the girl, turning her head away. 'I told you we should 'ave waited till we got home.'

'Is it hell the police. It's some bleedin pervert!'

For a few seconds I stood rooted to the spot while the horrible realization of what was happening sank into my brain. I had not come upon the blackout strangler attempting to provide the police with another victim; instead I had encountered a couple indulging in a bout of impulsive domestic coitus in which I had played the role of Mr Interruptus. Dried egg was on my face.

The man now was pulling up his trousers. He was a big strapping fellow and I could see his hands were huge.

There was nothing for it but to scarper. If I wanted to escape the pain and indignity of a busted nose, I had to leg it. 'Sorry to disturb you,' I said, lamely. 'I thought you were someone else.'

And then I ran, leaving the amorous couple hurling abuse at me down the empty street.

Ten minutes later I was in my flat, sitting on the couch trying to steady my hand while I lit a Craven A, my brow bathed in sweat. What a nightmare. In a matter of minutes I had metamorphosed from Ace Detective into creepy Peeping Tom. I took a deep drag and allowed the tobacco to surge into my lungs. I laid back, closed my eyes and breathed deeply, urging my body to relax.

In the darkness under my eyelids I ran the film again of my unfortunate encounter in Maple Street and in doing so I began to see the amusing side of it. It had all the elements of a silent comedy. An adult silent comedy. I chuckled. The mixture of indignation, fury and unsatisfied passion that registered on that big mutt's face caught in the wavering beam of my torch was, in retrospect, in the comfort and security of my own home, very funny. Well, at least that would teach them a lesson. In future, wait until you get home.

I laughed out loud. I realized that part of my amusement was relief – relief that I had managed to get away before the situation had turned nasty, or nastier than it had been. I imagined the man telling his mates in the pub all about the incident the next day:

'Well, me and the missus fancied a bit of the old love-making on the way home from the boozer the other night. Like we used to do in our courtin' days. Well, we came upon this empty doorway, like. That's nice I thought. Doing it there would give it a bit of an edge, a bit spicy like, you know what I mean. So we set to and I was in the middle of givin' her what for, if you get my meanin', when this geezer comes along and shines a torch on us like he wanted a front-row seat. It's a good job he hopped it before I managed to pull me trousers up or I'd have given *him* what for. Bleedin' pervert. I ask you, what's this country comin' to when you can't have a bit of the how's your father without some bloke coming along to take a gander at you at it?'

That night I went to bed smiling.

The next day I returned to Manchester Square. I walked through the invisible magic curtain and once more entered the enchanted land of serenity and elegance. Even the hubbub of nearby Oxford Street seemed muted and was hardly discernible.

As I approached the premises of the Britannia Club there was already a stream of visitors passing through its discreet entrance, each person flourishing a purple ticket before being admitted. I wasn't sure what kind of people I had expected to attend one of these meetings, but to my surprise, none of them exhibited two heads or sported bolts in the neck. In fact they seemed to represent a cross-section of the great British public: housewives, soldiers, men in business suits, shop-girls and those well-heeled souls who do not need an occupation. Normal folk in other words. To be honest, I think I would have preferred it if they had had two heads and bolts in the neck. It would have been easier to understand. And more comforting.

There were two sturdy unsmiling heavies stationed either side of the door, ready, no doubt, to repel boarders. With stern, no nonsense expressions, they scrutinized the visitors as they made their way up the steps.

I walked up nonchalantly and gave them a smile. They returned it unused. A little man with slicked-down hair wearing Arthur Askey glasses examined my ticket.

'Lady McLean invited me,' I announced loudly so the bully-boys on guard could hear.

I was ushered in by Arthur Askey and directed to the meeting-hall beyond the hallway. The room was more than half-full and yet everyone sat in silence. Whether this was out of embarrassment, apprehension or some kind of dutiful worship, I could not tell. However, apart from the occasional cough, the air was stiff with silence. It was like the waiting-room at Madame Tussaud's. All eyes were focused on the raised dais at the end of the room. Here four people sat behind a long table, chatting in hushed conversation. I recognized only one of them: Lady McLean. She was dressed in the same blue dress that she'd been wearing the day before and was in engaged in what appeared to be an earnest discussion with a tall, rosy-cheeked, silver-haired man wearing a tweed suit. I wouldn't have placed a bet on it, but I was fairly confident that this was her husband, the Right Honourable Fascist Swine MP. He certainly looked the type: narrow of eye and with a stiff, overbearing nature. This was a snapshot observation and based, to some extent, on biased pre-knowledge. But I was convinced that I was right.

I assumed that one of the other two men was our anti-Semite prophet for the day, Guy Cooper, the guest speaker.

I took a seat near the back on the aisle. I wondered if there were any observers in from MI5. If so I hoped they didn't clock me and put me down as a genuine sympathizer. Unfortunately, wearing a black eye-patch does make one stand out in a crowd. I'd hate anyone to think I was there in support of the cause. In fact, I wasn't sure why I was there at all really. Curiosity, I suppose – and we know what that did to the cat.

By 12.30 the room was almost full. And the doors at the back were closed. The fellow who carried out this task was none other than the little tough who'd had a go at Benny in the café, the arrogant strutting fellow with the slicked-back hair.

Heavens, I thought, if he sees me there could be ructions. As he made his way to the front of the hall I dropped my hat on to the floor and ducked down to retrieve it, scrabbling around, face out of sight, until he had passed. When I got up again, I heaved a gentle sigh of relief when I saw that he had taken a seat on the front row.

I was surprised at myself for being so nervous but these people, those sitting around me like wax dummies and those arrogant so-and-sos on the dais were so alien to me, alien to my beliefs and my understanding of the war and the causes of the war that they terrified me. I suppose part of me wondered whether perhaps they were right and I somehow had got it all horribly wrong. In reality, Hitler really was a nice chap and the Jews were the rats in the wainscot, nibbling away at the structure of Europe. But, more important, I saw myself as so very vulnerable in their midst, like a black at a Ku Klux Klan meeting. If someone could see under my sheet I was done for!

Suddenly there was movement on the dais which helped to shake me out of my paranoiac reverie. The white-haired chap in the tweed suit rose, came round the front of the table and smiled benevolently at the audience.

'Good afternoon. I am Sir Howard McLean, President of the Britannia Club, and I bid you welcome. It's so encouraging to see so many of you here at this private meeting. I know that amongst you there are those already committed to our cause but there are also those who have yet to be fully convinced. You are equally welcome because I am certain that after you have listened to our speaker today no doubts will remain in your mind as to which path to take, which cause to support, which course of action to follow in order to restore this country's greatness, this country's purity, to make Britain great again.'

His voice rose passionately and his pale features flushed as he reached the climax of his rally call. Sporadic applause broke out, which he acknowledged with a gentle wave of the hand.

'I would now like to introduce to our guest speaker for today, Mr Guy Cooper. Guy has been a silent but powerful force within the Fascist movement since the early 1930s. He fought in the First World War as a captain and was awarded the Military Cross for his bravery. So it is fair to say that he knows all about the horrors and futility of war at first hand. For a time he was on the committee of the British Union of Fascists and he has worked tirelessly for our cause since the outbreak of the current conflict. I sure that in listening to him you will be enlightened and enthused. Ladies and gentlemen, Mr Guy Cooper.'

We all applauded this time, including me. Well, I didn't want to draw attention to myself. I was already feeling like a mouse in a cat's home. In such situations you miaow and hope for the best.

Guy Cooper came to the front of the stage and waited for the applause to die down. He was a tall, good-looking man in his early fifties, with an easy, relaxed manner. His long, intelligent face was topped with a thinning mop of blond hair. He smiled benevolently at us with a sweet Father Christmas smile. He could have been addressing a meeting of the Women's Institute on dead-heading your roses to encourage more luxuriant summer blooms. And then suddenly the face grew stern. A cloud had drifted across the sun.

'Friends, fellow countrymen ... and countrywomen, of course ...'

An embarrassed ripple of laughter.

'... What I am going to say this afternoon is probably the most important message you'll ever hear. It concerns your lives, your well-being and your future. It concerns the kind of country you want to live in. The kind of country you want to call yours. The kind of country you wish to be proud of. Let me make one thing clear from the start: I speak to you today as a patriot.'

He paused, allowing the import of this statement to sink in, pacing up and down the dais, stroking his chin as though in thought. It was a precisely timed, calculated and well-rehearsed performance. Eventually, he turned to face us again.

'War is a terrible thing and there isn't a person here present who is not suffering under its yoke. But, you know, war is not inevitable – certainly this war was not inevitable. It is not even necessary. We are where we are through the incompetence and contrivance of our own government. From the start they rejected – out of hand – the very notion of appeasement. They preferred to send our young men out as sacrifices on the bloody altars of their own making.

'There are some people who say that Hitler is mad. I ask you, is it a madman who in seven years has been able to restore Germany to its position as one of the foremost nations of the world? Is it a madman who is leading his forces across Europe and who is even now knocking at our door? Let me ask you this question: who are the real benefactors of this war? Mmm? Look around you on the streets of London and you will see damaged, crippled soldiers returned from the conflict, invalided out of the army, left to survive by their own means in a crumbling society. Cast aside. Thrown on the scrapheap. Have they benefited from this war? I think not. They have been used as cannon fodder in a conflict that we should never have begun.

'So who is the real enemy? I will tell you: the Bolshevik and the Jew. They were the enemies of Germany and now they are Britain's enemies. They are the only beneficiaries of this.

'I say again, this is an unnecessary war and not our war. That is the truth the British government is determined to hide. And because I hold this belief I am pilloried by the establishment and called a sympathizer, an agitator. Well, believe me, I am not a violent man, this organization, the Britannia Club does not believe in violence ...'

'Liar. You bastard liar.'

The cry came from a young woman sitting several rows in front of me. It stopped Guy Cooper in his tracks. This wasn't part of the performance.

The woman jumped to her feet. 'You're evil lying bastards, the lot of you,' she cried. 'If it wasn't for you my brother would still be alive.'

All heads turned in her direction. And a sense of disquiet filled the room. I saw the heavies on either side of the dais make a move towards the woman, but they stopped in their tracks when she pulled a revolver from her handbag and aimed it directly at Guy Cooper.

eight

Inspector David Llewellyn read PC O'Connell's report again as he waited for the constable to arrive. It did not take him long: it was very brief. It did not make encouraging reading. According to O'Connell, every landlord of every pub in the vicinity where the two murders had taken place had claimed that they knew nothing of prostitutes operating on their premises, and to a man, on being shown photographs of the murder victims, had failed to recognize them. As O'Connell observed in his notes: 'They were, no doubt, frightened of losing their licences.'

'Brilliant bit of deduction, Watson,' Llewellyn muttered under his breath as O'Connell entered.

'Sit down, lad,' the inspector said wearily.

The constable did as he was told.

'Not very inspiring reading, this.' Llewellyn held up O'Connell's report and dropped it down again on his desk.

'No, sir. I seemed to have drawn a blank.'

The inspector ran his fingers through his hair. 'You saw no chink of light at all? Didn't you show the pictures to the regulars, likely-looking potential punters in the bar?'

It was clear from O'Connell's expression that he hadn't thought of that.

'What about instinct, then? Did you at any time feel that you'd hit a nerve, made someone a little uneasy? Averted glances, twitching, sweating a bit? Anything?'

The constable struggled to come up with something. 'Well, it may be my imagination ...'

'Yes, yes.' *For God's sake use your bloody imagination,* thought Llewellyn, desperately. Even a straw in the wind would be welcome now.

'I did think that the feller at the Barley Mow was rather

uncomfortable when I showed him the picture of Molly Yates, the second victim. He hardly glanced at it before he came out saying he'd never seen the girl.'

'The Barley Mow is on…?'

'Boynton Street. Landlord's name is Peter Walker.'

Llewellyn rubbed his chin. Meagre though this lead was, it was something, he supposed. 'Anything else?'

O'Connell looked back at him blankly.

'OK, lad, get back to your duties.'

'Yes, sir. I'm sorry I was not more successful … but you can't manufacture evidence, can you?'

Llewellyn could have said a lot in response to the constable's lame excuse, but he was too tired. It was quite clear that this dim-witted excuse for a copper was destined to remain a constable for the rest of his career. Initiative, foresight and intuition were all missing from his make-up. Well, it was partly his fault for sending O'Connell in the first place, although he hadn't realized just quite how dull the lad was. He should have sent Blackstock instead. He had more about him. Still, he'd know in the future. He dismissed O'Connell with a curt nod and a wave of his hand.

Left alone, he consulted the map on his desk with a Sherlock Holmes magnifying glass. The Barley Mow was less than a quarter of a mile from where young Molly had been found. It was a possibility. What the hell, he grimaced, one had to start somewhere.

He went to the door of his office and called in his sergeant.

'Sunderland, boyo, if you have any plans for this evening, cancel them.'

Sunderland frowned. He certainly did have plans, which involved going to the pictures with his girl, but he knew better than to admit that to his superior. 'Something come up, sir?'

'You and me are going for a quiet pint at the Barley Mow.'

nine

With a gun pointing directly at his heart, Guy Cooper lost all his confidence and his relaxed *savoir-faire*. His face suddenly becoming shiny with perspiration, he just stared at the weapon, open mouthed, while his hands flapped nervously at his side.

The heavies had halted in their tracks like a movie image when the film sticks in the projector. They could see that if they rushed the girl with the pistol she might panic and fire, and there would be one less fascist in the room. The audience, too, had become paralysed, whether it was with shock, amazement or some other fleeting emotion I couldn't say, but they just sat there, static shadows in the silence.

However, on the dais Lady McLean showed no such reticence. She rose from her chair and addressed the young woman directly.

'My dear, whatever is troubling you, the answer is not violence. I'm sure it can all be sorted out if you'll just put the gun down.' She spoke in quiet, controlled, even tones but she was not able to remove the patronizing note in her voice and that sense of command in her delivery. She was obviously a person who was used to getting her own way. Her confident stance and her unwavering glance told me that.

'Nothing can be sorted out. You can't bring back the dead. Now sit down or I shoot now,' came the curt reply.

Lady McLean hesitated for a moment as though she was going to respond, then she thought better of it and with a careless shrug she did as she was told.

This interchange had been a convenient diversion, allowing me to slip quietly from my seat at the back. Crouching low, I crept swiftly and quietly down the aisle towards the girl without her being aware of me. Her attention was firmly focused on the group on the stage. The gun she held in her hand did not waver.

I had to stop her before she did something stupid. To be honest, I wasn't terribly bothered about an arch-fascist getting his head blown off, but I didn't want this angry, determined but sadly misguided girl to do something she would regret for the rest of her life. These people were not worth it.

On the stage Captain Guy Cooper, hero of the First World War, was showing his true colours – various shades of yellow.

'Please don't shoot,' he moaned, finding his voice at last.

'I'll give you the same chance as my brother got,' cried the girl. 'That's no chance at all.'

Cooper shook his head desperately. 'But … I don't know your brother. I don't know what you're talking about.'

'You're a member of the Britannia Club, aren't you? Then you're responsible for his death. All that stuff you were spouting … that makes you guilty and it's just your bad luck you're the one I've got in my sights.'

I had come almost level with the girl now. She was on the aisle seat, second row from the front, about five feet in front of me. She had obviously planted herself here to get a good shot at her target. As I edged my way closer I could see that despite her tough stance she was terribly nervous. Her eyes were moist with tears of anger and frustration and the hand that held the gun was shaking with nerves. In such a state she could fire at any time, I thought, and then, as if to prove me right, she cocked the pistol.

Cooper emitted a guttural croak but seemed transfixed, rooted to the spot by fear.

If she was going to shoot him, she would shoot him now. I couldn't wait any longer. I had to act or it might be too late. I flung myself at the girl, pushing her to the ground with all my weight, while at the same time knocking her arm upwards, spoiling her aim. The gun went off as we crashed to the floor, the bullet ricocheting somewhere up in the rafters. We hit the ground with some force, wooden chairs skittering in all directions. This seemed to break the spell and suddenly there was a cacophony of noise: shouting, screaming and a stampede of footsteps as people rushed to escape from the mad gunwoman. I heard Guy Cooper telling everyone to 'Leave now, leave as fast as you can.' They didn't need a second telling.

Just as I snatched the gun from the girl's limp hand, I was hauled to my feet by one of the heavies. The other took hold of the girl.

I shook myself free and pushed my assailant away.

The other heavy had his arms round the girl's neck, constricting it tightly. I raised the gun. 'Let her go,' I said.

He narrowed his eyes, uncertain what to do. He didn't know whether to take me seriously. Or just ignore me. To prove my point I held the gun out at arm's length, aiming at his head. 'Let her go,' I repeated.

'Do as the man asks,' came a voice behind me. It was Lady McLean. Reluctantly the heavy obeyed her instructions.

The girl slumped down on to a chair and put her head in her hands.

'That was a very brave thing you did, young man.' Guy Cooper, who miraculously had regained his former demeanour, patted me on the back. 'I think you saved my life.'

I attempted a shy grin. I didn't think it was appropriate to tell him that I had acted for the girl's sake and not to save his scrawny fascist neck.

'Shall I get the police?' asked the heavy who had attacked the girl.

'No, no. That will not be necessary,' said Sir Howard, who had come down from the dais now that he saw that the danger was over. 'We do not want to make a fuss about this, draw attention to such matters. It can't do us any good.'

'You mean you're just going to let her go.'

'I suppose I do.' Sir Howard looked around the empty room littered with upturned chairs and scattered cushions. 'It's a great pity ... that the meeting had to end like this. But it can't be helped.'

He was talking as though a careless soul had spilt a cup of tea and upset some cucumber sandwiches at the vicarage fête, rather than that someone had tried to blast a respected member of the club to kingdom come....

'What do you think she was raving about? Her brother being killed by the Britannia Club? ' asked Sir Howard.

Lady McLean put her arm around her husband's shoulder. 'It's obvious that the poor girl is not right in the head. She was raving.'

'Best place for her is in the nut-house.' The heavy offered his medical opinion.

While this conversation was taking place I studied the girl, who was sitting hunched up on a wooden chair. She was barely into her twenties and pretty, but bore the haggard expression of one who had suffered a great deal in her young life. She now seemed to have slipped into some kind of trance and gave the impression that she was unaware of what was being said or even where she was. She had put so much mental and physical effort into her plan that now it was over, now it was scuppered, she was a spent force and had retreated within herself.

'What are we going to do with her?' asked one of the heavies. 'Surely we can't just let her go? She tried to commit murder.'

Sir Howard looked unsure. 'What do you think, Guy?'

Cooper stroked his chin thoughtfully, the restoration of his confident public persona now complete. 'I think that's the only thing we can do. If we get in touch with the police, it will bring the club unwanted attention from the authorities. They might well decide to close us down as a danger to public order.' He sighed theatrically. 'In the end, nothing happened. No real harm was done. We know her now; she'll never gain admittance to the club again. Sanderson, look in the girl's handbag and see if she's carrying an identity card.'

The heavy who had manhandled me obeyed orders and within moments withdrew the card. He read the information aloud: 'Barbara Cogan, 34 Balaclava Street, Aldgate.'

'Cogan,' repeated Cooper, curling his lip. 'A Jewess. That explains it all. Get her out of here.'

'I'll see she gets back where she belongs,' I said firmly. 'If we put her out on the street in the condition she's in now, who knows what trouble she could stir up. She needs to get back with her own kind. They'll see the sense of preventing her doing anything like this again.'

'I think the young man's right,' said Lady McLean.

Sir Howard and Guy Cooper stood aside and engaged in an urgent whispered conversation.

Lady McLean came close to me and touched my arm. 'It's John Hawke, isn't it? I remember you from yesterday,' she said.

I nodded.

'You were very brave. We have to thank you for your actions.'

'Indeed, we have,' agreed Guy Cooper, having finished his conflab with Sir Howard. 'Yes, Hawke, we think you are right. Take the girl, deliver her to the bosom of her family and if you get a chance, warn them of the direst consequences if she should attempt to interfere with us again.'

'You can be sure of that,' I replied firmly.

'Can we trust him?' snapped my favourite heavy.

'Certainly,' said Lady McLean coolly. 'I'm a good judge of character and I know that we can trust him, can't we, Mr Hawke?'

'I'm eager and happy to do all I can for the club,' I said to underline my worthiness to the cause.

Sir Howard came forward, grasped my hand and gave it a firm shake. 'We can't thank you enough, Mr Hawke. I think it would benefit all of us if we met later for a chat.'

'Indeed,' agreed Lady McLean, coming close and laying her hand gently on my arm. 'My husband and I have organized a little drinks party this evening. We should be honoured if you'd come along. We could talk further and maybe interest you in taking an active part in our organization.'

What the hell was I getting myself into? Curiosity had led me to the edge of the mire – now I was beginning to sink into it.

'Thank you, that would be very pleasant.' What else could I say?

'Good, we'll expect you at 8.30.'

I nodded. 'I'll be there. And now I'll get this creature out of here and back to her filthy ghetto.'

The three fascists exchanged gentle smiles at my nasty witticism.

I leaned forward and took the girl's arm and gently pulled her to her feet. She came without any resistance. As she stood, the others automatically took a step back as though her Jewishness was infectious and they might catch it. They watched in silence as I led the girl up the aisle to the exit.

As we passed into the entrance hall, I breathed a sigh of relief and then suddenly realized how much I was sweating, sweating with fear. If I'd known I was due to play a central part in such a dramatic incident with a bunch of fascists, I think I would have stayed at home.

We were just about to pass into the street, when I felt a tap on my shoulder. I turned and came face to face with the rough I'd first encountered in Benny's café.

'Bravo, Mr Hawke. That was most impressive.' The words escaped in a sneer. 'I must say I am most surprised to see you here. I really didn't think your sympathies lay in our direction – not after your performance in the café the other day.'

'Performance. Yes it was,' I replied without missing a beat. 'Don't always judge a book by its cover, it could get you into a lot of trouble.'

He was about to respond to this taunt and for a moment his fingers curled themselves into fists, but he managed to restrain himself. 'Off you go with your little Jewish girlfriend. Make sure she gets home safely.'

'She will. I hope you do, too,' I said pointedly and ushered the girl out of the building.

Once outside, I took a deep breath and let the cool air fill my lungs. I wanted to expunge all traces of the contaminated atmosphere of the Britannia Club. Somehow I felt dirty. Just being in the building, close to those people made me feel like some sort of traitor. I abhorred their views, their corrupted vision of the world and now I was being welcomed into their midst. The thought of it turned my stomach.

The fresh air also brought some animation to my charge. 'Where are you taking me?' she asked quietly.

I smiled at her and squeezed her hand. 'For a cup of tea and a cream bun,' I said.

ten

We left the magical, pampered world of Manchester Square and headed for Soho and Benny's café. Barbara Cogan, my little would-be assassin, walked quietly by my side as though she was a docile schoolgirl. She didn't ask questions such as where we were going and why and she didn't resist when I took her arm to guide her through the throng of pedestrians. All the fire and ferocity which she had demonstrated in the meeting-room had dissipated. It was as though part of her brain had shut down, not really wanting or caring to know any more. It was my job to revive her, to summon the real Barbara Cogan from the limbo into which she had retreated.

'My name's Johnny,' I said, leaning close to her in my best Doctor Hawke bedside manner. 'There is something rather important that you ought to know.'

There was not a flicker of interest on her serene features.

Undaunted, I continued: 'I am not really a member of the Britannia Club. I'm not a fascist sympathizer. And I'm not an anti-semite. I am your friend. Please believe me.'

I must admit that it was a pretty tall order for her to believe me – to accept this story coming from a chap whom she had seen attending a meeting at the Britannia Club; a chap who had stopped her killing one of the club's top brass and a chap who had agreed to pop back to join his fascist friends at a drinks party later that evening. I wouldn't have believed me.

I tried a different tack: bending the truth. Only a little. 'You see, I am a private detective and I've gone undercover to investigate the activities of the Britannia Club. Look ...' I rummaged in my wallet and extracted a dog-eared business card. 'This is who I am,' I said, waving it in front of her with a kind of manic desperation.

She looked at me for a moment and then took the card. She read it slowly and then looked at me again. 'Is this ... true?'

'Cross my heart and hope to die.'

A flicker of a smile ghosted itself across her features.

'Then ... why ... why did you stop me?'

'Because in the end you would have only hurt yourself. Where's the sense in being hanged for murder? And if you succeeded in shooting that chap Cooper, that's first degree murder and hanging would have been a certainty. After all you weren't exactly short of witnesses.'

The phantom smile made another brief visit. 'I suppose not.'

'If you want to damage the Britannia Club, shooting one of its senior members won't do the trick. They'd soon replace him. There are plenty more bigots waiting in the wings, I can assure you. They're like that monster from Greek mythology, the Hydra, isn't it? You cut off its head and another two grow in its place. Something like that.'

She frowned, confused by my classical allusion. I was losing her again. I should learn to keep things simple.

Fortunately we had arrived at Benny's café and without further reference to Greek mythology I ushered her inside. Although the lunch-time rush was subsiding, the café was still pretty busy and there were only two tables spare. I took the one nearest the window. Benny and his waiter Carlo were scuttering about delivering plates of hot steaming somethings to hungry customers and scooping up empty dishes to return to the kitchen. Eventually Benny spied me, and gave a cheery wave; then he noticed the girl. His face split into a broad grin. It was rare for Benny to see me with a member of the opposite sex and when he did he behaved like a clucking mother hen. He was already writing out the wedding invitations, picking out the church, happy in the thought that I was to become a respectable married man at last. Benny regarded the state of bachelorhood as only one notch up from being a slave-trader. He had married young himself but his wife had died from pneumonia before they had had a chance to have a family. Since that time Benny had dedicated his life to his little café. On the occasions when we were alone together late at night he would talk about his Sadie with more than a wistful glint in his eye. The old boy was a romantic and in a way he sometimes thought of me as the son he never had. And, like all Jewish fathers, nothing would have pleased him better than for me to settle down into the quagmire of married bliss from which he could vicariously breathe in the fumes of happiness. Before I knew it he had manoeuvred his way through the tables and was standing by my side.

'So secrets you have from me now,' he announced with a mock frown, then he smiled at Barbara. 'Lovely secrets.'

'This lady is just a friend.'

'I should be so lucky to have such a charming friend.'

'You have me.'

Benny ignored the remark and continued to smile at Barbara. 'So, you going to introduce me to your "just a friend"?'

'Benny, this is Barbara. Barbara, this is Benny, who is famous for his salt-beef sandwiches and jumping to conclusions.'

'Charmed, my dear.' He bowed.

Barbara seemed bemused by Benny's performance but she managed a gentle 'Hello.'

'Now, you'd like some food, yes.'

I nodded. 'Yes.'

'May I recommend today's special—'

'I'd like one of your famous salt-beef sandwiches,' Barbara said.

Benny raised his eyebrows. 'Of course.'

'Make that two and a dish of potatoes to share.'

'It shall be done.' Benny turned to go, but as he did so he leaned close to me and whispered in my ear. 'Oh, Johnny, you've hit the jackpot here: a lovely Jewish girl.'

After he had scampered away to the kitchen, out of sight, I leaned forward and took both of Barbara's hands in mine. Looking at her closely for the first time I realized how young she really was. Despite her height and the grown-up make-up, she couldn't have been more than twenty years old.

'Barbara,' I said and repeated her name three times until I had her full attention. 'Tell me about your brother.'

'Isaac. My brother, Isaac?'

I nodded. 'Yes. What happened?'

'He died.'

'How did he die? How was the Britannia Club involved?

Suddenly she lost the dreamy expression and her eyes shone brightly. She gripped my hands tightly. 'They killed him. The Britannia Club. Some of them came down our way causing trouble. It happens from time to time. We have learned to live with it. We had the Blackshirts before the war. It's a Jewish area and we're used to trouble – but not like this. Usually it's just louts who've had too much to drink and they want to do some Jew-baiting. They're cowards really, because most of our men are away in the war and there's no one around to fight back. My dad's dead and I live with my mum and my kid brother. We just close our doors, pull our curtains and wait until it's over. And then clean up the mess.

'About a week ago about a dozen men from the Britannia Club came down late at night'.

'How did you know they were from the Britannia Club?'

She gave a grim smile. 'They don't disguise the fact. One of them carried a placard and they all wore the club badge. They were young men really. Immature ... but inspired by their leaders to behave in such a way. That's the way they seem to operate. They were out for trouble. They carry so much hatred in their hearts....'

Barbara turned away and took a deep breath in a brave attempt to hold the tears back. I waited until she was ready to start again.

'They marched up the street shouting, "Yids out. Yids out." They threw bricks through windows and hurled a lighted torch into Bernie Solomon's, the butcher's shop. Isaac, my brother, couldn't stand it any longer. He ran from the house, shouting at them, warning them off, telling them that he'd call the police if they didn't go. They turned on him, roaring like animals. They knocked him to the ground. They hit him ... kicked him. They beat him about the head. One man in particular ... he ... I saw it all. I was watching from my bedroom window.'

She snatched her hands away from my grasp and buried her head in them and sobbed quietly.

What could I say? What could anyone say? I just sat there while the anger and disgust welled within me. Despite all the nastiness I had experienced in my life, I was still not immune to the cruelty that one person can inflict on another, that strange darkness that infects the heart of man. I felt like weeping too. Instead, I passed Barbara a fairly clean handkerchief which I'd extracted from my trouser pocket.

'The bastards,' was all I could think to say. Eloquence is not my strong point in such situations.

'They left him for dead. But he wasn't dead. I could see that he was still moving. I ran downstairs to go out and help him. As I came out into the street, I saw that one of the bastards had come back to him. He was leaning over Isaac's body chanting ... chanting, "Die, Jew, die." He snatched at Isaac's jacket. He took his wallet. Then he saw me and ran off. When I got to Isaac I saw that there was blood all over the front of his shirt. He had been stabbed several times. The man who stole his wallet must have done it. Isaac died later than night.'

Eventually she mopped her tears and dried her eyes, smearing away most of her make-up. Now that her face was clean she looked younger than ever.

'You informed the police...?'

She shook her head.

'There was little point. They can never do anything. People are too frightened to say anything in case these monsters come again. We're only Jewish scum after all. What does the death of one little Jew-boy matter? A little boy of seventeen.'

There was a world-weary maturity in the manner of this young girl that was both impressive and sad. Life had caused her to grow up and experience grown-up pain far sooner than she should.

It was true that there were regular skirmishes in Jewish enclaves in various parts of London, particularly the East End. Misguided zealots, frustrated by the war, needing scapegoats, went on the rampage. The police were virtually helpless in dealing with them. You cannot arrest a mob and the victims were reluctant to give evidence for fear of further repercussions. I knew of these things but now, coming close to the reality of it, I began to realize how terrible it really was.

'So you thought you'd carry out some retribution.'

'I had to damage them, for Isaac's sake.'

'We'll damage them, Barbara. Believe me. But we'll do it properly and legitimately. And we won't settle for cutting off a few branches, we'll aim for the root. Dig up the whole damn freakish growth.'

'Are you serious?'

'Cross my heart and hope to die.'

'Don't say that. Don't say "hope to die"...'

I nodded. 'You're right. OK, sensible answer. Yes, I am serious. We'll put an end to the Britannia Club.'

This started Barbara crying again.

With perfect timing Benny arrived with our food.

'What, your first tiff already.' He glowered disapprovingly.

I glowered back at him.

'What did you say to the girl to upset her, Johnny Hawke?'

'I told her that you were my father.'

Benny nearly dropped his tray.

eleven

The Barley Mow was fairly crowded at six o'clock that evening when Inspector David Llewellyn and Detective Sergeant Stuart Sunderland entered, lightly disguised as punters.

'I suppose we ought to stick to shandies in order to keep a clear head,' said Llewellyn as he shouldered his way to the bar, 'but as this is unpaid overtime, I'm kicking that idea into touch. I'm having a pint. Same for you, eh?'

Sunderland nodded. He knew it was best to go along with his governor. It made for a quieter life.

Drinks purchased, they sat at a small round table by the door with a good view of the saloon bar.

'You know, Sunderland,' began Llewellyn expansively, after his first sip of beer, 'once upon a time, there would have been little point in coming into a pub on a whore-hunt much before 9.30 in the evening. That's when they used to descend like a bloody plague of locusts, ready to pick up the miserable buggers who'd been drinking all night to forget their troubles. These saps were not only easily seduced but because they'd be fairly squiffy with ale they were not so sharp at spotting the odd fiver being lifted from their wallets. Now, with the war, there are so many desperate randy bastards out there wanting a quick one you can find a prosser at any time. Take that little gel over there.'

Sunderland followed Llewellyn's gaze. At the far side of the room was a woman sitting on her own. To the sergeant in that lighting and at that distance she could have been anywhere between twenty-five and fifty. She had peroxide-blond hair and harsh make-up and smoked a cigarette with a kind of nervous desperation.

'How do you know she's on the game?' he asked.

Llewellyn grinned. 'Tell-tale signs: tight, revealing jumper, skirt hitched a little higher than is respectable, heavy make-up, no wedding-ring, and look how she scrutinizes every feller who comes in.'

'She could be waiting for someone.'

'She is. The likely lad. One who's got enough dosh for a quick knee-trembler outside' He took a large gulp of beer. 'You stay here while I have a word with the little lady.'

As Llewellyn approached the woman she looked up at him and smiled. He drew a stool up to her table. 'Mind if I perch myself here?' he asked in a friendly fashion.

The woman smiled showing a row of brown teeth. 'Help yourself, love. It's a free country.'

This close up, Llewellyn observed that she would never see forty again.

'You wouldn't like to buy a lady a drink, would you?' she said with no hint of coyness or shyness in her voice.

Llewellyn grinned. 'Be pleased to. I just wonder if you could help me first.'

The woman looked apprehensively at him, her smile fading. 'Depends on what kind of help.'

Llewellyn pulled a photograph from his jacket pocket and handed it to her. It was a picture of Molly Yates, the most recent victim.

'Do you know her?'

The woman gave a snort of indignation. 'You're a rozzer, aren't you? Should have known.'

'Have a look at the picture. Do you know her?'

She gave a cursory glance and shook her head.

Llewellyn pocketed the photograph and sighed. 'Look, love, I believe she frequented this pub. She was murdered by one of her punters. It could be you next. All I'm after is a bit of information, information that might help to catch the bastard who did it. That's all I want. I'm not about to delve into your personal activities, if you catch my drift.'

The woman thought for a while, biting her lip. 'I thought you were buying me a drink,' she said at length. 'Rum and pep, since you ask.'

Llewellyn nodded and retreated to the bar. When he returned with the drink moments later the woman looked more relaxed and had lit another cigarette.

'What's your name, love?' he asked, handing her the rum and pep.

'Let's say I'm Nancy, shall we?'

'Suits me. Now then, Nancy, take another look at the photograph. Are you sure you've never seen that girl before?'

Both Llewellyn and Nancy knew this was a charade, but she glanced once more at the picture and nodded. 'Yes, I think I have seen her in here. Not often. She's new on the game, I think, but I don't know her personally. Despite what you cops might think, we don't have a bloody union, y'know. We don't have meetings and socials; we just work on our own.'

'Can you cast your mind back to last Monday? Did you see her in here that night? Did you see her getting off with any bloke?'

Nancy shook her head again, but this time Llewellyn reckoned it was a genuine response. 'I'm too busy keeping my eye out for my own punters to notice such things. Your best bet is Eva; she's a bit of a mother hen, especially with the young ones. She's been on the game since the year dot.'

'Where will I find this Eva?'

'She'll be in later, around eight usually. Sits on the stool over by the piano. Big woman, black hair – dyed of course. If I'm still here, I'll tip you the wink.'

'Thanks, Nancy. And watch out for yourself.'

'Yeah, yeah. What am I supposed to do? Starve?'

Llewellyn threw some coins on the table. 'Buy yourself another drink.'

When he returned to his own table he found Sunderland in deep conversation with a young girl who could easily have passed for Nancy's daughter: she was of the breed. The girl was giggling and tickling Sunderland under his chin with her forefinger. The sergeant seemed to be enjoying it.

'Pardon me for intruding,' grunted Llewellyn, parking himself down next to Sunderland.

'That's all right,' chirped the girl, fluttering eyelashes heavy with mascara. 'I was just going.' She turned to the sergeant again. 'Bye for now, Stuart. You know where to find me.'

Sunderland blushed. The girl giggled and left.

'Seem to be having a nice time there ... Stuart,' Llewellyn observed pointedly.

'Just doing my duty, sir, I was asking about Molly, but I drew a blank.'

'I wouldn't exactly say that, boyo.'

Sheepishly, Sunderland took a large gulp of beer.

'Just be careful, lad. You sometimes get more than you see in the shop-window with these girls, y'know. Morally, I've no problem with them but they can carry a lot of trouble.'

Sunderland frowned, unsure what his governor was on about.

'VD, boyo. The dreaded clap,' he explained. 'One quick shag with an infected whore and your old man drops off. You have been warned.'

Sunderland shuddered at the thought. 'How did you get on with the lady over there?'

Llewellyn told him.

'So we wait for this Eva then?'

'That's about it. A big woman with black hair, sits by the joanna.' Llewellyn glanced at his watch. It wasn't seven o'clock yet. 'Looks like we might have a long wait. I reckon we'll have to go on to shandies after all'.

The two men waited impatiently, sipping their shandies slowly. Apart from their work, they had little in common and gradually their sporadic conversation dried up. To his disappointment and chagrin, Llewellyn saw that his contact, the peroxide-blonde who called herself Nancy, had clicked with an ARP warden around seven o'clock and had disappeared into the night. He wondered where they had gone. Had she a shabby gaff nearby or was she going to take him to her favourite doorway for the deed? What a life, he thought. He pictured his wife at home, probably listening to the wireless and knitting. He knew she'd wait up for him and they'd share a cup of tea before going to bed. He'd be too tired for real passion, but they'd hold each other under the covers and fall asleep in each other's embrace. How far removed from this domestic normality was the life of these girls whose lovemaking was soulless and, indeed, sexless. Men used them and they used men, neither really engaging in loving emotions. It was need or greed on her part and lust on his. It made Llewellyn feel sad.

Sod it, he said to himself, if this Eva creature doesn't come in the next five minutes, I'm going to get a proper drink. A nice bottle of Mackeson, most likely.

As was his luck, Eva did arrive in the pub within the next five minutes.

'Isn't this our lady now?' asked Sunderland, nodding in the direction of the large, black-haired woman who made something of an entrance as she flounced into the saloon bar, nodding and smiling to the regulars who returned her welcome gestures with broad grins. The landlord already had a gin and tonic on the bar waiting for her as she heaved her considerable backside on to the bar stool.

'I'll pay for that,' said Llewellyn sidling up to her. She raised a sooty eyelid.

'Blimey, Arthur,' she said, addressing the barman, 'when did you start letting gentlemen into this boozer?' She laughed at her own joke in a wheezy, stertorous fashion, while her large bosom rippled like a giant jelly.

Llewellyn studied this old tart – and old she was. Her make-up, he assumed, had been applied with a trowel, filling in the cracks on her raddled visage. In fact it wasn't make-up so much as a mask. Her eyes were ringed with thick mascara and her cheeks had been rouged in such a fashion that she looked as though she was experiencing a permanent hot flush. It was the nearest thing Llewellyn had seen to a pantomime dame in real life.

'Cheers, mate,' she grinned, raising her glass.

'Cheers,' responded Llewellyn. 'There's another if you can help me.'

The sooty eyelids narrowed. 'The bleedin' cops, is it? Since when have you started buying tarts like me a ginny bribe? You're usually round here running me in or after a quick fumble for free.'

'Neither in this case.'

Eva drained he glass. 'There's a relief. Here, Arthur, get another in here. Make it a double. The gentleman's paying.'

Llewellyn nodded to the barman.

Nursing her replenished glass, Eva turned full on to the inspector. 'So what is it you want, officer?'

'You've heard about the murders. Two girls strangled.'

'It happens sometimes. Occupational hazard. Some men are bastards.'

'We want to catch this particular bastard before he does it again. You can help.'

'How?'

Sunderland, who had been hovering in the background, stepped forward and handed Eva a picture of Molly Yates.

'Blimey, there's two of the blighters,' she cried in mock surprise. ''Course, you lot go around in pairs, don't you ... to hold each other's hand? Two of you, eh? I reckon that means another drinkie.'

'Look at the picture first, eh love,' said Llewellyn.

She gave the photograph a cursory glance and handed it back. 'Yeah, seen it,' she said. 'It's poor Molly.'

'Yes, it's poor Molly. You knew her.'

'As well as you get to know any of the girls. She was fairly new on the game. A bit naïve....'

'In what way?'

'She really didn't treat it as a business. She saw it as a step-ping-stone to happiness and married bliss, poor cow. She thought that she would meet her Mr Right one day and he'd whisk away to a nice semi in Brighton or some other such place. She tended to give the ugly blokes a miss. She only wanted to do it with a good-looking feller, especially if he was in uniform.'

'Did you see her in here last Monday?'

Eva screwed up her putty features. Her make-up cracked in several places. 'The night she copped it? Yes, I think so. I saw her chatting with a bloke near closing-time. Monday's always a slow night for some reason. I can't remember when I last had a punter on a Monday.'

'What did this man look like?' Sunderland asked.

Eva pursed her lips. 'Can't rightly say. Didn't take much notice really.'

'Come on, Eva, think. Anything, any detail at all would help. Bring a picture to your mind....'

She screwed her face up once more and bit her lip. Well ...' she said at length, 'he was a good-looker. Dark features. And tall. I do remember he was tall. He towered over little Molly.'

'What was he dressed in? Was he wearing a uniform?'

'A raincoat. A black gabardine. Yes, that's it. He kept it on all the time. I thought it a little odd 'cause it was fastened up to the neck. And big boots.

Llewellyn almost laughed. 'Big boots?'

'Yeah, big, shiny boots. Just like your mate's got.'

Instinctively, Llewellyn glanced down at Sunderland's feet.

'Anything else?'

Eva shook her head? 'Nah. Honest. I'd tell you if I knew. I'd be very happy if you caught the devil, but you don't want me to be making things up do you?'

Llewellyn sighed. 'No.'

'Right, then, what about that other drink?'

twelve

Barbara devoured her salt-beef sandwich and most of the potatoes as though she hadn't had a meal since the outbreak of the war. As she cleared her plate she grinned at me in an embarrassed way.

'Sorry, I'm not usually such a glutton, but I've not eaten much in the last few days. I was knotted up inside knowing what I intended to do.'

'As long as you're not building up your strength to try it again....'

She laughed. It was a genuine, unfettered laugh, her eyes sparkled and her features lit up with a natural exuberance. It was as though she had been in a dark tunnel and was now just emerging into the light.

I smiled back. With all the worry taken from her face, I saw that she was very pretty. Steady, Johnny, a voice within me cautioned, she is just a kid. Yeah, you're right, I agreed. But a very pretty kid at that.

'What happens next?' she asked.

'I think you should retain me as a private detective to find your brother's killer.'

'What a great idea,' she said, enthusiastically but then her grin turned to a frown. 'But I could never afford you.'

'Oh, I come very cheap. I could do the whole deal for ... say a coffee and a salt-beef sandwich.'

'Don't be kind to me. I can't bear kind right now.'

I shook my head. 'Not really being kind. After what you've told me, I can't just leave the matter there. It's part of my character, I'm afraid. I've just got to find out for my sake as well as yours. A crime has been committed, someone must pay. It's as simple as that'.

'In that case, you're hired.' She gave me a gentle smile and squeezed my hand.

'Give me a few days to do some digging and I'll see what I can find out. I've got the drinks party tonight to start with ... that should prove illuminating. We can meet up so I can report back.' It was business, but I did want to see her again.

'OK. I could meet you for lunch here the day after tomorrow. I work in the haberdashery department at Bourne and Hollingsworth in Oxford Street which is not too far away.'

'Shouldn't you be there now?'

'I took a few days off this week. I'm due back tomorrow.' She glanced at her wrist-watch. 'I'd like to go home now. I'm feeling a little tired after ... everything'

Suddenly she did look tired. It was as though her body had reminded her of the strain she had suffered. Her shoulders slouched and dark circles appeared under the eyes which widened with disbelief. It was little wonder, for the girl had been through a terrible experience. Her desire for revenge, for retribution, had propelled her into actions that were alien to her. She wasn't a cruel-hearted killer but for a while she had entered a twilight world and it seemed to me that only now did she realize the full implications of what she had tried to do: to shoot a man dead in cold blood. Suddenly she was aware that had I not been able to stop her she would probably be sitting in a police cell now, charged with murder, rather than sitting in Benny's café with me. The appalling realization of what might have happened drained her dry.

I offered to take her home but she begged me not to. 'I don't want my mother to know anything about today. She'd only worry me with questions and she'd want to know all about you. I just ... I just couldn't cope with that just now. She's still grieving for Isaac and I don't want to bring her any more trouble. She knew nothing of what I planned to do. I see now that I was crazy....' Barbara shook her head with wise disbelief.

I knew she was right and I didn't want to put her under any pressure. 'That's fine,' I said easily and gave her hand a squeeze.

I paid the bill and popped her in a taxi. 'See you here, the day after tomorrow at 12.30,' I said.

She nodded and waved as the taxi drew away. I saw her mouthing the words 'Thank you,' through the grimy window before the taxi went round the corner and out of sight.

As I turned to make my way back to my office I noticed Benny standing in the doorway of his café, grinning at me.

When I got back to Hawke Towers I lay on the bed and took a rest. I reran the events of the day in my head, trying to isolate incidents in an attempt to make some sense of them. Such brain-work befuddled my mind and it sought an escape. I soon drifted off into sleep.

When I awoke, it was dark. I clicked on my bedside lamp and checked the time. It was 7.30. I'd been out for over three hours. Now I really had to get my skates on if I were to get to the drinks party with my new set of admiring friends at the Britannia Club.

After the very basic ablutions – a splash wash, a fresh application of Brylcreem and a rub with the curtains to shine my shoes – I was out on the street heading back to Manchester Square.

Dusk was falling fast as I approached the premises of the Britannia Club. This time the door was closed and there were no bruisers standing on guard outside. I rang the bell and waited. The door was opened by a butler-type chap in evening dress with a stiff white collar and a bow tie which was so tight at the fellow's Adam's apple that it looked like some vibrating satanic butterfly on the verge of flight. I gave my name and he checked it on a list.

He gave me a sepulchral smile. Apparently I was expected; he led me into the hallway and up the staircase to a salon on the first floor. Here another penguin-suited minion handed me a glass of champagne and ushered me into the brightly lit room. Immediately I was aware that I was the only man there in a lounge suit. The place was awash with fellows in smart black dinner suits and crisp white shirts and ladies in evening dresses. I felt as though I was walking into a black-and-white film.

I took a big gulp of champagne.

'Mr Hawke, how wonderful.'

I turned and saw that it was Lady McLean, dressed in an elegant flowing black gown made of some shiny material which no doubt was very expensive.

'Good evening, Lady McLean,' I said, giving a little bow.

'Just call me June. It makes me feel less old.'

Before I was able to respond with some candy-floss flattery I found myself surrounded by about half a dozen of the other guests. Sir Howard and Guy Cooper were among them and some faces I did not recognize. One fat, greasy fellow with a walrus moustache borrowed from a very large walrus prodded me gently in the chest.

'I say, young feller, I gather you're the hero who saved Guy from buying a packet from some Yiddish tart this afternoon?'

This comment seemed to amuse the group and I joined in with their chuckling.

Walrus-man stuck out his chubby hand in my direction. 'Pleased to meet you. Lord Alfred Wordsworth.'

It was a name I knew. He was a respected industrialist.

I shook his hand. 'John Hawke,' I said, part of me wanting the earth to open up and swallow me whole.

Guy stepped forward and took me to one side. 'We must have a talk later, Mr Hawke, but I think that Jocelyn is about to entertain us now.

As though on cue a piano struck up at the other end of the room. The crowd gathered round in a semicircle and the pianist, a young blond-haired man with the staring eyes and the shiny features of a ventriloquist's dummy, gave a little bow and struck up with his song:

> As I go rolling down The Strand
> I see them strolling hand in hand
> And I really don't, just don't under-stand
> Why are there so many Jews around in Lon-don?
> Why can't the Jews just simply disappear?
> Hitler's got them on the run in Ger-many
> Why can't he do the same thing over here?

The assembled throng beamed with beatific smiles and nodded knowingly at each other, while tapping their fingers in time with the music. I looked around at the faces of my fellow guests as the pianist rendered this foul ditty. They all seemed amused, these apparently intelligent, well-heeled individuals, all oozing an air of charm and sophistication and yet obviously carrying within them a burden of hate and disdain which my poor brain could not understand. I found myself feeling sorry for them as well as despising them.

'Again!' someone shouted and the pianist gave a reprise, allowing the members of the Britannia Club to join in this time, especially raising their voices for the last two lines.

There was laughter and applause. I grabbed another glass of champagne from a passing flunkey. If I was to survive this evening I needed some anaesthetic.

'What a nasty little song.'

I turned in the direction of the voice and found myself looking at Anna Neagle's twin sister. Well, someone who looked as though she'd used the same mould at least. She was gorgeous: tall, elegant, with blond hair moulded in great curves and waves around her beautifully alluring face. Her clear blue eyes dared me to respond to her observation.

I could not have agreed with her more about the 'nasty little song' but I was aware that it wasn't my place to admit to it in a room full of rampant fascists. In fact I was surprised the girl had the nerve or the foolishness to do so.

'You really think so?' I said evenly, sipping my champagne.

'I certainly do,' responded the attractive young woman in the same forthright tone. 'It trivializes the situation. The Jewish problem is not a suitable subject for a music-hall song. Their hold on this country is far too serious – too tragic – to sing silly ditties about it.'

'You could be right.'

'I am'. The matter was not up for discussion. 'You're John Hawke, aren't you?'

'Yes. And who are you?'

'I'm Eunice – horrible name. My father is Sir Howard McLean.'

Oh, so it runs in the family, I thought. I knew it would be naïve of me to wonder why on earth this pretty young woman, the daughter of the head of the Britannia Club, held such strong, perverted racist views – why, rather than enjoying a night out on the town having fun, dancing at a night club, she preferred to mingle with a bunch of narrow-minded fascists. But in some ways I am naïve.

'What do you do?' she asked, her eyes peering into mine with a devilish intensity.

'Do?' I asked warily. I had to be careful here. I really didn't want to give too much away about my real life, but I was also sure that if I spouted a pack of lies they would easily be found out. I tried to deflect the question.

'Why are you interested?'

She smiled, brushing her body against me and slipping her arm through mine. 'Because I like the look of you, if you know what I mean.'

I felt my libido stand to attention. I did know what she meant. I wasn't *that* naïve.

'That's gratifying,' I said, feeling both flattered and rather frightened at the same time. If this conversation had been taking place in the Velvet Cage with a stranger I would have been at ease and confident, but getting the come-on from the attractive daughter of the leader of a fascist organization was a new experience and was making me somewhat hot under the collar.

'We should get together, away from here. I'm sure we'd have a good time.'

My libido was now starting to draw pictures.

I took another gulp of champagne. As I drained the glass I saw Sir Howard approaching with Guy Cooper. They looked serious, wearing matching frowns. For a fleeting moment I wondered if my cover had been blown. If it had, what on earth would they do? Put me up against the wall and shoot me?

Sir Howard took my arm gently. 'John, I wonder if we could have that quiet talk now?'

I found the words 'What about?' trembling on my tongue but I managed to keep them to myself.

'Of course,' I said.

Sir Howard turned to his daughter. 'Would you mind leaving us, my dear? It's business.'

Eunice groaned. 'Just when I was enjoying myself.' She pulled away from me and then gave me a little peck on the cheek. 'I'll see you later,' she said before slipping away.

'I see you've made the acquaintance of my daughter,' observed Sir Howard drily.

'I think it's more the other way around.'

'Remarkable girl, if ... unpredictable.'

'This little talk ...' I prompted, in an attempt to get the conversation back on track. The last thing I wanted was Sir Howard thinking I was lusting after his daughter.

'In private,' said Guy, taking my arm.

The two men exchanged glances in a conspiratorial way and then led me through the throng of guests into a side room.

I felt a growing sense of unease. I really had no idea what I was letting myself in for now.

thirteen

It had been a good day.

He had been active and involved in normal duties. At times he had almost forgotten the gnawing ache. Almost. The searing discomfort when he visited the lavatory was always there to remind him in spades. Pissing broken glass with throbbing pains in the gonads was the Devil's aide-memoir of his condition. But he was resolved that he wasn't ready to give up just yet.

He had more work to do. More tarts to see to.

And it had been a good day. The best for ages.

He had functioned normally and the place had been buzzing with the details of the murders. They really had made an impact. *He* had really made an impact.

It thrilled him. If they only knew his secret. Well, they would be amazed. Not him, they would cry. Not him, he's not capable of that.

Oh, but he was.

As he lay on his bed in the darkness, smoking a cigarette, despite his discomfort, he was smiling. In a strange way, he pondered, this condition is perhaps not such a curse after all. I am making my mark on the world. I'm important.

It had been a good day.

And tomorrow would be better. Then he would kill again.

fourteen

Sir Howard McLean and Guy Cooper led me away from the party into a side room which was illuminated only by two table-lamps.

'It's better in here if we are to talk business,' said Guy, slipping a silver cigarette-case from his jacket pocket and offering me one. I could see that they weren't my usual cheap Craven As but posh, imported handmade jobs. I took one and Sir Howard flicked a desk-lighter for me.

'We assume that you are a staunch supporter of our cause,' said Cooper. 'I trust we are right in our assumptions?'

'If your cause is to get rid of the Jews, I'm certainly with you,' I replied with some vehemence, the words almost sticking in my throat.

Both men smiled. 'A succinct summation, I should say, eh, Guy?' observed Sir Howard, his stern features relaxing.

Cooper nodded. 'You have already proved yourself to be a quick thinker and an able sort of chap. This afternoon's performance was first class. We know that you were invalided out of the army and now work as a private detective.'

Homework had been done.

I nodded and blew smoke casually into the air.

'You're just the sort of fellow we need in the club. We feel you might be very useful to us.'

'I'm not much of a talker. I'm afraid. I couldn't get up and spout, make speeches.'

Sir Howard sat at a desk, his face thrust forward and bleached by the harsh rays of the table-lamp. 'That's not what we we're after, at all, John. In the current restrictive climate words are simply not enough. We need action.

'Let me put you in the picture. We in the Britannia Club are a very vulnerable species at present. These days being an outspoken or organized fascist can easily lead you into jail. Since Mosley's incarceration and the forced dissolution of the BUF, it's not safe for self-respecting people like ourselves to raise our heads above the parapets for fear of being arrested. We are only tolerated because our meetings are private, by invitation only, and we do not express our anti-Semitic beliefs in public. In other words this foolish, ill-advised government has effectively tied our hands and gagged us. It expects us to stand silently on the sidelines while our country is destroyed.

'So you see, if we are not able to act within the law – the law doled out by the Jewish-sympathizing government – we have to make our own laws, our own rules. We are men and women of principle after all, and our aims are of the noblest: Britain for the British. What, I ask you, is wrong with that?'

After a moment's pause I realized that this was not a rhetorical question.

'There is nothing wrong with that. In fact it is our duty,' I responded earnestly.

Sir Howard grinned. 'I told you, Guy, this was a fellow after our own hearts.'

Cooper blew smoke into the air and nodded. 'Good man.'

'You see, we don't think that it will be very long before Hitler will be here....'

'In Britain?' I could not keep the shock out of my voice.

'Indeed. The Führer has already conquered Europe. All he has to do now is cross a little stretch of water to add Britain to his conquests. The man in the street has no real concept of what is happening. In simple terms, John, we have to mobilize our troops, help to cleanse the capital in readiness for what will inevitably be German rule.'

Guy placed his hand upon my shoulder. 'Behind the docile front of the Britannia Club, we organize vigilante groups: young men who feel the same as we do and are not afraid to use their fists or any other forms of violence to help cleanse our city. With the Jews you knock them down and kick them when they are down.'

I could hardly believe what I was hearing. Veiled and to some extent circumspect though their language was, these smooth, well-bred thugs were talking about lynching-mobs. They were talking about murder.

I stubbed my cigarette in a large ornate ashtray and prayed I would say all the right things. I was certain that if I didn't, I wouldn't see another sunrise. I knew I had to play it cool.

'That sounds fine by me, but where exactly where do I come in?'

'Do you want to come in?' said Cooper gently, as though he were asking whether I took sugar in my tea.

'If it helps the cause, of course. I want to see a brighter, better Britain. A Jew-free Britain.'

'Excellent. We'd like you to help co-ordinate some of our groups in the East End. Their strikes must be brief and brutal and they must be able disperse before any counter action can be taken by the Jews or the police are called in.'

'And we'd like to target some of the synagogues too,' said Sir Howard. 'A few well-placed torches should do any damage the *Luftwaffe* fails to carry out.'

'Just tell me what to do,' I said with a fervour to match their mood and expectations. I felt that I had turned into some kind of automaton, mouthing exactly what they wanted to hear, while I was squirming inside with fear and disgust.

'However, this is small beer to what we believe will happen in the next six months. By Christmas things will be very different in this country. And we shall need all the good men we can get on our side.'

'I am on your side,' I snapped, almost giving a Nazi salute.

Cooper smiled. 'I know. Now, we hold planning meetings once a week. I think it would be useful for you to come along to the next one, this Saturday. It promises to be rather special. It would give you a chance to meet some of the other lieutenants, as we call them. We could then plan the specifics of your involvement.'

There was no turning back now. I had to go further down this crazy, dark path that I'd stumbled upon. Barbara had been right.

The Britannia Club was responsible for Isaac's murder, and probably others, too. If I could accumulate sufficient evidence, I'd get this lot behind bars for the duration and see that the killers faced the hangman. Noble stuff, Johnny, old boy. However, I was also aware that if I put a foot wrong before I'd got enough information my life wouldn't be worth a pin's fee.

Well, you wanted danger, you stupid bastard. Now you've got it.

'Count me in. I'll be there,' I heard myself saying.

'One further thing,' said Cooper, 'this is our private arrangement. Do not discuss it with anyone else.'

'Sure.'

'We mean it,' added Sir Howard brusquely. 'No one else. Not all the members are aware of our … extra curricular agenda, shall we call it? My daughter, for instance, has no knowledge of these activities. On this occasion I would advise you adhere to the government warning about careless talk…. You catch my drift I hope.' The eyes narrowed into a cold stare.

I caught his drift all right. He was circumspect no more. I could recognize a threat when one was thrust under my nose.

'As I said, I'm not the talkative type.'

'Good. We meet at 7.30 on Saturday evening.'

Both men extended their hands and I shook them firmly, sealing the bargain. My God, it seemed that I had sold my soul to the fascists.

Sir Howard rose casually, slipping once more behind the mask of bluff *bonhomie*. 'I suggest that we return to the party now. I am sure John would welcome another glass of champagne.'

Once back in the brightly lit room where the party was at full throttle the two men left me to my own devices. My initial instinct was to run for the hills. I felt a kind of stifling claustrophobia, being trapped in a room with these smartly clad traitors. I also felt dirty, contaminated, as though I had come into contact with some unpleasant disease. But I suspected that an early departure would have seemed suspicious. Looking around the room, I was reminded that in fact there were two types of fascist present: those misguided souls who held the

belief that the Jewish nation were to blame for all the ills beset-
ting this country, and those vicious zealots who were determined
to go to any lengths to destroy them.

While I was pondering my next move, Lady McLean appeared
at my side. Again I was struck by what an attractive woman she
was for her age. She must have been a gorgeous head-turner as a
girl. She gave me a gentle, beguiling smile and took my arm,
leading me to a quiet area of the room. 'I hope you realize and
respect the trust we have placed in you, Mr Hawke.'

I nodded seriously. 'Of course.'

'If this movement is to succeed, if we are to reach our goal –
a unified and British Britain – we need young men like you with
vision, dedication and drive. You could go far. Don't let us
down.' She raised her eyebrows prompting me to respond.

'I am with you all the way,' I lied in the most convincing way
I knew how.

She squeezed my arm tightly, flashed a brief smile and left me.
It was a warning. A polite, civilized threat.

I grabbed another glass of champagne from a passing flunkey.
A little alcoholic anaesthetic was needed. I was just about to
take a sip when I saw a face heading towards me through the
throng. It was none other than my friend from Benny's café.

'Good evening,' he said briskly. I half-expected him to click
his heels and go into the *Heil Hitler* routine.

'Good evening.'

'We keep bumping into each other.'

'Don't we. Do you think people are beginning to talk?'

There was no change in his expression. I hate people with no
sense of humour. Especially those with Jew-baiting tendencies.

'Are you giving another performance tonight, like the one in
the café?'

'No, tonight we are both on the same side.'

'Really? That's good. I saw you go off with Guy and Sir
Howard. Does that mean you are joining our little army?'

I grinned and put my finger to my lips. 'Mum's the word.'

This time a faint flicker of amusement registered in his eyes.
He held out his hand.

'Ralph Chapman.'

I shook his hand and nodded.

'Well, John,' he said conspiratorially, as though somehow we had become old friends in a matter of seconds, 'I look forward to your first blood.'

'So do I.'

'There's nothing like it, I can assure you. Gets the old adrenalin going like nothing else.' He winked and patted me on the arm. 'See you later, I've no doubt.'

With that he turned and merged with all the other dinner-suited bastards.

To hell with it, I said to myself, I'm leaving. If I have to play dumb to one more of this crowd, I'm liable to burst or smack someone very hard in the face.

I had just made it to the door and the flunkey was on the verge of opening it for me, when I felt a tug on my elbow.

'You're not going without saying goodbye, are you?'

It was Eunice.

'I guess I was.'

'You naughty boy.'

She leaned forward and gave me a long hard kiss on the lips. It did make me feel like being a naughty boy – a very naughty boy.

'I'll be seeing you,' she said, her eyes full of wicked promise, then she too melted away into the throng.

As I hit the street and the cool, refreshing and untainted night air, some words of Sir Walter Scott floated into my brain from I know not where:

Oh what a tangled web we weave when first we practise to deceive.

fifteen

The soldier stepped from the train on to the platform, wiped the sleep from his eyes and smiled. He was here, back in London, safe and sound. The great noisy cathedral of King's Cross station, echoing with the various sounds of trains and travellers, seemed so wonderfully, reassuringly normal to him. One could almost believe that there wasn't a war on.

Indeed, he reaffirmed in his own mind that for the next few days or so there was no war, no dead comrades, no unit for him to return to, no guilt. And no bloody Nazis. There was just freedom and as much fun as a reasonably full wallet could secure. He was frightened to look beyond that.

The shriek of a train whistle made him jump and he smiled at his own nervousness. He shouldn't be nervous, he told himself, not in London. He was glad he had come back here. There was so much more to do and see than in his adopted home town on the coast, and less likelihood of his being apprehended. It was easier to lose oneself in the teeming capital. And that's what he wanted to do above all: to be anonymous. Of course, being here also gave him the opportunity, if the spirit moved him, to catch up on the past. But for some inexplicable reason he wasn't sure that the spirit would move him. Maybe it was because he really didn't want to reach back. Maybe.

He would wait and see how he felt.

The important thing now was to grab a large breakfast with eggs, bacon, the whole lot, to set him up for the day and then find a night's lodgings before he went off to enjoy himself. To crowd his mind with new sensations in order to blot out yesterday, all those bloody yesterdays.

With a grim determination he hauled his kit-bag on to his

shoulder and made his way up the platform towards the exit, merging very quickly into the vast sea of milling humanity.

sixteen

The next morning I woke up with my head in a vice that was slowly being tightened by an unseen hand. Well, that's what it felt like anyway. I just prayed that my skull would split open and allow my brains to escape, thus putting me out of my misery.

I'd had hangovers before but not one quite like this. It was, I supposed, the result of too much champagne, not my normal tipple, and too close a contact a with bunch of loony fascists: a deadly cocktail. Even the usual remedy of back coffee and a couple of Craven As failed to release the vice.

Slowly I rose from my pit, washed, shaved and dressed, each operation being carried out with strained, awkward, painstaking motions. I gave a fair imitation of Boris Karloff as Frankenstein's monster.

By the time I'd downed another coffee and consumed a further two fags I sensed that a kind of normality was on its way. While I waited for its return, I cast my mind back over the events of the previous evening. In the cold light of day they made me shudder. It seemed that I had been signed up as an assassin-in-chief for the Britannia Club, an association that secretly organized vigilante groups to harm and indeed kill Jews in London. My immediate instinct was get on the phone to David Llewellyn at the Yard, spill the beans and let him take over, thus letting me off the hook. His men could raid the place and that would be that.

Only it wouldn't.

I knew that I had to have actual proof before I involved the police. Conversations were hardly proof and could easily be denied. I needed concrete evidence in order to make the charges stick. At the moment it was only my word against theirs and I'm sure Messrs McLean and Cooper had enough clout in high places to squash my testimony. And me along with it. No, I was stuck with my role of fascist supporter for a little longer yet.

Great.

I breakfasted on a cup of tea and a couple of stale digestive biscuits; then I moved next door into the room I laughingly call my office. Consulting my appointment diary I was relieved to note that I did have a prospective client due at ten o'clock. It was a bread-and-butter job – something to do with an apparently errant clerk who was helping himself to the petty cash – but it would help to keep my mind off other matters for a while.

By lunchtime I was feeling almost normal. The vice had evaporated and I could move my head quickly without my vision blurring or my brain hurting. I had dealt with my client, a Mr Goodall, whose problem was, as I suspected, a simple one. I was able to advise him on a course of action to trap the pilfering clerk. All he had to do was mark the notes that went into the petty-cash box, and when they appeared to go missing simply ask the clerk if he would be kind enough to change a pound for two ten-shilling notes from his own wallet. If the exchanged notes were the marked ones, hey presto, he had his proof. That seemed to satisfy Mr Goodall; I was able to extract a small consultation fee and that was that.

Somewhat at a loose end, I decided to take myself off to the pictures for the afternoon. They were showing Ronald Colman in *The Prisoner of Zenda* at the Astoria in Tottenham Court Road. I'd seen it before but I thought an afternoon of Ruritanian romance and derring-do was the ideal antidote to murdering fascists and pilfering clerks.

I was just reaching for my hat and coat when there was a knock at my office door. Surely, not another client? I thought. Two in one day was riches indeed.

However my visitor was Eunice McLean.

'Hello, darling,' she said, leaning provocatively against the doorframe. 'Aren't you going to invite me in?'

Before I could reply she came in anyway.

'How did you find me?' I asked, failing to keep the irritation from my voice.

'I thought you were a detective and would know such things. There aren't too many John Hawkes in the telephone book. And I sort of knew that "John Hawke – Private Detective" was you. And it was.'

'And why are you here?'

'Now that is a silly question.' She slipped her coat off and draped it over a chair. She was wearing a tightly fitting black woollen dress that hid no secrets about her figure.

I was unaccustomed to this sort of attention and I did not have any previous experience to guide me through the minefield which I saw clearly before me. This girl meant business and I was flattered. Under any other circumstances I would have welcomed her advances, but I was not about to get emotionally entangled with the daughter of Sir Howard McLean, an unscrupulous fascist with blood on his hands, and she herself a girl whose own moral outlook was diametrically opposed to mine. No matter how alluring she was.

And she was alluring.

'Miss McLean, I'm sorry but—'

'Oh, you're not going to play hard to get, are you, Johnny?' She pouted and drew so close that I could smell the heady aroma of her expensive perfume.

I was about to push her away when it struck me that this might be some kind of test. She might have been sent here to find out more about me, to see if I really was suitable material for the Britannia gang. All that stuff her father had spouted about keeping the information regarding the vigilante groups to myself, that his daughter was ignorant of such activities, might well have been a pack of lies. After all he was a specialist in deception.

I stared into the beautiful face of Eunice McLean, searching for some signs of betrayal. I could find none. She seemed very earnest in her desires. Wasn't I the lucky boy? Or was I? I really didn't know, but I was sure that if I did not respond in kind it would seem to be suspicious. Who could resist this creature and why on earth would they want to?

On impulse, I took her in my arms and kissed her fully on the lips. I felt her body relax into my embrace and she returned my passion in spades. I couldn't help myself: I really was enjoying the experience. Part of my tired brain was asking me when was the last time a beautiful woman had kissed me in this fashion. In fact I didn't recall a last time. I didn't think there was one.

After a while we paused for breath and Eunice pulled away a little, smiling.

'You're quite a kisser, Johnny boy,' she said, her smile broadening.

'That makes two of us.'

She came close again and we repeated the procedure. I must admit it was a struggle to keep my wits about me. It would have been so easy to give in to the moment, but I had to keep reminding myself while I was holding and kissing this beautiful young girl that I didn't trust her.

Eventually I broke the clinch and reached inside my jacket for a pack of cigarettes. I offered her one.

She shook her head. 'Why smoke when we can neck?'

'I think I need to come up for air for a while and I'd like to talk.'

She seemed puzzled. 'What about?'

I lit my cigarette and stared at those wide, innocent eyes. 'Why this? Why me? A pretty girl like you from a privileged background chasing after a poor one-eyed guy like me … it doesn't make sense.'

She giggled. 'You do yourself no favours, Mr Johnny Detective. There's something dangerous about you that appeals to me. You're real. You should see some of the soppy individuals my parents try to hook me up with.'

I could imagine.

'Do your parents know you're here now?'

'What do you think?' She pouted her lips and blew me a kiss.

'I think that you could get me into a lot of trouble with your father and I don't want that to happen. I respect him and his views—'

'You can still respect him and make love to me, too.'

'Whoa, young lady, let's take one thing at a time here.'

'OK, kiss me again.'

'Not just at the moment.'

'Oh, Johnny ...'

The real, spoilt immature girl was emerging now, slipping out behind that worldly, confident façade, a girl who was used to getting her own way and sulked when she didn't. A girl who was allowed to follow her whims and, strange as it seemed, I had become one of those whims – a passing fancy. It would have been so easy to tell her to grow up and not to throw herself at comparative strangers no matter how 'dangerous' and 'real' they seemed. But she would have ignored me or worse. I knew I had to keep her sweet for the sake of my mission. I didn't want her turning against me and moaning about me to her dad.

I took her in my arms again and kissed her. It was a hard job, but I knew I just had to do it.

'Listen, Eunice, you're a sweet girl and I find you very ... very ...'

'Attractive.'

'Yes, but don't you think we should take things a little more slowly? We hardly know each other.'

'There are ways of changing that ...'

'Yes, but not now. I'm afraid you have to go. I have work to do and then I've got an important appointment this afternoon.' I didn't add that it was with Ronald Colman at the Astoria cinema. 'Let's meet up for a drink sometime at the weekend, maybe a meal.'

'You do like me, don't you?' She frowned and looked thoroughly miserable.

I couldn't help grinning at the sudden change in her demeanour.

'Of course I like you.' And strangely I did and that worried me. 'Now run along and I'll be in touch with you before Saturday to arrange things.'

'You'll ring me. Promise.'

'Of course.'

'But you don't have my number.' She scribbled it down on the pad on my desk. 'There. And if I don't hear from you by Friday evening, I shall come round here and bang on your door until you show yourself.'

Without another word I helped her on with her coat and guided her to the door.

'I will ring,' I said, gently pushing her into the corridor. 'I am a man of my word.'

She grinned, her beautiful face lighting up again. 'I knew you were.' She kissed me on the cheek. 'I'll miss you Johnny Detective. See at you the weekend.'

I nodded and waved her goodbye.

After she'd gone I stood for some time in kind of trance. Had all that happened, or had I imagined it? I sank in my chair dazed. An encounter like that was so unfair on my emotions and my male urges. The memory of those kisses stirred me. Eunice was an added complication to an already messy situation.

seventeen

He stood by the window in his tiny room, holding back the blackout curtain and the shabby, discoloured net curtains so that he could see the sky. Already the day was retreating and the first faint glimmer of the stars had begun to prick the slate-coloured canvas.

He was eager to start but he had the stoical patience that allowed him to wait until it was time. This restraint gave added pleasure, a sensual anticipation to the night's deeds. He smiled. Come the dark, and the killing could begin.

eighteen

The soldier studied the froth on his pint of beer in an absent-minded manner. He was somewhat despondent. His first day in London had not lived up to his expectations. He had not been in the city since before the war and he had been dismayed and shocked at the changes he had seen – the damage and destruction that the blitz had caused. There were now great wastelands of rubble where smart buildings had once stood. Hardly any street or thoroughfare seemed to have escaped some scars of the bombing. Ugly damaged structures were shored up with little hope of surviving the next blast and there was a general dusty atmosphere of gloom everywhere. Even the faces of the crowds that passed him by seemed somehow damaged by the war. Cheery words and flashing smiles appeared to be on ration too. And even good old Eros had been boarded up to protect the little fellow from the Hun. There were hoardings everywhere instructing the populace what to do: 'Wear or carry something white'; 'Go through your wardrobe – Make do and mend'; 'Keep Mum – Careless Talk Costs Lives'; and 'Dig For Victory'. This was not the lively capital of his youth but a city held in thrall by the conflict.

He had escaped these reminders of the war by spending the afternoon at the pictures, then, on a guilty impulsive whim, had rung his brother from a telephone box outside the cinema. He knew that he should have got in touch with him earlier – even sent him a letter informing him that he would be in London 'on leave', but something, some inexplicable feeling, had prevented him. He hadn't fallen out with his brother; they had somehow just drifted apart. There was nothing in their separate lives that bonded them any more. But after such a dispiriting day he had the sudden urge to see him again, to engage with someone who knew him. He had tried to ignore the need to talk to someone about his problems for long enough. His escape hadn't been successful but he now realized that he couldn't escape from himself.

He stood in the dank call box listening to the telephone ringing and ringing at the other end. There was no reply. Another disappointment in a day of many.

He grabbed a bite to eat in a dingy café, then wandered the streets for a while until dusk fell and the lights of the Saracen's Head caught his eye. Well, at least he could get drunk, he thought. No point in being on leave and not getting pie-eyed.

But here he was, staring at his first pint without much enthusiasm.

'Penny for 'em, soldier.'

The voice broke into his reverie. He looked up and saw a slim young woman wearing a saucy beret which was pulled almost over one eye. She looked French but her voice was pure East London.

He looked puzzled for a moment.

'Your thoughts,' she added with a wink. 'Penny for your thoughts.'

'Ah, you wouldn't want to know.'

'You could always try me,' she said, dragging up a stool and sitting at the same table. 'I'm a very good listener ... among other things.'

The girl wasn't pretty and she was heavily made up, particularly for someone of her young age, but he thought there was something attractive about her and she seemed friendly.

'You on leave?' she asked.

He nodded.

'That's nice.' She raised her glass as though in a toast to his temporary freedom, then looked dismayed when she saw that it was empty. 'Oh, dear,' she said.

He was sharp enough to know this was part of a well-practised routine to get a free drink, but he didn't mind. In fact it entertained him.

'What can I get you?'

'Oh, I'd love a large gin and tonic', she said, apparently surprised and delighted at his offer. 'And I wouldn't mind a bag of crisps neither. My tummy's rumbling a bit.'

'OK,' he said, strangely charmed by this flighty bit of stuff. He had no delusions about what she was and what she was after, but he didn't care. She was beginning to brighten up his dispiriting day and that was all that mattered. With a grin he wandered over to the bar to carry out his errand, returning a few minutes later with the drink and crisps.

'You're a sweetie,' she said, after taking a gulp of her gin and tonic. 'On leave, are you? Where you been?'

He shook his head. 'Can't tell you that. Careless talk, y'know.'

'Oh, yeah. Careless talk,' she sneered, stiffening slightly. 'I could be a German spy, right.'

'You could.' He smiled. 'I believe the Germans are very good at disguises.'

This amused her and she relaxed again. 'Well, if you can't tell me where you've been, what are we going to talk about?' she asked just before stuffing a handful of crisps in her mouth.

'How about you?'

'Lord help us. That's a bleedin' boring subject, I can tell you.'

'It doesn't look boring from where I'm sitting. What's your name?'

'I'm Mary. Sweet and contrary, that's me. I was named after that film star Mary Pickford. What's yours then?'

He told her.

'Ooh, that's nice. That's a real manly name.' She reached across the table and laid a hand on top of his, rubbing it gently. 'Mind you, I could tell when I saw you that you were a real man.'

He couldn't help but chuckle at this corny routine.

Her face clouded over again. She didn't take kindly to being laughed at and withdrew her hand.

'What's so funny?'

'Nothing, Mary. Nothing at all,' he said with genuine warmth. 'You're lovely.' He took hold of her hand. 'Just lovely.'

The cloud dispersed and the sun came out once more. 'Do you really think so? Lovely? Really?'

'Of course'

'Well, you're not half tasty yourself,' she said without an ounce of shyness. She took another large gulp of gin to celebrate their mutual attraction. 'You couldn't put another in here, could you darling? I'm real thirsty tonight.'

He drained his own glass and went up to the bar again. While he was waiting to be served he looked back at Mary. She had her handbag open and was checking her appearance in her make-up mirror. As she did so, a tall, dark man in a black belted raincoat came up to her and engaged her in conversation. It looked very much as though he was trying to do a little business. Why wouldn't he? She was a prostitute after all.

Although he couldn't hear what they were saying, it was clear that she was telling the man to get lost. The man persisted but she shook her head and raised her voice. This seemed to anger him and he turned his gaze on the soldier at the bar. There was fierce hatred in those eyes. So much so that the soldier felt a cold shiver run down his spine.

After a moment the tall stranger moved away through the crowded bar-room and was swallowed up amongst the other customers and the thick smoky miasma that pervaded the pub.

'What did he want?' the soldier asked as he plonked two drinks down on the table, his own beer slipping over the sides of the glass.

Mary huffed. 'Well, it wasn't the time, I can tell you.'

'He tried to pick you up?'

'Cheek of the bastard. I told him to sling his hook. I said was with my boyfriend.'

He raised an eyebrow. Boyfriend? That seemed like some kind of promotion from potential client.

She eyed him seriously. 'After this drink, why don't we go back to my place and we can really relax there?'

'Why not?'

'You got some money?'

'Some. How much will I need?'

She reached out and ran the back of her hand down his cheek. 'I like you ... so we'll say two quid eh?'

He didn't reply but took a drink of beer instead. He wasn't

bothered about the money. It was no indignity for him, having to pay for love. It was what red-blooded single men did, or so he'd been told, especially if they didn't know how long it would be before they copped it from a Jerry sniper. Anyway, he liked the girl and she was attractive.

However, he did wish that it was real. That there was someone warm and loving wanting to hold him and kiss him – someone who had genuine affection for him, affection that didn't come with a price-tag. He gave a little self-indulgent shrug. Well, that was how it had been all his life. An orphan from infancy with no experience of parental love or real caring, he had always found it difficult to connect with people, to form meaningful, loving relationships. He had even drifted away from the one person who had really meant something to him, his younger brother.

'Where are you now?' Mary prodded him gently. 'Dancing with the fairies?'

'Sorry,' he smiled. 'I just went off. Miles away.'

Mary smiled sympathetically. Soldiers were often like that. They'd be having a good time and then all of a sudden for no apparent reason they would be reminded of something, the fighting, a dead comrade, a loved one lost maybe and they'd drift off for a few moments with sadness seeping into their features.

'Now then,' he said cheerily, 'where is this place of yours?'

'Not far. A five-minute walk.'

'Come on then, Mary. Let's go.' He grinned broadly.

As they got up to leave, at the far end of the bar the tall dark stranger in the black belted raincoat watched them with interest. After they had passed through the swing-doors he waited about thirty seconds, drained his glass and headed for the door.

The soldier found that Mary's place was just one dingy room in a cheap boarding-house. There was a smell of damp and a general air of staleness hanging about the place. The room contained a bed, a wardrobe, a chest of drawers and one moth-eaten armchair – nothing more.

As they entered she clicked on a small table lamp which cast a pink glow over the depressing surroundings.

'I never put the main light on,' said Mary, hanging her coat on the hook on the back of the door. 'Make yourself at home.'

The soldier slipped off his coat but stood awkwardly, not quite knowing what to do next. He had never been with a woman in this way before. A woman like this – a stranger who did it with lots of men for money.

'Pardon me a minute, love. I'm bursting for a pee.' She pulled a metal basin from under the sink and without any sense of embarrassment hitched up her dress and crouched down at the far side of the bed.

He heard the rush of urine splatter into the tin bowl and winced. He knew he was not in for a romantic evening, but this was rather too basic for his sensitivities.

'That's better,' she said, sliding the bowl under the bed. Then she proceeded to take her dress off. 'You got any johnnies?'

He shook his head dumbly.

'You men!' she puffed, and pulled a packet from her handbag. She extracted a silver-foiled condom and threw it over to him.

With an instinctive reflex he caught it.

'Come on love, slip your things off, I'm freezing here.' She stood before him in black stockings and a bra, with her hands on her hips. The gentleness and coquetry had disappeared from her demeanour now. This was business, she seemed to be saying. This is assembly-line work.

He did as he was told and when he was down to his vest and pants she came over to him and pressed her body into his. Her smell, her touch, her smooth flesh aroused him instantly. He sensed that despite everything she liked him. He kissed her passionately as he might do with the love of his life, ran his fingers through her hair and then down her back where he unhooked her bra. They embraced for a few moments more and then, gently, he lowered her to the bed. The recalcitrant springs protested but by now his mind was on other things and he hardly noticed the noise.

nineteen

He had followed the soldier and the tart from the Saracen's Head at quite close quarters. He kept to the shadows, but they had been too engrossed in their silly banter to notice him anyway. He'd managed to catch that her name was Mary, which would be a useful piece of information for later. He watched them go into the dingy lodging-house.

He secreted himself in a doorway across the street and waited. These things didn't take too much time. She was a businesswoman where time and motion meant money and he was a sex-starved soldier more than eager to spill his seed. He gave the whole process twenty minutes at the most. He checked his watch and made a little bet with himself.

He lost his bet. It was over an hour before the soldier emerged from the building. The boy must be quite a stallion, he mused, either that or the lad was having trouble getting started. However, for a fellow who had just indulged in a passionate and prolonged session of love making, he didn't look happy. His shoulders were slouched and he wore an expression of grim bleakness. Ah, well, that's sex for you. It's like throwing yourself off a high building. Initially you feel exhilarated, a wonderful sense of bodily freedom and then, before you know it, you see the ground hurtling towards you and it's time to pay heavily for the experience. He should know.

He watched the soldier walk away down the street with his hands dug deep in his pockets, no doubt in search of a compensatory drink. Clearly the experience had been an empty and dispiriting one. And then he returned his attention to the building across the street. Not long now, he thought. It was a thought that excited his senses. Not long now.

*

After the soldier had gone Mary lay on the bed for some time. She had a cigarette and a glass of gin from the bottle she kept hidden in the wardrobe. She was a fool. Only two quid. Just because she fancied him. Silly tart. Two quid! She could have got more. Then a smile crept over her face. Well she had, hadn't she? Propping herself up on the pillows, she examined her new treasure: the soldier's wallet. On impulse, she'd half-inched it from his jacket while he'd been swilling his face at the sink after they'd made love. There wasn't much inside, just his identity card, a scrap of paper with the address of a hotel and – more important – ten pounds in cash. She grinned. Now that was a good night's work.

Then the grin faded. Suddenly she realized that he might discover his loss sooner than she thought and be back knocking on her door in quicksticks. She knew he had some loose change in his pocket and had hoped that might supply his needs for the rest of the night. She'd been banking on his not noticing until he got back to his hotel at least, but then he might have needed to check the address on the bit of paper. What the hell! She'd feign ignorance. London was full of pickpockets. He couldn't prove anything. And he wasn't the type for violence. She'd just brazen it out if she had to. She'd done it before.

Quickly, she took some cash from the wallet, stuffed it in her own purse and then hid the wallet in a shoebox in the wardrobe. She caught sight of herself in the mirror on the back of the door. She looked rough. Not the smart young thing she had been when she'd set out that evening. That's what this life was doing to her: slowly but surely robbing her of her youth. The features grew puffier, the lines increased and the eye-bags became more defined day by day. But what could she do? It was a road she had chosen. Easy money and better pay than working in a factory. Just lie there and think of the money, girl. That's all you have to do. Yes, it was a road she had chosen – and so there was no turning back.

'Come on, girl,' she said to herself out loud, 'let's put on the war paint and get out of here. You need to cheer yourself up.'

The thought of the garish lights and smoky atmosphere of some pub or other did brighten her spirits. It was her way of blanking out the terrible truths. Within ten minutes, with her make-up repaired and a splash of cheap cologne, she was ready to go to work again. She smiled at herself in the mirror and winked. 'Hello, darling,' she said.

As she stepped out on to the pavement, someone called her name.

'Mary. Hello, Mary.'

Her first thought was that the soldier had returned already and she stiffened with anticipation of a scene.

But then a figure stepped out of the shadows and she saw that it was too tall for the soldier.

'Hello, Mary,' he repeated. 'I thought we might do a little business now that you're free.'

As he grew near to her, she recognized the man as the one who had tried to pick her up in the Saracen's Head earlier that evening.

Her immediate instinct was to tell him to get lost but something stopped her. He was quite good-looking in a craggy sort of way and it certainly was an easy way of earning some more cash. If they were quick she could still get to a pub before closing-time.

'I don't know,' she said, playfully. She was certainly going to screw this eager beaver for more than two quid.

'I can be very generous,' he said, moving even closer.

'How generous?'

He pulled a note from his raincoat pocket.

'A fiver.'

Blimey, she thought, this chap is desperate. She could hardly turn down a fiver and besides he's so keen, it'll be all over in ten minutes.

'All right,' she said. 'For a fiver. Come inside.'

She led him up to her room and clicked on the pink light again.

'Cosy isn't it?' he said. She thought there might have been a touch of sarcasm in his voice, but she ignored it.

'Take your kit off,' she said, as she slipped out of her dress.

The sight of the young woman in her bra and panties genuinely aroused him and for a fleeting moment he wished that he could just make love to her and leave. But he couldn't, so he wiped such thoughts from his mind.

'Come on,' she said with some impatience when she saw that he was still standing there in his raincoat. 'We can't do anything with your clothes on.'

'Let me ... let me kiss you first,' he said, awkwardly. 'It works better for me that way.'

She shrugged. 'All right.'

He put his arms around her and hugged her closely to him. Mechanically, she closed her eyes and then, in her darkness, she felt his hands around her throat.

twenty

Frank Hall wasn't sure whether it was the effects of the beer or the arthritis that made climbing up the stairs more of a challenge these days, but certainly it took him longer to reach the landing than it used to. He reckoned that he'd have to throw old age into the frame as well. He wasn't getting any younger.

With much puffing and panting he hauled himself up to the top. As he paused to catch his breath his eye was caught by the pink glow emanating from a room further along the landing. Someone had left their door open.

'That's a silly thing to do,' he muttered to himself.

Curious, he went along to investigate.

He stood on the threshold of the room. There was no sound or movement within. 'Hello,' he said politely and tapped gently on the door.

There was no reply.

Instinctively, he put his head inside the room and the sight that greeted his eyes made him gasp. His old heart thudded with the shock and he felt unsteady on his feet. Grasping the door for support, he stared transfixed at the tableau before him.

On the bed lay a young woman. She was dressed only in her bra and panties. Her mouth was agape, the tongue protruding lifelessly, while her eyes, wide with fright, were held in a rigid, fixed stare focused on some point on the ceiling. On the girl's forehead was a red smudge; it looked like the number three.

Frank was sure that she was dead. Dead as a doornail.

twenty-one

Somehow the charms of Ruritanian adventure and the dashing exploits of Rupert Rassendyll failed to weave their magic for me this time round. As I sat in the darkened auditorium watching *The Prisoner of Zenda*, my mind kept slipping back to the more dramatic scenes in my own recent life: Barbara's attempt to shoot Guy Cooper at the Britannia Club; the conversation I'd had with Cooper and Sir Howard McLean inviting me to join their gang of murdering thugs; and the lovely Eunice and the problem she presented. All these things seemed far more engrossing and disturbing than Ronald Colman's attempt to impersonate the King of Ruritania at his coronation.

Despite my wandering attention, I did stay to the end of the show, even enduring the inane antics of The Three Stooges in a noisy and unfunny supporting short, because I really had nothing better to do. When I came out of the cinema I grabbed a cuppa from a tea-stall in Leicester Square and then wandered the streets for some time, turning events over and over in my mind again, trying to formulate a plan of action. It wasn't a fruitful exercise. I wasn't good at planning. I was a spur of the moment man.

By the time I had grown weary of my thoughtful perambulations it was dusk and I found my feet leading me to the Velvet Cage. Perhaps some jazz and a few shots of Johnnie Walker would help ease my worries. That was my usual excuse anyway.

It was still fairly early when I padded my way down the stairs into the club, yet it was quite busy. Tommy Parker and the boys were on their first set and I saw that Beulah White was sitting by the band ready to warble. Beulah, a coloured girl, had been a fine singer with a sexy, smooth voice but unfortunately she had a fondness for a certain white substance which had played havoc with her vocal chords and had raddled her once pretty features. She was probably still only in her thirties but looked at least ten years older. She still knew how to handle a song, but listening to her I was constantly reminded of what she could have been and this added a tinge of melancholy to all her performances.

She gave me a wave as I headed for the bar and then got up to sing 'Every Time We Say Goodbye'. As she clung to the microphone, eyes closed, the hubbub of the club quietened. The lyrics, half-whispered, half sung, were moving and poignant. With the war pressing against the window-pane of all our lives, they meant some thing to everyone:

> Every time we say goodbye, I die a little
> Every time, we say goodbye, I wonder why a little ...

For a short while the audience were caught up and bonded in a common experience by the sentiment of the song. We all had our private realities and sadnesses touched by the lyrics and by the singer's simple but telling delivery. Couples leaned in towards each other, holding hands on the table, reminded of the frailty of love and the uncertainty of relationships in the time of war.

I waited until Beulah had finished singing before ordering a drink. By the time I'd been served she was on her next number, an up-tempo version of ''S Wonderful'. It was as if she had pulled a switch: the audience relaxed once more and the hum of conversation had returned. For them the moment of introspection had gone, but it had touched me deeply. The song had reminded me of how alone I was in the world. I had no one to care for me, to be concerned about and equally there was no one to worry about my safety, to hold me tight in the darkness while the bombs were falling. Although a grown man, I was still an orphan.

Suddenly the whisky tasted sour and I wanted no more of it. I wanted my bed. I wanted to pull the covers over my head and escape from my own reality.

twenty-two

Detective Inspector David Llewellyn gazed down at the dead girl, his eyes focused on the red smudge of lipstick on her forehead, marking out the number three.

'He leaves us in no doubt it's the same man, doesn't he?' he said, almost to himself.

Sergeant Sunderland, who was rummaging through a chest of drawers, searching for clues, did not reply. He realized that he could add nothing constructive to his superior's observation.

'He's been bolder this time,' continued Llewellyn, still airing his thoughts to himself. 'Coming indoors with the girl, risking being seen.'

Sunderland gave a non-commital grunt and dropped to his hands and knees to search the floor. Surely a man could not come into a room, murder a girl and leave nothing behind. There must be some trace of him here, something, however small. He would have appreciated a little help in his search for that something but his boss remained resolutely rooted to the spot mumbling to himself.

Llewellyn was gazing around the dingy room, bathed in a garish pink light, a sense of angry despair starting to grip him. The killer had struck again and there appeared to be no more clues to his identity than there had been with the other two murders. The bastard was laughing at them.

Outside on the landing the old codger who'd found the body was being interviewed by a constable, but Llewellyn knew instinctively that he would not be able to add anything fresh to what they already knew, which was, in the inspector's estimation, close to bugger-all. At this rate the murderer could go on killing for years with impunity. He could litter London with the corpses of strangled girls.

He snatched up the girl's bag from the chair and examined it again. There was not much in there: some lipstick and other make-up, a pack of johnnies – tools of the trade – and quite a bit of cash.

'That's all he does it for. The kicks he gets from killing. Money doesn't interest him.'

'Got something here, sir,' cried Sunderland excitedly, extracting a small object from the bottom of the girl's wardrobe. He thrust a leather wallet at his boss. 'What do you make of that?'

The two men exchanged serious glances.

Llewellyn took the wallet and examined the contents. He grinned. 'Yes, I think we do have something here: ID card and the address of a guest-house. Paddington area. A virtual treasure-trove. Someone up there has been listening to my prayers.'

'D'you think it's possible that our man dropped it?'

'Oh, oh, boyo, we can only hope so. We can only hope. The wallet's empty but the girl's purse is full of cash. Too much of a coincidence, I'd say. Seems like she pulled a fast one before he did the poor cow in. We'd better act quickly on this and get over to The Mount guest house in Paddington right away. We don't want our man to do a bunk. PC Anderson can take charge here until the pathologist turns up.'

'Right ho, sir.'

Llewellyn afforded himself a little smile as he slipped the wallet into his pocket.

A lady in a blue candlewick dressing-gown and her grey hair in curlers eventually answered the persistent ringing of the door-bell at The Mount guest-house.

'What on earth do you want? Can't you see the sign in the window: we're full up.'

Llewellyn held up his badge. 'Police.'

'Lord above!' cried the woman. 'What d'you want? This is a respectable house.'

'I've no doubt, but we need to speak to one of your guests.'

Her face dropped. 'I suppose you'd better come in then.'

*

The soldier was vaguely aware of a sudden bright light and strangers in his room. He tried to rouse himself from his drink-fuelled slumbers but his mind desperately sought the comfort of sleep. Someone shook his shoulder and called out his name. He nodded vaguely and his head thundered when he moved it. It was like a surreal dream. Strange shadows crept up the wall as two dark shapes crowded his blurred vision. He tried to speak but his mouth was dry and his tongue felt like a piece of old carpet.

His recent past came floating back to him. He really had drunk far more than he should have. After leaving Mary he had headed for the nearest public house and started drinking. Strangely, despite having spent time love-making with a pretty girl, he had felt more dispirited than he had done before. It really had been an empty experience and had brought no joy to him. Neither did the alcohol but it did act as a kind of anaesthetic. When he left the pub to return to The Mount guest house he was well and truly drunk. He knew he was too far gone to attempt flagging down a taxi so it took him an hour to stagger through the darkened streets to the Paddington address. On reaching his room, he had flung his coat off and flopped, fully clothed, on to the bed and immediately fallen into a drunken coma.

Now he was being roused from it. He heard his name being called again and then suddenly one of the dark shapes was shaking him violently in an attempt to bring him into the land of the living. His brain swished around on a sea of stale alcohol and nothing seemed to make any kind of sense any more.

He licked his lips, running his tongue along the cracked, dry skin and tried to speak but his mouth had ceased to work properly and his words came out in an indistinct and slurred fashion.

'Whaddya wan' wi' me? Who are yuh?' he heard himself say.

'Police. We are arresting you on suspicion of murder.'

'Murther? What yuh talking 'bout?'

'We've got to get this bastard back to the Yard and sobered up before we can get any sense out of him,' said one of the dark shapes.

The soldier didn't hear the end of this sentence. He had slipped back into inebriate slumber.

twenty-three

Eunice leaned over and gave me a full-blown kiss directly on the lips. It was a sensuous, pleasurable experience but it couldn't eradicate the worry I felt about the coronation. Sir Howard McLean stepped forward with the crown of Ruritania ready to place it on my head. I tried to look as regal as possible but as he approached I could see that his eyes grew suspicious. Oh, my God, I thought, he's seen through my deception. I would be denounced as an impostor.

And then there came the almighty screech, an insistent, high-pitched irregular screech which pierced my brain and shattered the dream like a broken mirror. Bright shards of light splintered my mind. I sat up with a start in the darkness. The cathedral, my regal robes and Princess Eunice had all vanished and like little Dorothy I was back home again. Back home in my poky bedroom in my lumpy bed with the telephone ringing fit to bust.

I clicked on the bedside lamp and shook off the fragments of sleep and the unsettling dream. 'John Hawke,' I muttered into the receiver. My brain wasn't really sharp enough yet to have formulated any thought as to who this caller could be, but I hoped that whoever it was they had a damn good reason for interrupting my coronation at three in the morning.

'Good morning, boyo. Rise and shine,' came a voice crackling out of the receiver.

It was Llewellyn, sounding as bright as a button.

'David? What the hell do you want?'

'Sorry to interrupt your beauty sleep, I know how desperately you need it.'

'David, you've heard of the point. I would be obliged if you'd get to it,' I growled with some irritation.

'There's been a development in the blackout strangling case.'

'I'm pleased for you.'

'I think we've got our man.'

'At last we can all sleep safely in our beds. Good-night.'

'Hang on, Johnny. I'm not just ringing to tell you that. There's something more.'

Suddenly his voice sounded serious, apprehensive. The joviality was replaced by a kind of dark awkwardness which was unsettling. The little antennae in my brain which usually pick up danger signals started receiving messages.

'What is it?' I said warily.

'Look … this isn't something to discuss over the phone. I'd like you to come down to the Yard.'

'You mean now?'

'Yeah. It would be best.'

I glanced at my watch. 'At 3 a.m?'

'I wouldn't be asking you if it wasn't important.'

I ran my fingers through my hair and sighed. 'Now I'll never know if I was crowned or not.'

'What?'

'Nothing, I'm just rambling. I'll be there within half an hour.'

'Thanks Johnny. See you then.'

The line went dead.

What on earth was that all about? I wondered as I dragged myself out of bed. Whatever it was, the phone call left me feeling very uneasy. I was sure that it must be serious and urgent for old Llewellyn to want me to go down at the Yard in the early hours of the morning. What increased my feeling of disquiet was David's tone of voice. I knew him well enough to sense that he was very uncomfortable about something – something that involved yours truly. Like a terrier, this thought worried at my nerves as I scrambled into my clothes.

Ten minutes later I was out on the dark silent streets. It seemed, apart from a couple of cats rehearsing for an evening at Covent Garden, that I had the city to myself – for a while at least. I hurried as fast as I could on to Tottenham Court Road where I hoped I might spy a taxi. I was out of luck. All self-respecting Londoners were curled up in their beds at this time of day, or were down in the underground stations on makeshift mattresses and, so I reckoned, were all the taxi-drivers too. I hurried down Charing Cross Road as far as Cambridge Circus, where I spotted the lone cab, the desperate cabbie searching for fares in a deserted city. I had no trouble in flagging him down.

The policeman on duty at the entrance to Scotland Yard directed me to a little office just beyond the gates of the great building. Here a grizzled old sergeant, who seemed to be expecting me, rang through to 'Inspector Llewellyn' and then told me to take a seat. I did so and waited in a nervous feet-shuffling mode for about five minutes until a young dark-haired man came for me. I recognized him as David's sergeant. I'd met him briefly once before.

We exchanged nods and brief tight smiles of recognition, then he took me off along a maze of dimly lighted corridors and up several flights of stairs until we arrived at David's office.

My old friend shook my hand gravely. 'Glad you could make it,' he said without a trace of his old trademark *bonhomie*.

'I hope I'll be glad too, after you've told me what this is all about,' I said, plonking myself down on a chair opposite his desk.

'As I said on the phone, I think we've got the blackout strangler....'

'Yes, yes ... and?'

'Another girl was murdered tonight. Another prostitute. The killer changed his tactics somewhat. No doorway, this time. He carried out the deed at her own place. They'd gone back for sex and he strangled her on the bed.'

'How did you catch him?'

David pursed his lips and thought for a moment. 'It was as though he wanted to be caught. After he'd done the girl in, he left the door of her room wide open so the body would be discovered pretty quickly. And she was. An old bloke who lives in the same house found her. We were there within a couple of hours of her death.'

'Then we got lucky,' intervened the sergeant. 'We found the wallet.'

'The wallet?'

David picked up a small brown wallet from the desk. 'This. It belongs to our man. It contains all the details we needed to pick up the owner. We found it in the dead girl's wardrobe'.

'Her wardrobe?'

'We think that she took the wallet from his jacket before ...'

'Surely he would have noticed.'

David shrugged. 'Not necessarily. But maybe. Yes. Maybe.' He leaned forward over the desk. 'Maybe he wanted to be caught.'

This was fanciful. Claptrap, in other words. What murderer wants to be caught? I wasn't convinced at all. It was more wishful thinking than sound psychology. It was rare for a killer on a winning streak to feel the need to give the game up. However, I could be wrong. I let it pass for the moment.

'So you caught him,' I said, with a touch of sarcasm.

David nodded. 'We caught him. We've got him under lock and key.'

'And you all lived happily ever after! Now where the hell do I come in? Why have you dragged me down here in the middle of the night?'

Llewellyn grimaced and looked away. 'Sort of out of courtesy, I suppose.'

'What the hell are you talking about?' Whatever the game was, I wanted it to be over.

'I think it would be best if you see for yourself,' said David, pushing back his chair and standing. 'Come down to the cells and have a look.'

Without any further conversation I followed the two policemen along another set of corridors and down different flights of stairs until we were in the land of the choky, the lock-up. Outside cell three a burly constable was standing guard. He saluted at David as we approached.

'Constable,' said David wearily. 'I just want have a gander at our likely lad.'

'Yes sir,' came the muted reply.

David pulled back the metal plate of the spy-hole and stared into the cell. He muttered something to himself and then turned to me. 'Have a look for yourself, Johnny. Feast your eyes on our murderer.'

I looked through the spy-hole and saw a man sitting on a low camp-bed. He was staring ahead of him with an expression that I can only describe as bewildered despair. But it wasn't his expression that made my blood run cold. It was the man's face. It was one I knew well. It belonged to my brother.

twenty-four

As the sky lightened the rain came. Heavy, slashing, cleansing rain. He awoke to the sound of it beating against his window. As always it took him a while to remember the pain, to remember his fate. In those few precious waking moments before his consciousness kicked in he was his old self, his old unsullied relatively carefree self once more. The clock had been turned back. He was an innocent again. The future was his to grasp and mould into whatever shape he wished. It was like a small miracle.

And then the miracle faded. His mind and his body brought the truth back into focus. The ache made itself known again. It too had woken and, it seemed, had renewed its vigour. Nevertheless, he would cope with it. He had to cope with it. It was part of him now.

For a while he lay on his back listening to the rain, the insistent rhythmic thrash against the glass; then gradually his thoughts drifted back to the events of the previous night. Images, almost like faded photographs, slipped into his mind: the garish pink room, the pattern of the girl's hair spread wildly on the pillow like tendrils of some exotic underwater creature, the way she had struggled, her body undulating, almost like the sex act itself; and her wax dummy stare of terror after he had killed her. He had never seen these things in such detail before. The first two murders had been hurried affairs carried out in darkened doorways. Last night he had had the luxury of observing the process clearly and having the time afterwards to view the scene and appreciate things. He smiled at his use of the word 'luxury'. It seemed so ridiculously incongruous and yet so apt.

He couldn't go back now. No more doorways. He would kill the next one on her own bed too. It would be so satisfying.

The sharp sudden pain in his groin wiped the glee from his features and he grimaced. He waited for the ache to subside and then he got out of bed, padded into the little kitchen to make himself a cup of tea. He swilled down a number of the pills that the doctor had given him, along with some aspirins, hoping that they would ease the pain. Then, he sat down and lit a cigarette.

The rain still beat against the windows.

After a time he washed himself and shaved. He stared at the gaunt, tired features in the shaving mirror. The illness was taking its toll. His face was beginning to melt. For a moment a wave of futility swept over him. What was the point of anything really? Why bother? Why struggle on? It would be so much easier to have done with it all, to retreat for ever into that great unwaking sleep. He gripped the razor tightly pressing it gently against the jugular vein. Should he? He stared hard at his reflection, daring himself. And then his hand began to shake.

He closed his eyes and the moment passed.

Despite the rain and the ache, the day was calling. He had commitments to fulfil. He had to appear normal to the outside world – a little longer at least.

He finished shaving quickly before any more unsettling thoughts could come to him, dried his face and returned the bedroom. Glancing at the clock on the bedside table he saw that it was later than he'd thought. He'd better get a move on. He didn't want to be reprimanded for being late. He must not do anything which would draw attention to himself.

He opened the wardrobe and reached for his uniform.

twenty-five

I was in some kind of daze. Seeing my brother in London was surprise enough when I thought that he was serving overseas somewhere, but to find him banged up in a police cell on a murder charge just twisted up the notches on my emotional dial into shock mode. It was as though I was taking part in a play where everyone else knew the plot but me. As I gazed through the spy-hole, I shook my head in disbelief, not able to come up with anything coherent to say, so I just swore.

David Llewellyn nodded grimly and placed a hand on my shoulder. 'Let's have a cup of tea in my office, eh? I've got a spot of brandy up there and then I'll put you in the picture.'

Without a word we returned to his office, leaving behind my brother Paul in that small grey cell in the bowels of Scotland Yard.

Over tea, enlivened by the brandy, David explained in detail about the murder of Mary Callan, the prostitute, the discovery of Paul's wallet in her room and how they'd picked him up at a hotel in Paddington. Apparently he'd still been too drunk to say much, but he had admitted – David used the word 'confessed' – that he'd had sex with the girl that night.

'But it's all circumstantial evidence,' I said, still trying to make sense of this whole mad scenario. 'Just because he'd been with the girl doesn't mean he killed her. She could have had other punters after Paul.'

'It's possible, but unlikely. We still have a lot of investigating to do but he's the main bloke in the frame at the moment.'

'But Paul wouldn't kill anyone. He's not ... he's not a murderer.'

'What is he doing in London?' It was Sergeant Sunderland who asked this.

I shook my head. 'I've no idea. I didn't know he was here.'

'That's not surprising,' continued Sunderland in a smug manner. 'It would seem that Sergeant Paul Hawke is absent without leave and has been missing from his regiment for over three weeks.'

My shock dial went up another couple of notches and I found myself repeating the phrase: 'absent without leave' with a growing sense of unease. My certainties were flying out of the window.

''Fraid so Johnny,' said David. 'Soon as we got him back here I checked with the War Office. The night staff were remarkably efficient. Apparently Paul had been granted ten days' leave but he didn't return to his regiment. He's been away almost a month.'

'Just about the time the murders started,' observed Sunderland.

'This is ridiculous. It doesn't make sense. Why would he want to kill these girls…?'

David shrugged. 'Well, that's a question I've never been able to answer about murders of this kind. There are those who kill for gain or for hate or in anger, that's understandable I suppose, if not acceptable. But this type of murder, cold-blooded, motiveless…. Who knows what's going on in the disturbed mind of a fellow like that?'

Anger flared within him. Paul wasn't 'a fellow like that'. He wasn't some homicidal maniac. There must be some mistake here. And yet what the hell was he doing in London and not contacting me? Why had he not returned to his regiment when his leave was up? That didn't make sense either. There were too many uncomfortable questions hanging in the air.

'Can I talk to him? Perhaps I can get some sense out of him? I'm sure there's going to be a simple explanation for all this.'

David stroked his chin thoughtfully. 'I suppose so,' he said at length. 'It might help both of us see a clearer picture. But I couldn't let you go in there alone at this stage, Johnny. I'd have to come in with you. You're a friend, but there are procedures and this is a serious murder case.'

'Whatever you say,' I shrugged impatiently. 'But can we get on with it?'

*

As the cell door opened Paul stiffened and his bleary eyes focused on the door. When he saw me his jaw dropped open. I could see that his befuddled mind was searching for a suitable emotion. His eyes flickered with uncertainty as he staggered to his feet and took a step forward. I did the rest. I hugged him tight, the way he'd hugged and comforted me all those years ago in the orphanage when I got frightened in the darkness of the night. We said nothing. Words seemed superfluous.

I felt his body shudder with emotion. How strange it was for me now to be the one who hugged more tightly, who gave the comfort.

David Llewellyn closed the cell door and stood at a distance waiting patiently while this emotional reunion ran its course.

'Can you get me out of here, Johnny?' Paul said at last, breaking free of my embrace.

'It's not going to be that easy,' I said. 'You've a lot of talking to do.'

He slumped back on to the bed. 'I guess so. Where d'you want me to start?'

I glanced at David and he gave me the nod to go ahead. He was letting me lead with the questioning. I knew he wasn't just being considerate. It was a wise move. Surely Paul would open up more easily to his brother than a stranger.

'They tell me that you're absent without leave.'

'I don't know what's happened to me. I just … I just couldn't take it any more. I lost friends…. Oh I don't know. It all seemed so futile. Day after day of it. I just needed to get away. To escape. I had leave … I thought that would help, but when it was over I just couldn't face going back. I just couldn't. I was sick, physically sick at the thought of it. I wanted to lose myself….'

This wasn't the strong, confident and resolute brother I knew. I had never seen him like this before.

'Why on earth didn't you get in touch with me?' I asked gently.

'What could I say to you? How could you help? The trouble was inside of me. In here.' He tapped his forehead.

'Where did you go? What did you do?'

Paul ruffled his hair and put his head in his hands. 'I don't know. Can't remember now.'

I glanced at David who rolled his eyes at me. He had been right. This wasn't going to be so simple. Even in the short time I'd spent with Paul I realized that I didn't know him now. In fact it seemed that he didn't really know himself. I felt the cold clammy hand of truth rest heavily on my shoulder. Seeing my brother in this confused condition, I no longer felt confident in my assertion that he could not have committed these murders. He was obviously very disturbed and in a state of mental instability. Who knew what he was capable of?

'How long have you been in London?' It was David who asked this question. He saw that I was lost for words.

'A few days I think. I'm ... I'm just a bit confused. I had a lot to drink last night. I need to rest ... I just want to sleep. It will be better when I've had some sleep.'

'Sure lad, we'll let you rest. There'll be plenty of time for questions later but before we go, just tell us about Mary.'

Paul turned his bleary eyes to us. 'Mary?'

'The girl you went with last night.'

'Mary ... yes. Mary.' His brow contracted as he desperately tried to bring the events of previous evening into focus.

'Where did you meet her?' continued David.

'In a pub.'

'Which one?'

He shook his head. 'Don't know. Never been there before.'

'You picked the girl up.'

'I suppose so. I think it was more the other way around.'

'You knew she was a prostitute?'

'Well, yes. I saw her with another customer.'

'When? When was this?' I snapped. I wanted to shake him. Shake him soundly until he pulled himself together, flipped out of this crazy act.

'I was at the bar. Someone came up to her ... but she was with me. I think she liked me. She told him she was busy....'

'And you went back to her place for sex?'

'Yes.'

David moved forward and crouched down by Paul so that their faces were on a level.

'And that's where you killed her.'

For a moment Paul stared dreamily at David. And then shook his head. 'Kill her? No. I didn't kill her. Surely ... I didn't kill her. Did I?'

I leaned sideways pressing my forehead on to the cold grey wall and moaned softly.

twenty-six

'Don't tell me the love-boat, she hit the rocks already.'
Benny stood by my table, frowning at me and flapping a damp tea-towel like it was a cat o' nine tails and he was about to administer some medieval punishment.

'Look, the love-boat never got launched. It's all in your romantic imagination.'

'You can't kid me, Mr Johnny One Eye. The way you looked at that young lady with the bumpity-bump of the heart.'

'Bumpity-bump of the heart! You should write lyrics. Jack Hilton could use you.'

'Don't try to change the subject. What have you done to that lovely girl ... that lovely Jewish girl?'

'I've done nothing to her....'

Benny nodded in what I assumed he regarded was a wise and perceptive fashion. 'That's maybe the trouble.'

'Look,' I said, lowering my voice, not wanting my private life to provide a floor show for Benny's early diners, 'the girl is a client. Just a client. She got herself into a bit of trouble and I'm sorting it out for her. That's all there is to it. No romance, no engagement-ring, no church service.'

'A client? No romance?'

'That's it. No romance.'

Benny wrinkled his nose. 'There should be. You'd be a mug to pass up on such a looker.'

'No romance,' I repeated emphatically, hoping to close down this particular topic of conversation.

'So why d'you look as though you're carrying the world on your shoulders this morning?'

I grimaced. 'Ah ... I got a few problems. Things on my mind. Life is a little ... grubby just now.'

'You want to tell me about it?'

I summoned a grin. I didn't want to hurt the nosy old beggar's feelings, he only meant well. At times I really appreciated his mother-hen concerns for my welfare but at present I was not in the mood to spill the beans about my brother being arrested for murder or to discuss my role as cheerleader for the Britannia Club hoodlums. 'What I really want,' I said conspiratorially, 'is to have a cup of tea and a bacon sandwich.'

Benny curled his nose up. 'OK. I can take a hint. Anything else?'

'A little peace and quiet?'

'There will come a time when you'll be more than happy to bend old Benny's ear. But don't be so sure that he will be so obliging.'

My reserves of *bonhomie* were running on empty that morning. I could hardly produce a thin smile to placate my old friend, so I just nodded.

Benny frowned and leaned in close. 'Say, you are down in the dumps today.'

I nodded again. Benny gave me a gentle pat on the back and disappeared into the kitchen.

I glanced at my watch; it was just creeping up to 8 a.m. I felt tired and miserable and at a loss for what to do. Tea and a bacon sandwich might help. It was too early for whisky.

David had agreed to let Paul have a good eight hours' kip before interviewing him again. At least then he'd be fairly fresh and alcohol free and, it was to be hoped, he would make more sense. But I was worried. Even allowing for the tiredness and the booze, brother Paul now seemed a stranger to me. I felt fear. Deep down in the pit of my stomach, I felt fear. Could he really have killed all these women? Surely not? Not my big brother. But if he'd had some kind of mental breakdown...? There was no certainty any more.

What the hell was I going to do?

Absent-mindedly I poured some grains of sugar on to the table-top and chased them around with my finger. I trapped the grains by the sauce-bottle and pressed down on them until they had stuck to my finger, then gently I sucked at the sweetness.

Benny returned with my tea and sandwich and plonked them down before me.

'There we are, Mr Detectiveman. Enjoy.'

I looked up at him and suddenly smiled. Trust Benny – he'd hit the proverbial nail on the head. 'Thank you,' I said with warmth.

'What did I do?' he asked, somewhat surprised.

'You answered my question.'

'What question?'

'It doesn't matter, but thanks.'

'Any time,' he said with a bewildered shrug, before leaving me to my breakfast.

Mr Detectiveman took a satisfying gulp of hot tea.

Mr Detectiveman, that's me, I thought to myself, that's what I do. And that's what I'll have to do, if I'm going to find out the truth about brother Paul.

I spent the rest of the morning visiting the little hotel where Paul had been staying when he was arrested. The place was run by an elderly couple called Parkinson who were reluctant to talk to me. I learned very little from them, mainly because there was very little to learn. Paul had only booked into the place the day before and had paid for two nights. He seemed a normal, quiet sort of a chap, but they realized how wrong they'd been when the police knocked them up in the middle of the night to cart him away. Where Paul had been before that remained a mystery. The police had taken all his belongings to Scotland Yard so there was no chance of my examining them.

As I travelled back to Hawke Towers on the tube I tried not to be too disheartened by my lack of success. There was so much I didn't know yet but I did think that it was significant that Paul had given his real name to the Parkinsons, which was not the action of a soldier on the run or, indeed, a murderer. A trawl of the public houses in the vicinity where Mary Callan had lived and operated was probably my next move, but before I could do that I had an appointment with a pretty girl. One that Benny would never forgive me for missing.

On arriving back at the office I shaved and tidied myself and the place up a bit. I was expecting Barbara at one o'clock and although there was no romance, as I'd told Benny, I didn't want her to get the impression that I was an untidy slob.

One o'clock, the time she was due to arrive, came and went. I smoked a couple of cigarettes, paced the floor and waited. Then it was two o'clock but still no show. The girl wasn't coming. At first I was puzzled, then apprehensive, and finally worried. At 2.30, I slipped on my coat and hat and decided to investigate. If she wasn't coming to my place I'd go to hers.

I hadn't been in the East End for sometime and I was shocked to see how much damage the Luftwaffe had done to the area. Great acres of land lay waste where rows of small terrace homes had been reduced to piles of grey doll's-house bricks. It was an alien landscape conjured up by a twentieth-century Brueghel. Children were playing, clambering over the rubble of what had once been someone's front parlour or back kitchen. Their incongruous innocent cries of joy made the scene all the more poignant.

Barbara lived somewhere in this no man's land, in Balaclava Street, in one of the remaining clutch of surviving districts south of Aldgate. Balaclava Street was a dreary anonymous thoroughfare embedded in a section of similar streets built in the early part of the nineteenth century for the influx of workers who flocked to London at that time. Cheap, cramped houses where the swinging of the proverbial cat was impossible. There were rows upon rows of these houses, identical, featureless and impoverished. Fagin would have felt at home here.

Barbara had given me her address as 34. I walked slowly down this dreary street, checking off the numbers as I went.

Eventually I reached number 34.

It was still smouldering.

Wisps of smoke were escaping through the darkened apertures where the lower ground windows had been. Blackened net curtains flapped gently outwards into the daylight and the stench of damp ash filled the air.

The charred front door was ajar. As I stepped forward a thin harsh voice assailed my ear.

'There's nobody at home, mister,' it cackled with barbed sarcasm.

I turned and saw an old crone standing in the doorway of the house next door. Her arms were folded across her thin chest in an aggressive manner and her dark brown eyes, set in her gaunt wrinkled face, viewed me with a mixture of suspicion and aggression.

'What happened?' I asked, letting my hand travel gently down the blistered wood of the front door.

'What's it look like? There was a fire, wasn't there?'

'How?'

'Well, it weren't the Jerries this time. Petrol bomb through the window. I saw the geezer running off.'

I felt sick. My stomach lurched as I realized with a cruel clarity the implication of what had happened. It was revenge. Of course it was. The damned Britannia Club. Their thugs had done this. I took a step forward and pushed open the blackened front door. It was like staring into a large ashtray.

'I shouldn't go in there, mister,' the crone advised. 'It's not safe.'

She was right, of course, and there was no point in my trying anyway. 'What about the family?' I asked, turning to face the old woman.

She shook her head and suddenly the taut, harsh features softened and the eyes moistened. 'Poor Mrs Cogan ... caught upstairs. Not a hope. I heard her screams. Rotten it was. The young lass was rushed off to hospital but ...' She shook her head again. 'She looked bad. Not much hope.'

'Which hospital?'

'St Bart's I think I heard the ambulance man say. Who are you anyway?'

'A friend.'

'Never seen you before round here.'

'No ... but a friend none the less.'

'You got a fag, then?'

I passed her one and lit it for her.

'Ta,' she said, her face disappearing briefly in a cloud of

smoke. 'It was those bleeding fascists if you ask me. They've caused trouble round here before. As if we ain't got enough trouble with bleedin' Hitler trying to bomb us to bits....'

The fascists it was. I should have realized that they wouldn't let Barbara return to her normal life after she had rippled their deep waters. They weren't going to let her get off that lightly. The Jewish bitch! They intended to make her pay. A red-hot wave of anger swept over me. If I could have got my hands on Guy Cooper or Sir Howard McLean at that moment I would have beaten their brains in with my bare hands.

'The bastards,' I barked, thumping the wall of the house in angry frustration.

'You said it, mister,' said the woman. 'You said it: bastards.'

And then she closed her door, shutting out me and the desolate, threatening world beyond the confines of her little house.

twenty-seven

The door of the locker-room opened. PC O'Connell, who was lacing up his boots, looked up and saw Lowe enter. He looked weary, with dark shadows under his eyes. He shambled in like a man sleepwalking. O'Connell had noticed a change in his colleague in the last month. He had always been a quiet, self-contained sort of a bloke, not easy in company and stilted in conversation, but recently it was as though he had become more isolated than ever. It was as though he had given up on life, given up trying and was merely going through the motions, waiting for something to happen. Death possibly. The war did strange things to people and certainly Lowe was not unique in seeming to be affected in this way. O'Connell just thanked his lucky stars that he never took life so seriously that it would interfere with his optimistic outlook. He could cope, if others couldn't.

'Hey, heard the latest? They've caught the strangler,' O'Connell said cheerily, expecting the good news to raise the spirits of his colleague, but Lowe stopped in his tracks and stared at him uncomprehendingly.

'It's true,' O'Connell added. 'No joke. Llewellyn nabbed him last night after the blighter had just done another girl in. Number three.'

Lowe felt dizzy, the room swaying before his eyes. With some relief he sat down on the bench next to O'Connell. 'That is ... good news,' he mumbled without enthusiasm.

'You can say that again. Takes a bit of pressure off us lot, doesn't it? Now we can stop watching our backs and return to our normal duties: nabbing the black-market spivs.' He chuckled to himself.

'Well, there are plenty of those about,' Lowe responded, raising a weak smile, while his mind was still coming to terms with the shock of hearing that someone had been arrested for the murders – the murders that he had committed. He had never contemplated this eventuality and he really didn't know how he felt about it.

'Who is this strangler character then? What do you know about him?' he asked as casually as his numbed brain would allow.

O'Connell shrugged. 'Some soldier who's gone a bit batty. He was AWOL. Apparently the stupid blighter dropped his wallet in the tart's bedroom.'

Lowe closed his eyes and remembered. The tart's bedroom: that garish pink glow, the squalid furnishings, the pale corpse on the bed and those dead staring eyes. This vision was vividly imprinted in his mind. Of course, he suddenly realized, they'd caught the young chap Mary had picked up in the pub, the one he'd followed to her flat.

'Where is he now?'

'Down below. In the cells, of course, waiting for ... "the big interview".' O'Connell laughed at his own dramatic delivery. 'The big confession, more like. He won't be able to wriggle out of this one. He's for the noose all right.'

Lowe looked blankly ahead and gave a ghost of a nod.

'Well, I'm off to the canteen for a cuppa before I brave the naughty streets again,' O'Connell said breezily. 'See you later.'

'See you later,' Lowe responded in a monotone.

On being left alone, Lowe ruffled his hair absent-mindedly and tried to assess the situation. What do I do now? he thought. What on earth do I do now?

Ten minutes later Lowe had made his way down to the cells. Sergeant Braddock was on duty and he raised a cynical brow as Lowe lumbered towards him.

'Not another one. This ain't a peep show, y'know,' he said.

'Sorry, Sarge?' replied Lowe, uncertain what Braddock meant.

'I've had a steady stream of 'em all afternoon.'

Lowe still remained puzzled.

'Coppers coming along to have a look at the new guest – our little strangler. I could start charging a penny a peek. It'd help supplement my pension. That's what you're here for, ain't it? To have a gander at the strangler.' He gave wheezy chortle in appreciation of his own wit.

Lowe nodded. 'Well, yes ... I just wanted to see what sort of person he was.'

Braddock emitted a strange tutting noise. 'Never seen a murderer afore, eh? Grown copper like you.'

Lowe shook his head shyly. 'Thought it might be useful to see what sort of man goes around killing young girls.'

'That's a new one,' beamed Braddock, his boozer's face wrinkling with amusement once more. 'Most of the lads just want a peek out of morbid curiosity.'

'Well, that as well,' admitted Lowe, trying not to let the growing frustration show in his voice. Why didn't the old bastard just let him pass?

'Be quick then. He's in cell three. He's nothing special, mind. He doesn't have horns or a tail. You'd never notice him in the street – but then that's like most killers and that's why most killers get away with it.'

'Thanks, Sarge,' said Lowe. Thanks also for the lecture on killers. If you only but knew ... eh?

Lowe pulled back the metal plate of the spy-hole and stared into cell three. He saw a man sitting on the edge of the bed, staring despondently into space. He was in his early thirties, of average height, with plain regular features and a mop of unruly hair which was already tinged with grey at the temples. He looked very normal, very average, very innocent. Braddock was right. You would pass him in the street without a second glance. But it was a face Lowe had seen before. It was the soldier from last night. The girl's last client. Poor bastard, he thought with some compassion, so they're pinning the job lot on you. This had never been part of his plans and he felt somewhat confused.

'Do you want a photograph?'

The voice came from behind him, whispered gently in his ear.

Lowe turned and found himself facing Detective Inspector Llewellyn.

'Sorry, sir. I just—'

With some irritation, Llewellyn held up his hand to silence him. 'I know, I know. You were just curious.'

A red-faced and embarrassed Sergeant Braddock stood in the background. Llewellyn had obviously had words with him.

'Seen enough?' asked Llewellyn.

'Yes, sir.'

'Well, you can see a little more.' He thrust a large key into his hand. 'Open up.'

For a moment Lowe thought the inspector was joking, but the steady glint in his eyes told him otherwise.

Lowe did as he was told. He turned the key in the ancient lock, the grating sound echoing down the grim corridor.

Llewellyn stepped forward, pushed the door open and entered the cell.

Paul Hawke jumped to his feet, his tired eyes anxious and desperate.

'How are you feeling, Mr Hawke?' asked the inspector, in the casual easy manner he might use when enquiring after a friend's health.

Hawke did not know how to reply.

'Are you up to answering a few questions? Sort things out a little, eh?'

'If it means getting out of here, yes,' came the reply, a little more assertive than Llewellyn had expected.

The inspector gave a grim smile. 'Can't promise that, I'm afraid ... but you never know.' He turned to Braddock. 'Come on in here, Sergeant and bring your note-pad.'

As Braddock squeezed past the tall, imposing figure of Lowe, Paul Hawke noticed the constable for the first time. As he moved to allow the sergeant through the door, his face emerged from the shadows into the garish light of the corridor. It was a face that made Hawke catch his breath. He blinked hard and focused on that large gaunt face. For a split second the two men's eyes were fixed on each other. And they both knew. Each recognized the other.

twenty-eight

I was never sure what the third degree was and why it was so much worse than the first and second, but whatever constituted the third degree, the two members of staff on duty at the admissions and enquiry desk at St Bart's Hospital gave it to me in good measure. They were a pair of ancient stern-faced harridans whose craggy scrubbed features looked as though they lacked the mechanics to activate a smile. A wide variety of scowls, yes; but smiles, no. I'm sure if they'd been given the opportunity, they would have bound me to a chair and shone a bright light on my face and administered drugs to drag the truth out of me.

All I asked was if they could tell me in which ward I'd find Barbara Cogan. My simple request was met with a barrage of questions delivered in machine-gun fashion. Who was I? Why did I want to know? What relation was I to this woman? How could I prove this? What did I know of the circumstances of her admittance to the hospital?

I spun them a tale about being her boyfriend and having only just heard that she was in St Bart's. The Gestapo sisters took down my details, examined my identity card with close attention as though it was some sort of coded document which when translated would give the details of the Allied troop movements in Europe. Then they withdrew into a huddle and engaged in a hurried whispered conversation, each in turn swivelling her head to stare at me suspiciously. Eventually, one of them told me to take a seat and wait, while the other goose-stepped off, no doubt in search of the firing-squad.

About half an hour later an elderly doctor in a rather shabby white coat approached me in a strange slouching fashion. The tired, rheumy eyes gave evidence of long working hours with little sleep.

'Mr Hawke, is it?'

'Yes,' I replied, standing up.

'I gather you are enquiring about Barbara Cogan?'

'Yes, yes, I am. May I see her?

The doctor stared blankly at me in a distracted fashion for a moment before replying. 'You are her boyfriend?'

I now felt like a cheap fraud for giving that lie. 'Yes, a friend,' I replied, modifying my untruth.

The doctor gave a sigh and gently placed his hand on my shoulder. Before he spoke I knew what he was about to tell me. I felt cold steel pierce my heart.

'I'm afraid it's bad news, young man. Barbara died about fifteen minutes ago.'

I shook my head not in disbelief but in a desperate attempt to dislodge his words from my brain. I wanted to reject them. I didn't want them to be real, to be true. Please, God, he must mean someone else.

'I'm so very sorry,' the doctor said gently, as he must have done to countless men and women with increasing regularity since the war began. His face registered a kind of exhausted sympathy.

For some moments I felt empty and numb. The thought that a bright innocent young life had been snuffed out by the blinkered hatred of the fascist scum seemed to drain the energy from me. And then suddenly, like a light switch clicking on, a hot tide of anger swept over me. I wasn't going to let them get away with this. They would pay dearly for Barbara's death. If only I could get my hands on whoever was responsible ... that's what I would pray for.

'Can I see her?' I asked at length.

The doctor shook his head. 'It wouldn't be wise. She suffered from extensive burns, you know. It would be better to remember her as she was.'

For a fleeting moment my imagination conjured up the vision of a blackened body, only vaguely recognizable as human, the intense heat of the flames having robbed it of any individuality. With a mighty effort I cast this ghastly image from my mind knowing that it would return many times in the future to haunt me.

I felt my eyes prick with tears. They were tears of sorrow and frustration.

'I am so very sorry,' the doctor repeated himself, and then paused as though he had run out of things to say. He gave me a tired smile, then shambled back down the corridor.

I stood for some moments clenching and unclenching my fists, desperately trying to keep my emotions in check. Somehow, I felt this was my fault. I should have realized that those bastards at the Britannia Club would not let the girl get away without punishment. I should have insisted that she went into hiding for a while, moved her away somewhere secret until my business with them was over. Well, I suppose we can all be wise after the event. Sometimes the brutality of my fellow countrymen shocks even a battered and shop-soiled soul like mine.

After a while I realized that the two harridans were staring at me, but their expressions had softened and were touched with sympathy. They knew. They knew that my so-called girlfriend was dead and they felt sorry for me.

Their pity only increased my sense of guilt.

I walked out of the hospital into the growing gloom of a spring evening.

Slowly I made my way back to my place on foot, taking a circuitous route in order to give me time to try to come to terms with the wild whirligig of events which had turned my world upside down in the last few days. I'd not only got Barbara's terrible death on my mind, burning grooves into my memory, but there was also the situation involving my brother. With Paul, I just didn't know what to think. In my heart I couldn't believe that he was capable of murder, but my logic told me otherwise. The mind can propel you to do the most awful things when it is disturbed.

I knew I needed to view things as dispassionately as possible and formulate some plan of action so I could try and find a way out of this mess. As I walked, I was oblivious of my surroundings, making my way by instinctive compass. I smoked several cigarettes, furrowed my brow at regular intervals and I thought until it hurt. When I eventually approached Priory Court all I seemed to have achieved was a headache.

Indoors, I undressed quickly, took a large slug of whisky and headed for the safest place in the world, where pain, worries and troubles are put on hold. I went to bed.

twenty-nine

Paul Hawke stared at the meagre helping of food on the tin plate. It was some kind of stew and looked disgusting, but he was hungry and so, with a slow reluctance, he spooned some of it into his mouth. It was lukewarm and tasted like soft cardboard. He forced himself to eat it all, despite the protests of his rebellious stomach. He must eat. He must keep his strength up in order to sort himself out.

He swilled the last of the glutinous mess down with a mug of tepid tea. He had no idea what the time was. There was no window in his cell and his watch, along with all his personal possessions, had been confiscated. He had been asleep a long time and when he'd woken up, although he still felt rough and slightly disorientated, his mind was clearer. The alcoholic fog had dissipated. However with this clarity came the stark realization of his precarious situation. A girl was dead and he was accused of her murder.

A further interview with Inspector Llewellyn had got neither of them anywhere. His memories of the previous night were still not clear and he still couldn't account for his movements since going on leave. He must, he reasoned, have suffered some kind of breakdown. He hadn't been aware that he had been so disturbed; it was just a growing, gnawing horror in the pit of his stomach at the thought of having to return. To return to the fighting and the futile loss of life he saw around him every day. He wasn't frightened of dying himself; it was the thought of the others – his friends, the men he knew, young chaps who one day would be laughing, joking, writing letters to their wives, girlfriends or mothers and the next they were dead meat – pale-faced corpses on makeshift stretchers and a stark entry on a casualty list. A sudden sense of the monstrous futility of life, of the war and its conse-quences, swept over him and, silently, he wept.

After a while he wiped his eyes with his sleeve. Ironically, the tears had made him feel better. This unexpected release of emotion had been cathartic. It had eased his pain and, more important, helped him to face his own dilemma.

With some determination, he forced himself, yet again, to go over the events of the previous night. They came to him only in snatches of images. There was no continuous scenario. He tried hard to link them. He remembered the girl in the pub, the garishness of her little room and he remembered the sex and the emptiness of the experience. Then the fog really descended. He didn't remember leaving her, the further drinks he had and his return to the little hotel where the police had found him.

His mind wandered back to the pub and the first encounter with girl. And then he recollected the man. The tall dark man. The man who'd tried to pick her up while he was at the bar getting drinks. He saw his jaded, sallow complexion, the melancholic eyes and the fierce jutting chin. And then he remembered that he'd seen him again. He'd seen him in the doorway of this cell. He'd seen him in a police uniform! What had Llewellyn called him...? Lowe. What had he been doing chatting up Mary?

Paul felt his pulse quicken and he began pacing the cell. What did this mean? It probably wasn't unusual for policemen to take up with prostitutes. It might mean nothing at all. But this pros-titute had been murdered. He recalled how furious the man had been when Mary had rejected him. His face was like thunder. And there was something in those strange dark eyes when they had seen Paul again in the cell. Fear certainly, but something more than that. This man knew something.

Paul ran his fingers through his hair in an agitated fashion. Maybe he was grasping at straws here – but straws were all he had at present. What could he do now? Telling Llewellyn might be a mistake. It did sound a little far-fetched and no doubt the police would close ranks. No, he had to speak to his brother.

His brother, the detective. He'd know what to do. He had to see Johnny.

As Constable Alec Jones was about to perform his routine inspection of the prisoner, he heard a loud groaning emanating from the cell. Jones slid back the spy-hole and peered inside. He saw the prisoner curled up on his bed, hugging himself and rocking gently while at the same time emitting a regular, rhythmic moaning sound. Jones observed this performance for nearly a minute, undecided what to do. He was unsure whether he should go and fetch a superior officer or find out for himself what was wrong with the prisoner. He noted the empty plate by the bed. The canteen stew was enough to give anyone the colly-wobbles.

Jones bit his lip with frustration. It was always being impressed on them at the Yard that one should use one's initiative and here was a case in point. Surely, there was no need to go running for an inspector in order to ascertain whether the fellow in cell three had a tummy-ache.

With a decisive nod, Jones slid the key into the lock and opened the cell door. The prisoner continued to moan and showed no signs of being aware that a policeman had entered the cell.

Leaving the key in the lock, Jones closed the door and advanced on the troubled inmate.

'Now then,' he said gruffly, 'what's up with you?'

He received no reply. He leant over the bed and put his hand on the man's shoulder. 'Now, come on, mate, what's the problem? Is it tummy-ache? How bad is it? Do you need to see the doctor?'

Jones attempted to pull the prisoner round to face him. As he did so, the groaning man turned swiftly and before Jones knew what was happening there were hands around his throat. He tried to pull back but he was held in their iron grip. The two men struggled for a while, then suddenly the prisoner released Jones and smashed his fist into the young constable's face. There was a dull crunch of breaking bone as Jones fell backwards, crashing against the wall, banging his head. Warm blood trickled down his face. The prisoner pulled the dazed policeman to his feet and hit him once again, consigning him to the land of darkness and dreams.

Paul worked speedily. He stripped the constable of his trousers and tunic and exchanged them for his own. They weren't a bad fit. The tunic was a little tight but it would do. Then he dressed the policeman in his own clothes and gagged him with his handkerchief. He hoisted the unconscious constable and laid him on the bed with his back to the spy-hole. He patted the head of the unconscious new inmate. 'I'm sorry, I hurt you but needs must, I'm afraid,' he said wryly.

He peered out into the dimly lighted corridor. It was deserted. He emerged, locked the cell door and, with some trepidation, set about finding his way out of the building. He was vaguely aware of the route he had taken when he had been brought into the Yard. He remembered being escorted down a spiral staircase to the cell and here at the end of the corridor there was the very same spiral staircase. He clambered up it at speed, his feet clanging on the worn metal steps, hoping he would not bump into a copper coming down. At the top he found himself facing another fairly featureless corridor which had several doors leading to what he assumed were offices. He felt in his trouser pocket and discovered a large blue handkerchief. He made his way down the corridor, holding the handkerchief to his face as though he was about to blow his nose, thus partly obscuring his features.

Two constables suddenly appeared round the corner. They were in deep conversation and hardly gave him a glance. They were wearing regulation raincoats which had a sheen of dampness on them, suggesting to Paul that they must have just entered the building. Therefore, he reasoned, there must be a door leading to the outside near by. Brightened by this thought he moved on, still holding the handkerchief to his face. Now he passed a series of frosted windows down the left-hand side of the corridor. He stopped and tried to open one but they were securely fastened.

'Hey you!' a voice called out.

For a moment Paul froze with fear and then slowly he turned in the direction of the voice. He saw a burly man in a tight double-breasted suit beckoning to him. He had just stepped out of one of the offices. 'Hey you, constable, come here,' he called again in a voice that suggested he expected instant response.

There was nothing Paul could do but obey the brusque command. It was pointless trying to make a run for it. He had no idea where to run. Certainly it was pointless going back in the direction he had come. He just had to try and bluff it out. Trying to keep calm he approached the man who he assumed was some kind of plain-clothes officer.

'What's your name, lad?'

Paul plucked a name from thin air. 'Carter, sir. PC Carter.'

'I've not seen you around before.'

'My first week, sir.'

The officer grunted. 'They never tell you anything in this place. Right, lad, I've got an errand for you.' He dipped his hand into his trouser pocket and extracted a few coins. 'Here,' he said, dropping money into the palm of Paul's hand, 'nip along to the canteen, there's a good lad, and get me, that's Chief Inspector Knight, a cup of tea – milk with three sugars – and a sandwich. Spam or cheese, whichever they've got left.'

'A sandwich?' Paul couldn't believe his ears.

'You've heard of them. Two pieces of bread stuck together with a filling inside.'

'Yes, sir.'

'And make it snappy, lad. OK. I don't want my char to be cold by the time you get back.'

'Yes, sir.' Paul forced a grin and, after attempting a half-hearted salute, he pushed past the large inspector and hurried along.

Inspector Knight retreated into his office, unaware of the fact that he'd never see his money again or a cup of tea and a sandwich.

Paul's successful encounter with Knight had given him a boost of confidence. He still kept the handkerchief to hand, but now he walked with more assurance. At last he passed a window without frosted glass which looked out on to an inner courtyard beyond which he could see traffic and pedestrians. There was no one about, no figures in blue who would question him as he made his way out on to the street. And he could see the grey sky filled with ragged, scudding clouds.

He could smell freedom.

And then he came upon it. The outside door. The thin wooden barrier that stood between him and escape. But it was locked. Sensibly it was locked. They couldn't have any Tom, Dick or Harry come wandering into the building, or wandering *out* of it either.

A thought struck him. That would mean that all employees of the Yard who used this access would have their own key ... surely. With some urgency he inspected the pockets on his borrowed tunic and sure enough the top left-hand breast pocket rattled. He unfastened the silver button and extracted a small key ring.

After three attempts he found the required key that opened the door. Nervously, he stepped outside. The air was cold and damp but it was like nectar to him.

With a broad smile wreathing his features, he stepped outside and breathed in deeply. Then he closed and relocked the door behind him.

He knew that his troubles were far from over, but for the moment at least he was free and able to set about proving his innocence.

Unfortunately for Paul Hawke, as Fate had designed her dark scenario, he was seen effecting his escape. He was not seen by anyone who would raise the alarm, someone who would be desirous of his recapture. He was seen by Lowe.

thirty

I went home with the intention of getting drunk. I wanted to set sail to the Isle of Oblivion on a sea of whisky. However, by the time I let myself in to Hawke Towers, the common-sense side of my brain had convinced me that such action was futile. Getting pie-eyed would not bring Barbara back, or unravel the tangled skein of my life; it would only wreck my brain, give me a mouth like sandpaper and fuel my depression. With a grimace, I decided to settle for a black coffee and a Craven A.

With these restoratives, I sat on my battered sofa staring into space, trying to work out what to do next, but my mind kept wandering away from its task as it has a habit of doing when faced with a difficult problem. My eyes were caught by the twisting column of smoke spiralling lazily up to the light-fitting. I thought back to a week ago when my life seemed much less complicated, less bloody and hurtful. That was the way of things, of course: you never appreciate how lucky you are until you aren't! Now it was too late.

Then I thought of Barbara. The image of her pretty dark-haired face filled my mind. I remembered our meal together at Benny's, how she had devoured the food with such enthusiasm. I smiled at the thought – but not for long though, for I also remembered the dark and smoking shell of her house, the black-ened banisters, the smouldering ash and the stench of murder that lingered there. I knew that her death and the manner of her death would haunt me for a long time. I felt guilt, too. Somehow I should have prevented it. Somehow I should have protected her. Somehow. I knew that her brutal murder had laid upon me the responsibility of revenge: an eye for an eye – a life for a life. It was a responsibility I would not shirk.

I took a drink of coffee. It had gone cold so I abandoned it and lit another cigarette. I was glad now that I hadn't hit the whisky bottle. The alcohol would have provoked both my anger and despair and propelled me into taking some foolish and reckless course of action. I had to move with caution especially where the Britannia Club mob were concerned. Behind that pseudo-civilized, upper-class respectable façade, lay a vicious, cruel and crazy bunch of murdering bastards.

I felt my pulse begin to race as I thought about the smug, oily countenances of Sir Howard and Guy Cooper. I didn't know how far they were involved in Barbara's death, but that didn't matter. Even if they hadn't arranged it, they had inspired and no doubt countenanced such action. I took a deep drag on my cigarette and cast them from my mind. They could wait. The most pressing business was my brother. As I considered his predicament I ached for a whisky. Surely one good slug would help, would ease the barbed wire I felt wrapping itself around my brain. I began to weaken at the thought of the smoky liquid splashing into a stout tumbler and before my mind had been completely convinced, I found my body getting up from the chair and heading for the filing-cabinet. I had just pulled the drawer back and spied the bottle of Johnnie Walker lying enticingly on its side, when the door bell rang.

With mixed feelings I slid the drawer to gently and answered the door. I found David Llewellyn and Sergeant Sunderland standing before me with expressions borrowed from some Greek tragedy.

I let them in without a word. What now? I wondered, but I reckoned I had no need to put such thoughts into words. I could see from their grim faces that they would tell me soon enough without any prompting from me.

David stroked his chin and sighed. 'Paul's escaped.'

At first I thought I had misheard. 'Paul's what?' I said, unable to find any word similar to 'escaped' which I might have heard incorrectly.

'He's bloody well escaped. Done a runner.'

'From the Yard?' I was still having difficulty accepting the statement.

Sunderland clarified the matter. 'He feigned illness, clobbered the constable on duty and, dressed in his uniform, he managed to get out of the building.'

It sounded like a scene from a Christmas pantomime of my youth, or part of the adventures of Mr Toad at least. I couldn't help but smile.

David sighed again. 'This isn't a laughing matter, Johnny.'

He was right, of course, but sometimes it helps to see the farcical side of life. I nodded, suitably chastened.

'Is he here?'

'Paul?'

David nodded wearily. 'Where else would he go? He has little money. He's wearing a policeman's uniform and as far as we know he has no other friends in the city.'

'No, he's not here.'

'I'm sorry but I've got to look around, Johnny. We've got to put our friendship to one side now. We're dealing with an escaped murder suspect – the fact that he's your brother is of no consequence in the matter.'

'Sure, I understand,' I said, rather more coolly than I intended. 'But he's not here – and I wouldn't lie to you.'

'Officially, I can't take that risk.'

I knew he was right, of course. I would have felt the same if our positions were reversed, but I couldn't help being nettled by his observation about putting our friendship to one side.

'Be my guest,' I said quietly, sitting on the edge of my desk. 'You know the layout.'

Without a word the two men set about searching the premises. They didn't just look in the wardrobe and under the bed and other areas where a grown man could secrete himself, but checked other places too, drawers, cupboards and the filing-cabinet for any evidence to indicate that Paul had been there. Unfortunately for them, the cupboard was bare.

The search over, Sunderland moved to the door ready to leave, while David came over to me.

'Sooner or later he'll come here. He'll be in touch. You can't help him, Johnny. Not in a reckless fashion, anyway. You must contact the Yard immediately. And hand him over. Don't try to be the detective hero. You'll only get yourself in trouble.'

'Is that your friendly advice?' I asked.

'I'm putting a plainclothes man on watch outside for the next twenty-four hours,' he said, ignoring my sarcasm. 'We'll know at the Yard within minutes when Paul turns up.'

Without waiting for any reply from me he moved to the door. 'Right, Sergeant, let's be off. Our job here is done … for the time being. Thanks for your co-operation, Mr Hawke,' he added before closing the door.

I didn't move for some time and when I did I went to the window and gazed down into the street. There he was. Straight from the central casting agency: a tall figure in a long regulation raincoat and felt hat standing in a doorway opposite the entrance to Priory Court.

And then the phone rang.

It was Paul.

'Have they gone? Llewellyn and his tame baboon.'

'Yes. Where the hell are you?'

'In a telephone box on Tottenham Court Road. I knew they'd come running to you as soon as they'd found I'd scarpered.'

'Well, you were right. They did, you idiot.'

'Idiot, be damned. I had to do something to prove my innocence.'

'Like slugging a policeman and escaping from police custody.'

'I'm not going down for something I didn't do.'

Paul sounded a lot stronger, more assured; in fact more like his old self. This encouraged me. 'So now you are sure you didn't kill the girl.'

'Of course I am. I may have been a little strange over the past few weeks but I know I couldn't kill someone like that.'

'Well, if it's any consolation, I never believed you could either. But you've been a bloody fool and escaping from the nick really doesn't help your case.'

'Spilt milk, Johnny. Spilt milk. Anyway, I need you to help me find the real killer and I think I've got you a lead. I have to see you to explain things. I'll come round to your place in about an hour after it's got dark.'

'Oh no you won't,' I growled. 'Thanks to your antics I've got a friendly copper watching the premises. You come knocking on my door and you'll be back in your cell before you know what's hit you.'

Paul swore softly. 'What the hell am I going to do? I've hardly any money and I'm stuck in this bloody uniform.'

Sometimes I have the ability to think fast and formulate plans on the hoof. This was one of those times.

'Listen carefully', I said with hardly a pause in our conversation. 'This is what we'll do.'

thirty-one

Paul Hawke replaced the receiver with a sigh. With Johnny on his side, he felt sure that things would sort themselves out pretty quickly. So many of the cobwebs that had shrouded his mind had dispersed and he was beginning to feel more like his old self again. At least he had a better chance of proving his innocence now than he would while being cooped up inside a police cell.

He was just about to leave the telephone box, when suddenly the door swung open with great force and a man pushed himself inside, knocking Paul back hard against the receiver.

'What the …' said Paul and then words failed him. He was staring into the face of the murderer.

'Who were you phoning?' Lowe snapped.

The question came so quickly, Paul hadn't time for subterfuge. He wasn't used to deception anyway. Orphanage life had taught him to be prompt and truthful when asked a question.

'My brother, Johnny,' he replied.

'Telling him all about me, I suppose?'

Paul shook his head.

Lowe smirked and pulled a revolver from his raincoat pocket. He jabbed it into Paul's stomach.

'Is there anyone else you've told about me?'

'What is there to tell?'

Lowe pushed the revolver harder into his flesh. 'Don't be smart. Just answer the questions.'

'You killed that girl, didn't you?'

'You know that already.'

'I knew nothing for certain … until just now.'

Lowe ignored the remark. 'Who else have you spoken to?'

'No one. I've only just left the Yard. You know that 'cause you must have followed me.'

Lowe's brain had slowed down over recent weeks. Facts needed longer to establish themselves in his consciousness. It took him a few seconds to weigh up what he was being told and to realize that he was being told the truth. What really dominated his thinking now was the fact that this man was a threat. He could expose him. He could bring his mission to a premature end.

Paul could see the confusion and uncertainty in Lowe's eyes, and another indefinable element that suggested to him that this man's mental stability was crumbling. His eyes fell upon the gun pressed into his stomach and began to feel very frightened.

'Look,' he said breathlessly, 'all I'm concerned about is getting out of London. Escaping. That's why I was ringing my brother. He's going to meet me. Bring me some clothes and money so I can scarper. I'm no danger to you. Just let me go, eh?'

'Where?'

'What?'

'Where's he meeting you?'

As luck would have it, there was no one passing by the telephone box when the gun went off. There was a brief muffled explosion which merged with the sounds of traffic outside. Moments later a tall man in a dark raincoat emerged and walked briskly away.

thirty-two

I wasn't naïve enough to believe that the raincoat man placed so prominently outside Hawke Towers was the only man on the job. David Llewellyn was a far shrewder operator than that. In essence raincoat man was the decoy. There would be at least one other Scotland Yard chappie nearby ready to follow me whenever I left the premises. As the suspect's brother and, as far as we were all aware, the only friend he had in London, it stood to reason that sooner or later Paul would contact me and I would rush to his assistance. I needed to be trailed wherever I went.

So it was clear to me that I had to lose my shadow before I could meet my errant brother. I wrapped some clothes in a brown-paper parcel, dipped into my emergency stash of cash and left the building as ostentatiously as I could. No point in being cloak-and-dagger about it. Sooner or later my tail would make his presence felt. I walked swiftly, dodging in and out of the stream of pedestrians coming my way. I was determined to make the fellow work hard. On reaching Tottenham Court Road, I leapt off the pavement without warning and hailed a cab. I instructed the cabbie to drive off at speed. However, at the second set of traffic lights, I slipped out of the cab and like a greyhound after the rabbit, dashed down a side street. I circumnavigated the block and then secreted myself in a darkened doorway and waited for ten minutes. I reckoned that my actions should have cut the umbilical chord.

When I eventually emerged from the doorway, I kept to the side streets as I made my way via this roundabout route to Cambridge Circus. I kept glancing over my shoulder to check that I had been successful in shaking off my shadow. It seemed that I had. There was no ominous silhouette dogging my heels. In the bustle of the circus I hailed another cab and gave him directions. As he pulled away from the kerb, I peered through the rear window in time to see a tall man standing by a waiting taxi and pointing at my cab. No doubt he was uttering the deathless line: 'Follow that cab!' My shadow had lived up to his name. This fellow was clever and as tenacious as a limpet.

What was I to do now?

I leaned forward to speak to my driver. 'I've got a problem.'

The cabbie shook his head. 'I don't accept cheques, food coupons or IOUs. I only take cash, mister.'

'Oh, I've got the cash,' I said quickly to reassure him. 'That's not my problem.'

'What is?'

'The taxi behind us is following me.'

The cabbie craned his neck to look in his rear-view mirror. 'I see him. Is it the lady's husband by any chance?'

'You could say that. Any possibility of losing him?'

'You naughty boy.' He chuckled like a cheeky schoolkid sharing a dirty joke. 'Yeah, I think I can do the honours. Cost you a bit more though.'

'That's OK.'

'In that case hold on to your hat, my son.' So saying he thrust the vehicle into a high gear and it lurched forward as though it had been shot from a gun.

The cabbie drove like a wild thing. He must have been a racing driver in a previous life. He swerved dangerously but skilfully in and out of traffic; he sped through red lights; he took tight corners with a squeal of brakes as I was flung hither and thither within the confines of the cab; he zoomed down narrow streets without a thought of encountering oncoming traffic; he mounted the kerb to avoid pedestrians crossing in front of him; and he whistled merrily constantly throughout this hair-raising journey.

After ten minutes of this funfair ride, he screeched to a halt on a quiet street which ran parallel to the Strand.

He turned to face me, a big grin lighting his features. 'That should have done the trick, my son. Doubt if anyone could have stuck with me through that little lot.'

I nodded in agreement. I had only just made it myself.

'Best fun I've had in years,' he beamed. 'Now then, where'd you like to go to?

'No offence but I think I'll go the rest of the way on foot.'

My racing cabbie seemed disappointed at this but said nothing. I handed over a generous fare and stepped out of the vehicle.

'Happy to oblige,' he said, still grinning, and with a cheery wave he drove off at a more sedate speed.

I waited until he had disappeared from sight, leaving me alone on the darkened street, before pulling up the collar of my raincoat and resuming my journey to rendezvous with Paul.

I made my way down to the Embankment. It was quite dark now and pretty cool, and there were few pedestrians about. There was a full moon which kept hiding briefly behind gently drifting clouds. It sent intermittent diamond ripples across the dark water of the river. Still clasping the brown-paper parcel I walked along towards Cleopatra's Needle, my rendezvous point. I glanced down at my watch. I could just make out the figures on the luminous dial. It was nearly 9.30. I was a little later than I had expected but I knew that Paul would wait for me – he had little alternative.

As I approached the Needle I saw that there was a figure loitering nearby. I quickened my step but as I grew nearer, I faltered. The figure was too tall and lean for Paul and his stance was unfamiliar to me. As I approached the man turned to face me.

In the filtered moonlight I saw his features. I recognized them: I had seen this man before. That long face with the thin prominent nose, those dark, glittery raven's eyes and the determined chin. But where had I seen him before? He was unexpected and out of context. A face from the recent past which had floated by me somewhere was now presented to me without a proper grid reference and while my brain reached frantically into the filing-cabinet of my memory it failed to come up with an answer. Instinctively, I knew he would speak to me. Instinctively I knew that he had been waiting for me. Instinctively, I knew he was dangerous. Suddenly I felt a cold, squirmy feeling in my gut. What now, Johnny boy? What now?'

I glanced around me. There was no one else in sight. The Embankment was deserted. There was just the faint hum of distant traffic, the slight swish of the gentle breeze rippling the trees and the occasional dark shape of some vessel sliding and sloshing by out on the dark waters of the river.

For what seemed ages we stood facing each other, this familiar stranger and I, as though in a scene from some Western gunfight, only I couldn't go for my gun because I didn't have one with me. I rarely carried one. After I lost my eye when a rifle exploded in my face I didn't trust guns. They killed people. However, I would have trusted one just now.

'Mr Hawke,' he said at length. His voice was low and calm with a trace of amusement in the tone.

'That's me,' I replied.

'You've come to meet your brother.'

I had some flippant remark ready to trip out but somehow I reckoned this was not the time to play the wise guy. 'Yes,' I said simply.

'He can't make it, I'm afraid.'

'Where is he?' I asked with some urgency, my stomach squirming all the more as a real sense of fear began to grow within me. Not fear for myself but for Paul.

'He just knew too much.' Now the man smiled briefly before his face resumed its sardonic mask. This shifting of his features did the trick. My memory clicked into place. I recognized him.

'You're a policeman,' I said, surprising myself. I had seen him at the Yard in a uniform.

'Oh, yes.' The smile returned again briefly. 'But you'll know all about me. Your brother will have told you.'

I wish he had, I thought. I shook my head. 'He's told me nothing.'

'And so that's why you're here,' he replied sarcastically.

My brain was now on overtime, trying to work out what this fellow thought I knew. It could only be one thing. And if it wasn't, it was worth a try.

'You're the killer,' I said.

There was a smile again. I am not a squeamish sort of fellow, but that smile made me shudder. It was alien, produced by a consciousness that was not normal. A smile that had lost touch with humanity.

'He did tell you, then.' The eyes glittered with a strange satisfaction.

By 'he' I assumed he meant Paul. 'He didn't tell me,' I said. 'You did.'

His brows rose in mild surprise.

'Why else would you be here?' I explained. 'What have you done with my brother? If you've harmed him—' I took a step forward, anger overriding my sensible self.

He stepped back and pulled a gun from his raincoat pocket.

'Stop there – now!' he snapped, the sardonic, languid pose disappearing swiftly. 'Stop there ... or I'll use this.'

I did as I was told.

'Where is Paul?' I asked quietly, in reasonable tones without emotion. It was a performance. I was acting cool and calm when in reality my brain and gut were rivals in a jitterbug competition. I feared the worst for my brother.

'You needn't worry about him. His troubles are over.'

My stomach lurched and I felt vomit rise in my throat.

'You've killed him?' I said eventually. I already knew the answer and my head began to spin.

'I silenced him, yes. And now I must do the same to you.'

There are times when I'm thankful for spending hours in darkened auditoriums watching movies. This was one of them. Escapism, it's called, but it can be educational too. From nowhere my brain snatched a memory of an old gangster film where the hero was faced with such a dilemma as I was: big brute with a gun about to shoot him. I remembered how the hero extricated himself from this life-threatening situation. But, of course, that was the movies and I was starring in real life. However, I had to do something and I had no ideas of my own, so I had to go with Hollywood.

My assailant took a step nearer and raised the pistol in readiness to shoot. In an instant I had snatched the hat from my head and hurled it with great force in his direction. It was only a soft trilby and certainly was not going to do him any harm, but a dark object flying towards him at speed distracted him sufficiently to allow me to duck down out of the immediate range of the gun and dive at his legs.

As I brought him down in a rugby tackle the gun went off, but I felt no pain and so I assumed the bullet had missed me. We grappled like schoolkids in the playground, rolling over and over on the damp pavement as though we were participants in some wild party game. He was a big man and strong, but he lacked my agility and in this way we were strangely matched. My aim was to get the gun from him but he kept his arm outstretched, ramrod-straight, beyond my reach, so I had to take a different tack. I kneed him in the groin. The effect was instantaneous. He bellowed in pain and folded before me, crashing to the ground and scrunching himself into the foetal position. For a moment he lay still, breathing heavily. I crouched over him and tried again to snatch the gun, but before I could do so he rallied. Rising up, he twisted round and brought the weapon crashing down on my head. A selection of pretty fairy lights paraded before my eyes as I staggered backwards. In the haze I saw him scramble to his feet. I launched myself forward and with both hands grabbed the arm that held the gun. The force of my assault caused us both to rebound backwards against the parapet. The gun spun from his grasp and dropped into the river below.

Frustration at losing the gun fuelled his anger and gave him an extra burst of energy and strength. He advanced on me like a madman, eyes wide with fury, mouth set in a crazed grimace. Before I knew what had hit me – he had. I received a solid punch hard in the gut – more fairy lights – and then he rammed his fist against my chin. It made an unpleasant sound. This time the fairy lights flashed brightly and then flickered fitfully before darkness came to entertain me. It slipped over my head like a black velvet hood. I was dimly aware that my legs were giving way and with a strange sense of relief I sank into unconsciousness.

thirty-three

I woke just as the sky was lightening. A new day was dawning and a blistering headache was making itself felt, like an irate landlord hammering on your door in the early hours of the morning while you are trying to sleep off a hangover. That wasn't the worst of it. My body seemed to have rusted up and I found it almost impossible to move. I was still lying on the damp pavement by the Embankment, still alive, thank God, but secretly wishing I were dead. As I prised my head from the wet stone paving my vision softened for a while, as though someone had thrown a veil over me. Gradually, with much flickering of the eyelids, it cleared and focused. I saw the occasional pedestrian pass by giving me a wide berth. To them I was just another drunk who could not take his booze. If only that had been the truth.

With infinite slowness I got myself into a standing position. At this time my mind was focused solely on my physical movements. My recent history, how I had come to be lying on the Embankment feeling like and probably looking like a dead fish on the slab and, more important, the whereabouts of my brother, did not at first impinge on my consciousness.

At last I was erect, though, I have to admit, rather stooping in my erectness. I was now aware that not only did my head ache, but my chin and my stomach were suffering equally. With much gritting of the teeth, I began walking, robotlike, in the vague direction of home, my full attention still concentrating on the mechanics of moving forward. One foot slithered in front of another. Slowly, the stiffness eased and I began to pick up speed. Time passed and I was almost moving normally when I spied, as though it were a mirage in the desert, a little tea-bar ahead of me. Its lights and cheery ambience beckoned. It was a small portable job, selling warming fluids to the early-morning ants on their way to work. This thought prompted me to glance at my watch. It was nearly seven o'clock.

I purchased a mug of scalding-hot tea and leaned against the parapet to drink it. Its medicinal warmth surged through my body bringing feeling and humanity back to my weary frame. I replenished the mug and repeated the process. The effect was close to miraculous; my headache eased and my limbs began to feel relaxed. Tea, I came to the conclusion then, is a wondrous elixir. I may never touch another glass of Johnnie Walker again.

Of course, with this revivification the floodgates of awareness also opened and vivid memories of my last waking moments came back to me. In a speeded-up movie in my mind I relived the events of the previous evening, starting with the wild Keystone Cops taxi-ride and then the encounter with the killer on the Embankment, our tussle and my descent into unconsciousness. A little voice within me told me that I was lucky to be alive but, I wondered with a sagging heart, was Paul? And I wondered why had I been spared. I remembered the gun spiralling over the parapet into the water. Maybe the killer, relieved of his weapon, panicked and headed for the hills.

'You want another tea, guv? On the house,' called the cheery tea-bar owner. I was his only customer.

'Set 'em up Joe,' I replied. 'You got fags as well?'

'Just Woodbines,' came the reply.

'Any port in a storm.' I realized that as I said this I was actually grinning. Where did that come from? I was as far away from the land of mirth as it was possible to be.

Another cup of tea and a harsh Woodbine later and I felt almost ready to join the human race again.

There were no taxis around at such an early hour and so I foot-slogged it back to Hawke Towers. Another raincoat-man was on sentry outside but I ignored him. I wasn't quite ready for that yet. When I got indoors I slumped down on the sofa for what I intended to be a five-minute rest, but very quickly I sank into beautiful, dreamless sleep. If it hadn't have been for my bladder I could have been there all day, but after about an hour the effects of three mugs of hot tea made their effect felt and brought me back up to the surface.

Reluctantly I went to the bathroom and washed, shaved and put on fresh clothes. Like it or not I had to go to the Yard and see David. I'd have to confess about going to meet Paul, but at the same time I now had proof that he hadn't murdered the girl, or anyone.

As it happened the Yard came to me. I was just knotting my tie when the doorbell rang. I prayed it wasn't a client. At present my mind was in no fit state to deal with someone's errant husband or a missing uncle.

I found David on the threshold. He was looking grim but at least he was on his own. In truth I was relieved to see him.

'And where did you get to last night?' The tone was neutral but there was something friendly, sympathetic even about the eyes. I could see he was still caught between his two roles: my friend and a professional policeman.

This was no time for beating about the bush. I told David everything. When I finished he remained silent for some time, fiddling with his hat, then he sighed.

'Here's another fine mess, Stanley,' he said ruefully.

'Do you know the copper?'

David nodded. 'Don't know him but I know who he is. Name of Lowe. Bit of a dark horse, I gather.'

'Much darker than you gathered. At least you now know who the killer really is and that my brother is innocent.'

'Yup. Well, we'll get the posse round to Lowe's gaff, although no doubt he's scarpered.'

'But I'm worried that he's hurt Paul.'

David looked grim and nervous. He hesitated a moment before he spoke. 'Your brother was found last night in phone box about a mile away from the Yard. He'd been shot.'

My stomach lurched. 'Shot! My God. He's not dead?'

David gave a weary sigh. 'He's not dead, but he's in a very bad way.'

'He's alive then,' I snapped, desperate for David to confirm the fact. For Christ's sake, my brain yelled, where's there's life there's hope.

'He's alive, but—'

'Don't give me your bloody buts. He's alive.'

David nodded.

'I want to see him. Where is he?'

'He's in Charing Cross Hospital. He's due for an operation this morning. He was shot in the stomach. He's lost a lot of blood. I know it's cliché, Johnny, but he's in good hands. You should be able to see him this afternoon if he's come out of the operating theatre.'

I slumped in a chair, tears springing unbidden to my eyes. I had never contemplated losing my brother. It was something that was not on my life's agenda. He had always been there. The only one who had always been there. He had been my mother, father, friend and protector in the dark days of my youth. He was the only family I had ever known. And, although, we had grown apart in recent years, I had always been conscious of that firm invisible link between us. Now that was in danger of being severed. I pushed back the tears with as much masculine force as I could muster while David turned away, embarrassed, and fiddled some more with his hat. Suddenly, my self-pity was swamped by a sudden hot tidal wave of anger, anger directed at the bastard Lowe.

I jumped to my feet. 'David, do me a favour. Let's go to Lowe's place together now. You're right, he's probably done a bunk, but you and I might be able to pick up a trail, rather than a set of your bobbies.'

David looked at me for a moment and then nodded. 'OK. Johnny.'

He used my phone to contact the Yard to obtain details of Lowe's address.

'Right, he said,' he said, replacing the receiver, 'Let's go'.

I nodded and grabbed my coat. As we left, David laid a friendly hand on my shoulder.

Robert James Lowe lived in a tiny bedsit in a sad little street in Pimlico. His landlady, Mrs Flynn, a thin red-faced Irish woman who could have been a stand-in for Old Mother Riley glared at us suspiciously as David presented his credentials.

'I'll have you know I keep a respectable house,' she whined, a pungent vapour of gin emanating from her virtually toothless mouth. From the way she said it, almost as a chant, I suspected it was a claim that she'd made many times before.

'That is not in doubt,' assured David. 'We've come to see your lodger, Robert Lowe.'

'Oh, him,' she grimaced. 'He's a silent one, I can tell you that. It takes him all his time to say "Good morning".'

'Is he at home now?'

'I couldn't tell you. He creeps in and out like a ghost and I never know when he's here or not. Still, he pays his rent on time so I can't complain.'

'When did you last see him?' I asked.

She screwed up her face with thought. It wasn't a pleasant sight. 'Now you're asking,' she muttered. 'I honestly can't remember.'

'Never mind, if you'll just show us to his room,' said David.

'Now you are sure you're the genuine police an' all.'

'Scout's honour.' David saluted.

The old crone led us up a gloomy staircase which smelt of a mixture of damp, old cabbage and rancid fat to a room on the second floor at the back of the building.

'That's Mr Lowe's room. He's not in serious trouble is he? I've my reputation to think of. I told you, this is a respectable house.'

'It's nothing you need worry about, Mrs Flynn,' David said. 'I assure you your reputation is safe. Now, if you'll just open up and leave me and my colleague alone....'

With a grimace and a sigh she pulled a large bunch of keys from her apron pocket, selected one and unlocked the door; then she retreated down the pungent staircase.

The room was cramped and dingy with a large window at one end and a kitchen area which was curtained off. It was, however, incredibly tidy. The bed was neatly made and there were no papers or any other everyday detritus lying about the place.

'A fastidious fellow,' I observed, pulling open the narrow wardrobe door. Inside was a suit along with two shirts hanging there along with several empty hangers. I went though the pockets but found nothing. An investigation of the drawers revealed a similar state of affairs at first, then I lifted up the old newspaper used as lining and discovered a plain brown envelope nestling underneath.

'What you got there?'

I emptied the contents of the envelope on to the neat counterpane of the bed. There was a series of newspaper cuttings and a folded sheet of notepaper.

I scanned the cuttings quickly. They had been taken from several newspapers and related to the prostitute murders. I passed them to David. I unfolded the notepaper. In tiny, neat handwriting there was a list of his victims, including the place where he had met them and the time and location where he had murdered them, including Mary. Precise, even in murder.

'His little *aide-mémoire* to his crimes,' I observed, showing David the sheet of paper. 'Obviously, now he's been flushed out he has no further need for his little museum.'

'The bastard,' said David with some emotion as he read it. 'Somehow it's worse when you find out the culprit is one of your own.'

I said nothing. I knew that men in the police force were as capable of being saints or sinners as the next man. A uniform did not change your morality. The fact that the murderer was a copper didn't bother me; I was just relieved that it proved that my brother was innocent.

'Well, he'll not be coming back here again,' I said looking round. 'It's clear he's done a bunk. Taken a few clothes – there's no suitcase – and gone on the run.'

'Looks like we've got a manhunt on our hands.'

We were just about to leave when I noticed what looked like a small rectangle of paper peeping out of the corner of the mirror which hung over the small fireplace. David was half-way out of the door, so I snatched the paper – which appeared to be some kind of business card – and slipped it into my raincoat pocket.

*

David dropped me outside Charing Cross Hospital. He wished me luck and promised that he'd keep in touch with me regarding Lowe. I nodded grimly and gave him a brief wave as he drove off.

After a lot of palaver inside the hospital I was eventually taken to a small private waiting-room and left for some ten minutes before I was visited by a tall, bald-headed man in a white coat who introduced himself as Mr Carruthers. In a mechanical fashion I shook his hand.

'I am Paul's surgeon,' he explained.

'How is he?'

'I will be honest with you, Mr Hawke. There is little point in being otherwise. He is in a very bad way indeed. The X-rays reveal that his internal injuries are more severe than we first thought and he has lost a lot of blood. We are unable to operate at the moment because he is too weak to survive the rigours of such an experience.'

'Will he die?'

'The odds are not good. But we will do our best. The next twenty-four hours are critical.'

'I'd like to see him, please.'

Carruthers nodded. 'A few minutes....'

I could hardly recognize my brother. There were so many tubes and pipes connected to him. Only his head was visible above the covers. It was still and pale and skeletal. He looked dead already. I kissed his forehead and left.

After leaving the hospital I felt numb for a while. I wandered the streets aimlessly, the image of that pale, lifeless face imprinted on my mind. Slowly, common sense, rationality – call it what you will – came to my rescue. I began to realize that whatever happened to Paul, I had to carry on, I had to function. Moping would do neither of us any good. I had to get on with things.

By now it was nearly noon and I realized that I'd had not had any food all day, so I wandered down to Benny's to treat myself to his 'serviceman's lunch', which turned out be corned-beef hash and cabbage. It was warm and colourful, that's all I can say.

'So how's the lovely lady? When are you seeing her again?' asked Benny with a sly grin and a suggestive wink as he cleared my plate away. I hadn't the heart to tell him she was dead. This would only prompt a wave of questions which I didn't feel up to answering and would, in the end, only upset the old chap.

I shrugged casually. 'I keep telling you, Benny, she was just a client. She has her own boyfriend. End of story.'

'But you made such a lovely couple.'

'What is this? A café or a marriage-bureau?'

'For you Johnny, it's both.' He grinned. 'You want another tea ... on the house.'

I nodded, returning the grin.

While I sipped the tea I took out the business card from the pocket in my raincoat, which I had draped over the chair beside me at the table. It was for a Doctor Anthony Baker of Ferris Street, London W1. It bore the motto: *Discreet consultations available.*

I was curious. I reckoned I ought to call upon Dr Baker without delay.

thirty-four

Ferris Street was a narrow thoroughfare not far from Harley Street. It was close to the prime medical area of London where the eminent and expensive medics held court, but not actually part of it. This undistinguished and rather dingy tributary was a sort of down-market adjunct where doctors of questionable principles practised. There was quite a number of them, as the preponderance of little brass plaques indicated. Certainly, the peeling stucco portico and shabby front door of Dr Baker's surgery suggested that this was a medical practice in the second rank – at best. I'd seen cards like Dr Anthony Baker's before. The phrasing 'Discreet consultations' usually meant, 'I carry out abortions'. It wasn't only the reckless working-class lass who finds herself in trouble after her eager soldier boyfriend has returned to his unit, leaving her in the pudding club. That kind of abandon may also be found in the supposedly higher echelons of society. These upper- and middle-class ladies, when similarly inconvenienced, can have no recourse to the local neighbourhood crone with her primitive and life-threatening methods of terminating the pregnancy. They have to seek out unscrupulous professionals who earn a fine living relieving such ladies of their unwanted foetuses for a tidy fee. These medical toads grow rich and fat on the distress of others. And so it has always been, I suppose.

The rather bleak waiting-room was empty when I entered. A matronly woman, who was knitting some amorphous garment in a vomit-inducing shade of green, took my details. I was told that I could have a consultation with Dr Baker when he had finished with the patient he was with at the moment for a fee of two guineas, payable in advance. I doled out the dough with a fixed grin.

I sat twiddling my thumbs for about quarter of hour while the knitting needles echoed like castanets all around me.

Dr Baker's patient eventually emerged. She was a smart young woman in a fashionable two-piece suit and it was clear that she had been crying. Her eyes were puffy and red and she hurried out briskly in a state of controlled distress. She seemed to confirm my suspicions about this not-quite-back-street practice.

The mad knitter showed me into Dr Baker's consulting-room. She passed him a form containing my simple details. The doctor himself was perched casually on the edge of his desk. He was younger and sleeker than I expected but there was still the air of the self-satisfied fat cat about him. He was tall with thick blond hair Brylcreemed back into a shiny yellow skull-cap. He balanced a pair of light-brown horn-rimmed spectacles on the end of his nose, spectacles which I suspected he did not need, but which he thought made him look more professional, more authoritative, more like a doctor. He read the form and then addressed me with a professional smile.

'So, Mr Hawke, how can I help you?'

I pulled out one of my business cards and slipped it on to his desk. He snapped it up and, as he perused it, the charm left his face.

'A private detective?' he said with some disdain, as though I was akin to a leper or a child-murderer.

'I need to know some details about one of your patients.'

Baker held out two arms, the palms of his hands outstretched as though he was attempting to hold back a large wave.

'Oh, oh,' he said. 'Just wait a minute. I'll stop you right now. There is a confidentiality between patient and doctor. I cannot pass on to you any information concerning any one of my patients. Nothing at all. It would be most unethical. You're wasting your time. If you yourself do not require medical assistance, I must ask you to leave.'

'I could be saving you a prison sentence,' I replied smugly.

His mouth twitched nervously into an uncertain grin. 'And how do you make that out?'

'I've a pretty good idea what kind of services you offer here. They are not exactly ethical either, are they?'

'I think it is time you left.'

'I'll leave when you've told me what I need to know, or—'

'Or what?' Baker snatched up a silver cigarette-box from the desk, pulled out a cigarette and lit it with a lighter he extracted from his waistcoat pocket. It was a nervous, somewhat dramatic gesture. My medical friend was beginning to get worried.

'You can tell me or the police will be round here like a shot.'

'The police?' His voiced edged up an octave and the hand holding the cigarette began to waver. 'What ... what on earth are you talking about?'

'One of your patients – George Lowe – is a murderer wanted by the police.'

'Murderer?' His face was drip-white now and all the bravado was melting away fast.

'He's been killing girls, prostitutes. You may have read about the murders in the papers. He strangles the girls for no reason at all. Or no reason that we can fathom at the moment. He's killed three up to now.'

'George Lowe?'

'That's the fellow. He needs to be caught and quickly. Now I want to know what he comes to see you about. What you know about him. Anything that will help me track him down. Tell me and I'll try and keep the police away from your files.'

Baker puffed aggressively on his cigarette and briefly his face was obliterated by smoke. 'How on earth do I know you're telling the truth? For all I know you could be a madman—'

'Not mad, just a little annoyed and frustrated. It is very possible that Lowe has killed my brother and as long as he's at large he is a threat to other women. Now I suggest that you tell me what I want to know or I may very well forget I'm some kind of gentleman.'

There was a silence. Baker stared at me for a while, his features twitching with uncertainty, then he stubbed out his cigarette and moved awkwardly to a filing-cabinet behind his desk.

'Mr Lowe has been seeing me for about three months now. He has venereal disease. VD. In his case it is very serious.' He opened the drawer, pulled out a file and consulted it. 'He'd been with some girl, some tart, I suspect, and caught a real dose of it.'

'How serious is serious?'

'The man is dying.'

'From the clap?'

'He is in a very advanced stage of syphilis. He came to me quite late, too late in fact. It is often the case that men who contract the disease go at first into a state of denial – do not believe it is actually happening to them. Then, when the rash and the ulcers come, they try to treat it themselves with creams and potions from the chemist. To no avail, of course. When Lowe first came to me a few months ago he'd been contaminated for nearly two years.'

I gasped. 'My God,' I said, the words escaping as barely a whisper.

'There are four stages to the spread of syphilis: primary, secondary, latent and late. By the latent stage the disease, which spreads in the bloodstream, has begun to invade the nervous system. This brings headaches, dizziness, sleeplessness and can bring about seizures. Lowe has gone beyond that. He is in the late stage. The syphilitic deposits are attacking his liver, his heart and his brain.'

'His brain?'

'Yes.'

'What effect will this have on his behaviour?'

'Eventually it brings about psychosis—'

'In simple terms?'

'He will become mentally disturbed – deranged.'

'I think he's already there. Does he know all this?'

Baker shifted his glance away from me. 'Not ... not exactly. Not in detail. He knew that his time was limited. He's intelligent enough to know that he's dying.'

'You couldn't help him?'

Baker shook his head. 'He was too far gone by the time I saw him. I gave him mercury injections which helped to slow the rate of deterioration, but eventually the body becomes immune to them. It is like trying to mend a hole in a dam with a few pieces of wood. At first you may reduce the leak to a trickle but eventually the force of the water will not only sweep the wood away but crack the dam.'

I got the picture. It wasn't a pleasant one. 'What do you know of Lowe?'

Baker shook his head. 'Hardly anything. I'm not a psychiatrist. I don't ask probing questions about my patients' lives. People come to me with an illness and I just treat that.'

'You must have some details, some opinions. Come on, Baker. This man is a killer. We have to catch him.'

Baker casually fiddled with his glasses. I wanted to punch him.

'Well,' he said at length, 'he was a man of few words. Taciturn, I would say. Clearly, he was oversexed. He saw women merely as objects to satisfy his appetite. He claimed that when he was well he needed sexual intercourse almost every day, which for a single man presents certain problems. No doubt he bought various magazines to help him ease the need and he talked of visiting the Windmill theatre to see "the girls".'

'Did he mention any pubs that he frequented to pick up prostitutes? The Barley Mow for instance.'

Baker shook his head. 'The topic never came up,' he said suavely. 'As I've already said, I concern myself solely with the ailment, Mr Hawke. I have neither the time nor inclination to indulge in chit-chat with the patients whom I see.'

The point this jumped-up medic was making was reasonable enough; it was the sneering manner in which he expressed it that irritated me.

'Had you no inkling that this man could be dangerous?'

Baker gave a theatrical sigh. 'I am a doctor. *You're* the detective. The man was obviously distressed and anxious. With his diagnosis who wouldn't be? But apart from gleaning some notion about his sexual appetite, I knew nothing about the man other than his medical condition.'

'Not even what he did for a living?'

'No. It wasn't relevant.'

'How long has he got?'

'Three months at the most, probably less. The disease speeds up in its latter stages, but this is unpredictable.'

'You told him all this?'

'Oh, yes, there is no point in concealing the truth. He seemed to take it very well. As I said, he was taciturn. He accepted my diagnosis without emotion. He just wanted me to keep the inevitable at bay for as long as I could. Recently I have provided him with some laudanum to help deaden the pain.'

'How often does he visit you?'

'It varies. On average once a fortnight.'

'And when was the last time you saw him?'

Baker consulted his notes. 'Early last week. I saw a definite change in him.'

'In what way?'

'He looked more haggard and mentally more distracted. He complained that the pain was getting worse. As it spreads through the body the limbs begin to stiffen and I could see that this was happening to him.' Baker gave a wry grin. 'I had to tell him that there was little else I could do for him apart from increasing the dose of laudanum. I did ask him if there was anyone to look after him when he became bedridden. He said, "No."'

It was good to get out of the surgery and breathe fresh air once again. I felt somewhat tainted after spending some time in Baker's presence. He was an uncaring, unscrupulous bastard who lined his pocket through the misery of others. The sad fact was that he was but one of a growing army of greedy medics setting up shop to deal with abortions and other socially unacceptable complaints. The war was a boon to such people.

The really disappointing aspect of my encounter with Dr Baker was that I had learned very little that would help me. It was clear that Lowe had not very long to live. Although this meant that he had less time to be active as a killer, it would increase his need to act more swiftly and more often. With his mind crumbling he was likely to take greater risks. Time was running out. Somewhere out there in the great city he was no doubt planning his next murder. The thought of it chilled me to the marrow.

I assumed that he had found himself some other gaff, cheap lodgings somewhere where he could hide away in the daytime, well aware that the police were now on his tail. If he was to kill again he had to do it fast. It was a race against time. His mental deterioration would have increased his desire to wreak his revenge on women – those women who had given him his disease, his death-sentence, before either he was caught or he was too ill. He was out there now and I felt sure that, come the dark, he'd try to kill again.

thirty-five

I had a faint idea. I couldn't grace it with the title of a 'hunch' because it was too fragile, too insubstantial, but in my present situation I was prepared to grasp at any straw that presented itself to me. It was something that my friend Dr Baker had said to me about Lowe's sexual appetite – and his visits to the Windmill Theatre to see the girlie shows. Wasn't it possible, even likely, that he'd go there today? What better place to become anonymous and what better place to stimulate your sexual feelings before going out on to the darkened streets to kill again?

What the hell, it was worth a try.

At the corner of Harley Street I hopped on a bus and reached Piccadilly Circus some ten minutes later. The great hub of the city was a shadow of its former self with old Eros boarded up for the duration and all the neon signs switched off.

The Windmill theatre was up a side street running off the Circus. It was the Mecca for all servicemen on leave in London eager to see some exposed female flesh. The shows ran from noon until midnight with barely a gap between performances. I had visited the place myself very early in the war, a mixture of curiosity and boredom leading me there one rainy afternoon. I found it a depressing and totally sexless experience. The show consisted of a number of second-rate musical acts and desperate comedians, interspersed with a series of tableaux of naked women in various naïve poses. The girls in question, holding their stances like goose-pimpled statues, were as erotic as an empty fag-packet. It was against the law for them to move at all and so the artificiality of their static appearance robbed the occasion of any sense of potent sexuality. And, without being unkind, many of the females on view had seen better, and in some cases, much slimmer days.

Obviously I was in a minority in viewing this spectacle with sadness rather than excitement. The eager fellows in the audience seemed to lap it up. While the variety acts struggled for attention, the lads in the stalls would chat, read newspapers or have forty winks, simply passing the time until tableau girls were back on stage. Then it was eyes front and tongues lolling, perhaps hoping one of the nude lovelies would have a coughing fit. When someone got up to leave, vacating his seat towards the front of the stalls, there would be an unseemly rush to fill it, to get a better view of the blotchy flesh.

As I approached the theatre there was a small queue by the box-office, mainly made up of lonesome soldiers and sailors, some giggling with their mates and others wearing expressions that seemed to be a mixture of embarrassment and boredom. I stood in line wondering what impression I made as I fumbled in my pocket for the admission fee.

Once inside the tiny theatre, much to the usherette's surprise I took a seat at the back. I wanted to survey the audience and keep an eye on all those who came and went.

I settled myself in the empty back row within easy reach of the exit. There was an ancient fellow on the stage attempting to make various animal shapes out of balloons. He was dressed as a tramp and heavily made up to try and disguise his greatly advanced years. He probably was a wow at a toddlers' tea-party, but in front of a girl-hungry male audience he was dying on his rather shaky feet, After each laboured operation he thrust his new creation towards the audience with a triumphant cry: 'Ladies and gentlemen – a giraffe,' 'Ladies and gentlemen – a horse.' His efforts were received with a barrage of boos and catcalls. He seemed impervious to the jeers and carried on until he manufactured his *pièce de résistance* – 'Ladies and gentlemen, an elephant,' then he shuffled off as the small group of musicians in the pit played his exit music. No one applauded.

Awkwardly, the curtains swung to and the musicians, flipping over their sheet music, began playing some unidentifiable tune while there seemed to be a great deal of clumping activity hidden from view behind the drapes. Obviously, we were about to be treated to a tableau. Suddenly the audience became alert. Newspapers were discarded, conversation ceased and almost in unison the male patrons leaned forward in their seats. After a few moments the curtains jerked back to reveal a group of six girls sitting on a collection of various-sized cardboard rocks in a range of supposedly decorous and enticing postures in front of a seascape backdrop. Not counting the tiny panties and the odd transparent wisp of tulle draped across pallid breasts, the girls were naked. Apart from wavering smiles and the nervous flickering of heavily made-up eyelids, none of the beauties moved. It was as though they had been frozen in time. It was bizarre rather than erotic. I suppose they were meant to represent the sirens luring men on to the rocks. I have to say, they didn't lure me, nothing stirred in my loins, but the same could not be said for the blokes in front of me. I've never seen as many craned necks in one room at the same time.

I even saw one fellow in the second row produce a small pair of binoculars and clamp them to his eyes to obtain a better view. I was half-way to reaching for a smile when it faded away. Something suddenly struck me about him. It was now my turn to lean forward and crane my neck. I was right. I recognized that profile, the shape of the head, the set of the jaw. Or I thought I did. In the gloom at a distance I couldn't be sure. If only he'd take those damned binoculars away from his face....

The girls posed for what seemed ages, but what I suppose in real time was only about two minutes. Towards the end of the session some of them actually started shivering. I wondered what the Lord Chancellor would say about that. Eventually the musicians reached some kind of collective culmination and once more the curtains moved across in a jerky, arthritic fashion, drawing a veil over the scene. There were groans and boos from the audience. My man lowered his binoculars and slipped them away in his pocket. As he turned his head sideways I gained a better view of his features. My heart gave a leap. It was Lowe. Large as life, sitting there about thirty yards away from me.

My God, I thought, with some short-lived elation, I've caught the bastard! Well, not quite, I told myself sensibly when my pulse rate steadied. He was in my sights, but that was all. That was a big difference. What was I to do now? If I went off to ring the police, he might well have disappeared by the time I got back. And certainly it would be foolish to try and apprehend him in the theatre. Think what chaos that would bring. These eager gawpers would make mincemeat of anyone interfering with their entertainment. I lit a cigarette to help me think. Didn't need the whole fag, really. My options were limited. The only practical course of action was to just stay put for the moment and wait for Lowe to leave the theatre and then follow, hoping that a situation would arise where I could either call for help or I could tackle him myself. Not an ideal scenario but then they rarely presented themselves.

There was a comedian on stage now – a cockney wide boy, loud pin-striped suit, large fedora and vivid tie – spilling out a stream of near the knuckle gags. He was getting laughs from the audience but I paid little attention to him or his material; my beady eyes were fixed on my friend Lowe.

Suddenly, I felt a movement at the side of me, then a voice whispered in my ear.

'So this is where you spend your spare time, eh? Eyeing up the girlies.'

I recognized the voice and the attendant sneer it carried. I turned my head to clock the speaker for confirmation. It was Ralph Chapman, my chum from the Britannia Club.

'The same could be said for you,' I said glibly. This was the last thing I wanted: this arrogant toad queering my pitch.

'Oh, I'm a regular,' he said smoothly, plopping down in the seat next to me. I turned my attention back to Lowe whose stern features were unmoved by the comedian's patter. His eyes glinted in the darkness. All he wanted was the next tableau.

Chapman leaned sideways towards me. 'I suppose you heard about that little Jewish tart, your friend with the gun?'

I didn't react, partly because I didn't know how to. I just let him carry on while I clenched my fists in an attempt to quell my feelings of anger and hate.

'Got burnt to a cinder for her pains.'

'Really,' I said, keeping my eyes focused on Lowe.

'Oh, yes. We always make sure that those who threaten us get their just desserts.'

I gave a brief nod, hoping that that was sufficient to indicate that I agreed with him – when in reality I wanted to yank his heart out of his chest and stuff it down his throat.

He chuckled obscenely. 'Yes, we organized a little torch-party for her. Tinderboxes, those houses in the East End.'

'You—' I gasped, turning to face him.

He shrugged. 'Well, not me personally, but, let's say I had a hand in it.'

Suddenly there was a roar of laughter from the audience as the comedian delivered a particularly obscene punch line. It helped me ride my anger and disgust. I had to keep in character as a hardened anti-Semitic or I was in real trouble and I knew Chapman was simply testing me, still suspicious of me, seeing if I would snap and expose my real feelings.

'Good for you.' I grinned and then pretended to join in the laughter at the comedian's next gag, something about a chicken and a gas-mask.

'I thought you'd be pleased,' said Chapman, settling back in his seat. I turned and looked at his cold, hard features. They were smug and self-satisfied even in repose. Oh boy, I couldn't wait to rattle his cage but I would have to wait. For the moment there were more urgent things to attend to. I returned my gaze to Lowe.

He wasn't there. His seat was empty. He had evaporated into thin air just like Claude Rains in *The Invisible Man*. Already some young sailor was attempting to clamber over the seat and take his place. A cold panic gripped me. Where the hell...? How could I have been so stupid as to take my eyes off him for a moment? In desperation I glanced round the auditorium, my eyes darting in all directions. The stage lights created flickering shadows along the walls, misleadingly masquerading as figures. I gripped the edge of the seat in front of me, a sense of despair already invading my senses. Then I saw him. Like a dark ghost, he was moving up the far aisle towards the exit. He was about to escape into the big wide world outside, soon to be swallowed up by the great London crowds and out of my grasp.

I rose from my seat.

'Not going already? You've not seen all the show. I can recommend Dante's Inferno. All the girlies wear horns.' Chapman giggled obscenely.

'Yes, I've got to go. Nature calls.' I said, rather more breathlessly than I intended.

'Oh, do stay,' he said with a note of seriousness in his voice, an undertone of a threat. The smile had left his face. He showed no signs of moving to let me pass. The bastard was being deliberately obstructive. Why don't you let him have it, my brain told me. A clenched fist between the eyes. How satisfying that would be. For a brief moment I imagined the crack of bone and the warm spurt of fresh blood.

Not now, I told myself, but soon.

I tried harder to press past him but he didn't budge.

'Just sit down, old boy, otherwise you'll miss the titties.'

'If you don't move to let me pass,' I said, 'I shall be forced to urinate all over that nice jacket of yours.'

He moved and I shot by him without another word. I glanced ahead and saw Lowe disappear through the curtains below the exit sign. I hurried after him.

By the time I reached the foyer he had disappeared again. I glanced around but nowhere was he to be seen. I swore sharply under my breath. And then I noticed the door to the Gents. Maybe ... I went inside. The place appeared empty but one of the cubicles was occupied. Pray God, its occupant was Lowe. The cistern flushed and I left quickly. I didn't want him to see me just yet. I needed to tackle him in a much less public place.

I returned to the foyer, stood in a dark corner and waited. Moments later Lowe emerged and without a glance in my direction made his way out on to the street.

I followed.

thirty-six

The show at the Windmill had failed to distract or stimulate Lowe. It was not like the old days when a couple of hours in the warm dark ogling the naked female flesh on show and rubbing his penis would have got the hormones racing and put 'lead in his pencil' as his father used to say. But then again this wasn't the old days, of course. Things had changed. The syphilis had seen to that. He knew that he was reaching the end. His body was crumbling, his mind was losing touch with reality and the police were on his tail. In his own stoical manner he accepted that he hadn't much time left. That was why, in the end, he hadn't killed the one-eyed private detective. It suddenly struck him that getting rid of him would not gain him any more time, would not prolong his life. It wasn't the authorities he was up against, it was the rot, the rampaging rot which was consuming the whole of his body.

In fact he looked forward to the end – to death. It would be a relief. There was nothing he could do now to stop the pain, to stop that rot. Dr Baker had told him that at some time he would reach this stage and now he had. Even the laudanum had no effect any more. But he just wanted to make one last gesture before he finally stepped into the dark. He just wanted to dispatch one more tart – to kill one more time. To experience the pleasure of some sleazy pro's look of frozen horror as he clamped his hands around her neck and squeezed the life out of her. As they had squeezed the life out of him. He wanted to see those hands fluttering in desperation liked trapped butterflies and to hear that final squeaky, agonized croak as her body slumped to the floor. These were the fucking creatures who had given him his death sentence, so why should they escape his retribution?

As these thoughts swirled around his diseased mind he gritted his teeth and grunted quietly to himself. He wasn't aware that he was doing this; it was a recent unconscious habit that he had developed. However he did realize that he found walking at a steady pace more of an effort than it used to be. Each day, each hour, things got worse. His legs ached and his heart thudded within his aching chest.

Dusk was falling and pedestrians were slowly turning into silhouettes, walking shadows that breezed by him only to melt into the gloom. He loved the night: it gave him confidence and comfort. He gazed at the sky. Already the stars were pinpricking their way through the darkening canvas. Somewhere a woman laughed, her high-pitched shriek momentarily catching his interest before he got lost in his own thoughts again.

He glanced at his watch. It was time for a drink and to chat up his final victim. He decided that in honour of the occasion he would go to the Coach and Horses, the pub where he had met his first victim. There would be a satisfying unity in that. With some effort he increased his pace, completely unaware that some fifty yards behind him, he was being followed by a figure in a belted raincoat and fedora pulled well forward to mask part of his face.

Fifteen minutes later and severely out of breath, Lowe approached the Coach and Horses. On the corner he stopped suddenly and leaned against the wall, breathing heavily, his vision blurred. He was surprised and alarmed at how much the brisk walk had taken out of him, sapping his energy. The thought struck him that he might not have enough strength to carry out his plans. If he got a lively one it was possible she could struggle free. He clenched his teeth with determination. That was not going to happen. He would rise to the challenge when it came. He had to. Pulling himself to his full height, he pushed his way through the swing-door into the pub.

It wasn't long before his eye landed on a likely candidate. As he leaned on the counter he had surveyed the customers in the saloon bar. Despite the earliness of the hour the place was fairly crowded: there were locals, a few servicemen, some office workers having a quick one before hurrying away to their suburban warrens and there was a sprinkling of prostitutes – or a least some over-made-up tarts whose eyes flickered expectantly as each new customer pushed his way through the doors.

There was one of these women who particularly appealed to Lowe. She was older and stouter than the rest. She looked raddled and shagged-out. Lowe grinned to himself. She would be a push-over and that was what he needed tonight. Literally. He knew also that with such an experienced hag there was less pretence, less play-acting. One got down to business more quickly. He ordered himself another pint and bought a large gin, and took the drinks over to her table. He plonked the gin down beside her and pulled up a stool.

'For me?' she batted her sooty eyelashes and smiled an awful smile. The thick red lips parted to reveal a row of brown uneven teeth. 'Why, thank you, kind sir,' she added, before taking a large drink of the gin, as though he might change his mind and ask for it back.

'How much?' he grunted.

She raised her eyebrows in surprise.

'How much for a shag?'

Her face froze for a moment. 'Why, you don't waste time, do you, ducks?' she said at last, her voice having lost the suspect veneer of gentility.

'How much?' he repeated.

'I don't come cheap, my lad.' She grinned her awful grin again in the mistaken belief that she was being coquettish.

Lowe refrained from asking her again. His sarcastic expression did that for him.

'You got your own place or what?'

'Or what, I'm afraid, darling,' he said without a trace of humour.

'A short time, eh? Well, that'll cost you two quid and another gin.'

'Have your gin after. Drink up, let's be off.'

'My, you are in a hurry. Still, I like an eager boy. Just let me powder my nose, if you know what I mean, and I'll be with you.' She grinned again and put out her heavily ringed hand to give him an affectionate stroke of the cheek but he pulled away. Oh, he's one of those, she thought. Mr mechanical man. He wanted no affection, no sense of relationship, however false. Just put it in like some part of a machine and perform the function. Well, she'd been on the game many years and had his sort before. At least they were quick. It was just that since the war had started most of her clients – she liked to think of them as clients – had wanted some warmth and emotion in the process. It wasn't really making love, but it was at least pretending. In fact some of the young soldiers almost seemed content just to be held and kissed passionately. The sex came as an afterthought. She liked this. It made her feel human and cared-for.

As she made her way to the ladies she glanced at her watch. Well, she thought, I'll be back in here in fifteen minutes, two quid better off and another gin to keep me company.

When they left the pub it was fully dark and a sharp wind had sprung up. She pulled her thin raincoat around her and shivered. Not for the first time in recent weeks she thought to herself that she was too old for this game any more. Having sex outside in all weathers with a lot of strangers....

Lowe walked beside her like a shadow. He said nothing and made no bodily contact with her. Inside his head, he was preparing himself for the kill.

'There's a yard,' the woman said, 'two streets away. It's quiet and private, but I want to see your money first, mister.'

Lowe pulled out two pound notes from his back pocket and passed them to her.

'That's lovely,' she said, stuffing them in her handbag. Happy at receiving her payment, she grabbed Lowe's hand. 'Come on, then, love,' she said with a smile, leading him down the street.

thirty-seven

Following Lowe, I began to experience a growing sense of frustration. I'd been a clever boy in finding the bastard. But what exactly was I to do now? I was like a big mutt of a dog who had been chasing a car and had now caught up with it. What next? I had no official powers of arrest, no handcuffs to clip on the fellow's wrist even if he were docile enough to let me. On top of this, I didn't carry a gun. He'd got the better of me last night and he could easily do so again. Madmen don't know their own strength.

What I needed was back-up. I wanted that police squad-car to squeal round the corner, siren shrieking, and six hefty coppers to leap out and rugby-tackle Lowe to the ground. That's what I wanted. But I wasn't going to get it. Or was I? Surely all I had to do was make a call to David Llewellyn at the Yard and he could arrange the kind of posse I required. The only problem was, if I stopped to pop into a phone box to make the call, I'd lose Lowe. He would disappear off into the dusk.

And so my frustration grew.

However, my hopes were raised when Lowe approached a pub called the Coach and Horses. There was a phone box on the corner of the road about a hundred yards away. I watched him go inside, then, after a couple of minutes, I peered through the saloon-bar window and spied him at the counter, a full pint of beer in his hand. I sprinted back to the phone box and dialled David's direct line at the Yard. It rang. And it rang. And it rang. I glanced at my watch. It was seven o'clock. Dammit! He'd probably gone home for the night.

Bugger and blast.

There was nothing left for me to do but ring 999. Whether they would believe that I was tracking down a murderer and needed their assistance was another matter. I just had to hope I could convince them that I wasn't a crank. Not an easy task with the story I had to tell, but I really had no other options. I took a deep breath and was just about to make the call when the door of the phone box swung open and a tall, wiry fellow squeezed part-way in.

'Excuse me sir,' he said with a marked Irish accent, 'but I was wondering if youse could help me. You see I've had no sustenance today whatsoever and I'm feeling awfully faint. If youse could see your way to lending me a few coppers to buy myself a cup of tea and a bun or some such, I'd be eternally grateful, so I would.'

It was a nicely judged performance.

'Not just now, eh? I have an urgent call to make,' I replied sharply, giving him a gentle shove to eject him from the box. But he resisted.

'Oh yes, now,' responded my little Irish friend with some ferocity, the Gaelic charm having disappeared from his voice. To reinforce the sentiment he produced a long, cruel-looking knife from the folds of his tatty overcoat.

'In fact,' he continued, 'I'll be needing more than a couple of coppers, if the truth be known. Hand over your wallet. I've no real desire to use my little friend here but I can assure you, I have no qualms about doing so if necessary.'

I swore. This was all I needed now. I glanced over towards the Coach and Horses and, to my despair, I saw Lowe emerge through the swing-doors accompanied by a woman, whose dress and demeanour clearly indicated what she did for a living and it wasn't charity work.

'Come on, mister. Hand over the wallet.'

My blood was really up now. If I was to lose Lowe because of this worm....

'Didn't your mother tell you it was dangerous to play with knives?' I bellowed with a voice full of Shakespearian fury, taking a step nearer.

My assailant flinched at such an aggressive reaction. It was as though Dr Jekyll had turned into Mr Hyde. In that split second of uncertainty my arm shot out and I punched him squarely on the nose. He crumpled to the ground. As he did so I grabbed the knife from his hand. Already two rivulets of blood were streaming down his face from both nostrils.

'You've broke it,' he was moaning. 'You've broke me nose.'

'You're lucky I didn't break your neck. Now beat it before I do more damage to those ugly features of yours.'

He didn't need a second warning. He scrambled to his feet and ran as if all the devils in hell were on his coat-tails. His comic departure brought a brief smile to my face before I remembered my dilemma. I turned to face the road down which Lowe and the woman had travelled. There was not a sign of them. They had melted into the night.

I swore again. And then began running.

thirty-eight

The woman led Lowe along a narrow passage off the main street which gave way to a small courtyard area. It was dark and smelt of damp but she assured him that it was private and would suffice for their purpose. She had used it many times before, often several times a night when the pickings were good. With practised ease she leaned against the wall and slipped her tight skirt up around her thick waist. Even in the gloomy moonlight Lowe could see that she was not wearing knickers. She had obviously prepared herself when she had gone 'to powder her nose'.

'Come on, big boy, let's be having you,' she said, matter-of-factly, as though she was offering to take her pet dog for a walk.

Lowe advanced on her, not unconscious of the significance of the occasion. This was to be his last victim, the last tart he would send to hell. The last time he would throttle the life out of one of these damned creatures. The last sacrifice. He wanted to savour the moment.

He got close to her. He could hear her breathing, a slightly wheezy rasp, and he could smell her cheap perfume. Suddenly he realized that he didn't even know her name.

'What's your name?' he asked as he pressed his body up against hers.

'Kathleen,' she said with a grin. 'Kath to you, big boy.'

He kissed her. This was something that he did not ordinarily do and his instinctive response surprised him.

She responded to the kiss and reached down to his crotch searching for his fly. He wanted none of that. He didn't want to be touched. It was time to make a move.

'Good night, Kath,' he said softly, his hands slipping round her throat.

At first she thought he was being affectionate and she smiled, but as his grip tightened, she quickly realized that something was wrong, that he meant her harm.

'Here ... you bastard, get off,' she cried, kicking him hard on the shins. The pain was sharp and seemed to spread throughout Lowe's ravaged body. She kicked him again. This time he groaned and staggered back, releasing his grip. She kicked him a third time with even greater ferocity and screamed.

The scream reverberated in Lowe's eardrums, blanking out all other sounds. The noise filled his head until he couldn't think, he couldn't function. It seemed to go on for ever. He put his hands to his ears to stop it while he gazed in horror at the woman's distorted open mouth before him, the thick, moist, red lips vibrating obscenely, filling his vision. He felt that at last he was going mad.

And then she kicked him again. This time her target was his groin. Now it was his turn to scream, partly in severe pain as his inflamed genitalia felt as though they had exploded, and partly with fury – a fury which helped to bring him back to reality. With a snarl, he rushed at the woman, his hands like claws ready to rip the life out of her, but now she had pulled a knife from her bag, her protection against awkward customers.

'Get back,' she cried, brandishing the knife. But he took no notice. How could he? He was past worrying whether he would be injured or not. She could stab him to death for all he cared now. As long as the cow died with him, it didn't matter. He reached for her, his hands clasping her throat one more time. Then he felt a sudden jolt of pain as the blade entered his stomach.

thirty-nine

As I padded down the empty street in search of Lowe and the woman while cursing the small time Irish crook who'd delayed me, I heard a scream coming from somewhere to my far left. I skidded to a halt and spied a narrow gap between two buildings. As I sped down the passage another cry punctuated the silence. It was short and deep like the cracking of a branch from an ancient tree. It was the cry of a man.

As I emerged into a kind of courtyard area the scene that met my eyes seemed to have been conjured up from one of my booze-inflamed nightmares. I saw Lowe struggling with the woman, both of them panting and rocking backwards and forwards as if in some drunken dance. But it wasn't sexual passion that appeared to bond the two figures together. It was aggression.

I leapt forward. Grabbing Lowe by the scruff of his neck I yanked him backwards away from the woman. To my surprise he offered no resistance and after my initial effort he staggered backwards a few steps before slumping to the ground. He lay on his back, his mouth popping open and closed like a fish out of water while his hands shook aimlessly. I saw that there was the sheath of a knife sticking in his stomach and blood was frothing out all round it, creating a dark stain across his shirt. By this time the woman had sunk to her knees and was sobbing uncontrollably.

For some moments I stood watching this grim scene, mesmerized, not quite believing that it was actually happening. At length, Lowe gave a guttural cough and then, with an eerie suddenness, he lay still, his face frozen in death, the mouth open and the tongue lolling lifelessly. Not unlike one of his own victims.

I stumbled forward to try and comfort the woman. I lifted her up from her kneeling position and she clung to me, sobbing bitterly.

'You're all right now,' I said, without any real knowledge or certainty that she actually was. I hugged her back and stroked her hair and gradually the tears subsided. At last she lifted her head and brushed the moisture from her mascara-besmeared eyes.

'I've got to give this game up,' she said wearily. 'It's far too dangerous.'

Detective Inspector David Llewellyn extracted a bottle of Johnnie Walker from the bottom drawer of his desk. 'I reckon we need something a little stronger than tea, don't you?'

I nodded and emitted an affirmative grunt. I felt that was all that I was capable of at the moment. It was about two hours later and I was sitting in David's office at Scotland Yard. When I had eventually telephoned the police he had been dragged from the comfort of his hearth and home to supervise events: the removal of the dead body of Robert James Lowe to the police morgue and the arrest of Kathleen Winters for manslaughter.

I had gone back with David to the Yard to make a full statement, in which I explained all that I had learned about Lowe's condition and how I had traced him. David refrained from saying that I should have got in touch with him straight away and let the official police deal with it. There was little point. It was all murky water under the bridge now. The man had been caught and as fate would have it, he had already received his sentence. David poured me a generous measure and passed over the glass.

'Usually, I feel like celebrating when we've nailed a murderer, but somehow this time round I can't find any sense of elation,' he said, with a grim smile, splashing a more generous helping of whisky into his own glass.

I took a gulp, happy that it burned my throat. It was a pleasant discomfort. 'I hope the Winters woman will get off lightly,' I said when the whisky had trickled down and was warming my stomach.

'I'm sure the court will treat her case with understanding. It was self-defence after all. If she hadn't stabbed the devil, she wouldn't be around now.'

'I'm rather glad she got to him before I did. It would have given me great pleasure to kill the bastard myself.' I gripped the glass tightly, my knuckles whitening, and took another drink.

'No news from the hospital?'

'It's a waiting game. Paul is too weak to be operated on at the moment.' I wanted to say more. I wanted to say that I didn't know what I'd do if he died. He was the person I'd known all my life. He was the one person who in a strange kind of way made some sense of my life. He was my touchstone with humanity. At the back of my mind I knew there was always a possibility that Paul could have been killed on active service, but somehow I felt that that would be easier to accept. Dying for one's country was a noble death. But to die at the hands of a deranged murderer on the streets of London … a useless, pointless death. All these things I would have liked to have said to David, but it just wasn't the sort of things men confess to men. It's our oyster mentality, I suppose. We're fine with women, mothers, sisters, girlfriends, wives – to them we can open up, expose our sensitivities; but not to men. It breaks an unspoken masculine code.

Suddenly I felt very tired.

'I assume that I'm free to go?' I asked with a weary smile.

David returned the smile. 'Anytime you like, boyo. I reckon you've earned a good night's rest.'

I rose to go and he put his hand on my shoulder. 'I hope everything turns out … you know … with Paul.'

'Yeah, thanks.'

'I'll pray for him.'

I slipped out of the office and minutes later I was on the cold streets of London once again, the real world pressing in all around me and yet I felt as though I was in a bubble, my own personal protective shell that kept the real world at a distance from me. I made my way to Charing Cross Hospital.

The nurse on duty informed me that there had been no change in Paul's condition. 'That is not as bad as it seems,' she said softly. 'It means that he is holding his own for the present. With more rest and constant medication, he should begin to rally soon.'

I couldn't tell whether she genuinely meant what she was

saying or whether this was the standard reassurance given out to visitors when they didn't know what the hell was going to happen to the patient. I just had to hope that it was the truth.

I sat with Paul awhile. He looked exactly the same as he had done the last time I had seen him. The pale face with the paper-thin skin looked lost on the giant white pillow, and the various tubes created a veritable spider's web around the bed. If only he'd open his eyes. But he didn't.

It was around midnight when I let myself into Hawke Towers. I felt like that fellow in the old poem I had learned at school: I was tired and sick at heart. Immediately, before I had a chance to turn on the light, I knew there was something wrong. I was aware that I was not alone in the room. There was an aroma in the air, a mixture of tobacco, a fine expensive blend, and something sweet. I had a visitor. My hand hovered over the light-switch, but I left the room in darkness. And then I saw the red glow of the cigarette. It pierced the dark like a warning signal. Someone was sitting at my desk.

'About time too. I've been waiting for over two hours,' came the sultry voice in the darkness and the end of the cigarette glowed brighter.

I clicked on the light. 'Sorry to have kept you waiting', I said casually, sloughing off my raincoat and throwing it at the hatstand. Habit had made me an expert at such a procedure. The coat landed safely but awkwardly and hung there like the skin of a dead and fairly repellent fish.

Eunice McLean rose from my chair and came around the desk to greet me. She carried with her that strong sweet scent I had noticed on first entering the room. It was both nauseating and addictive. Before I knew it, she had planted a long and passionate kiss on my mouth. At first I just stood there like a dummy, but that scent was doing things to my brain. I didn't fight it – I just responded. My arms circled her tightly and I returned the kiss. I was clear-headed enough to realize that it was warm human contact and comfort rather than affection that prompted my amorous actions, but what the hell! If it eased my pain, I was up for it.

'I've missed you,' she said, leaning her head on my shoulder. 'You've been a naughty boy. You said you'd ring me.'

'Well, things have been somewhat hectic around here in the last few days.'

'What's happened?'

I shrugged. 'Nothing that would interest you. Just tired old detective business.'

She gave me a peck on the cheek. 'And you look like a tired old detective.'

I nodded. 'That's me, all right.'

'Do you want a drink?'

I grinned. 'Actually I'd like a good strong cup of tea.'

She grabbed my hand and giggled. 'Lead me to the kettle.'

Fifteen minutes later we were both sitting on my rather lumpy sofa in the cramped and shabby room I used as my living-quarters, stretched out before an ancient electric fire, drinking hot sweet tea from large chipped mugs.

'You certainly know how to treat a girl,' Eunice observed, snuggling up to me. 'Hot Typhoo in the finest china.'

We clinked mugs before taking a drink and then we both laughed.

'Tell me,' I said, slumping further down in the sofa, 'how did you get in?'

'I picked the lock, of course. I did go to a very good girls' school and that was one of the things I learned there.'

'Along with forgery, deception and knitting, eh?'

'That's right. How's your tea?'

'Just right,' I grinned.

We sat quietly sipping our tea. I felt so much ache and tension flow out of me. The warmth of Eunice's body moulded into mine had burst that isolating bubble, that protective shell. I had been released and I felt human again and cared for. I thrust to the back of my mind the fact that this very desirable young woman was the daughter of a despicable fascist who was probably responsible, indirectly, for Barbara's death. It would be wrong, I told myself, to blame Eunice for the sins of her father.

I leaned over and kissed her, my hand gently running through her hair. She responded, her body pressing even harder against mine, rousing me. I knew then that we would make love. It was a natural progression from the passion of the moment. In such situations all sensibility, all fear of consequence is silenced. The emotions, selfish and self-satisfying appetites, take over. I was driven. The sexual urge was now in full command. I knew it was foolish and dangerous, but I wanted it, I needed it. My body ached for it and my poor old bruised and battered soul required the revitalizing power of a woman's love, a woman's passion to resurrect my tattered spirit.

We made love on the floor, in front of the electric fire. It happened naturally and without guile on the part of either of us. We were at one with each other, sharing each other's pleasure. Afterwards, we lay, our bodies entwined naturally, not speaking, not kissing, just content. In fact so content was as I that I drifted off to sleep. When I woke up, I was on the floor alone. Rather stiffly, I pulled myself up and found that the room was empty, but there was a note on the sofa. It said: 'When you're ready, turn off the lights and come to bed.'

I wandered into my bedroom to find Eunice fast asleep under the covers. I disrobed as quickly as I could and then slipped in beside her, hugging her tightly.

She roused briefly from her slumbers. 'Hello darling', she whispered, before drifting back to sleep.

forty

I woke early. Even before I was fully conscious I felt a sense of unease. As my eyes focused on the cracks in the ceiling my brain got around to remembering who I was, where I was and then it furnished me in kaleidoscopic fashion with chaotic details of my recent life. I wasn't best pleased. In fact I groaned, wishing I hadn't woken up.

I shifted my head and gazed at my beautiful companion. There she was; serene and sleeping. So it wasn't a dream: it was true. I had l slept with the daughter of the leading fascist in the country. I was ashamed and disgusted at myself. However, these feelings of self-loathing were mixed with those of embarrassment and guilt because I had to admit that I had enjoyed the experience. If I were a high-flown literary type I'd have said that it was 'cathartic'. But as I'm just a poor gumshoe, I'll settle for 'it was rewarding because it allowed me to be emotional and get rid of a lot of pain'. All those bottled-up emotions had spilled out of me – in more senses than one.

Nevertheless, having Eunice in my bed did put me in a difficult position. There she was, breathing gently, sleeping like and looking like an angel, and here I was investigating her father and his filthy organization with a view to sending the lot of them to prison. Sleeping with Eunice made me some kind of despicable worm. I had lowered my standards until they were on a par with those of the cold-hearted Britannia Club bastards.

I jumped out of bed and headed for the bathroom. Cold water and a severe shave would help me organize my thoughts more coherently and help me decide what to do. One thing was certain, I had to get the girl out of my flat and then out of my life. However much I liked her – and I did – the baggage she came with was tainted and dangerous.

185

I returned to the bedroom some thirty minutes later. I was shaved, dressed and very much awake but, sadly, none the wiser. I had brought my sleeping beauty a mug of tea. I shook her shoulder gently and gradually roused her from the realms of dreams. She blinked dozily at me, slowly pulling herself up in bed, draping the sheets around her so that they covered her breasts.

'Good morning, darling,' she said with a lazy grin.

''Morning,' I said, trying not to smile, but I did. 'A mug of tea for you and then I'm afraid you'll have to leave. I have a busy day ahead of me.'

'You're getting rid of me already?' she said, taking the mug and cradling it between her hands, breathing in the warmth of the tea. 'You're a nasty man.'

I gave her a kiss on the forehead. 'Nonsense. I've just got to earn a living, that's all, and you are a real distraction. Surely you've places to go?'

'I like it here.'

'Well you can't stay under the covers all day, that's for sure. Now, come on, get dressed and scoot. Or do I have to pull you out of the bed myself?' I spoke in a jokey-stern manner but my voice did have an edge of frustrated irritation to it.

'OK, spoilsport,' she said. 'Give me five minutes to drink my tea and I'll get out of your hair … for the moment.'

I kissed her again on the forehead and left the room.

Some twenty minutes later I was doing some elementary filing in my office, nervously passing my time while Eunice got dressed and did whatever girls do in the morning, when she appeared in the doorway. What is it with women? On waking they can look dishevelled and pasty-faced as though they've spent the night in a wind tunnel and then a short time in the bathroom with their magic make-up bag and they can emerge looking like a million dollars. Eunice looked like a million dollars. I wanted to hug her and take her to bed all over again.

'I'll go now,' she said with mock petulance, 'but you'd better ring me, Mr Hawke, or else.'

'I will. How could I not?' I felt as though I was dredging up old movie dialogue, saying anything to get the girl to go so that I could think.

We embraced and she left.

I slumped down in my chair, head in hands, and heaved the greatest sigh of my life.

After staring into space for some five minutes or so I decided to head for Benny's and get some victuals inside me. My stomach couldn't remember the last time it had had something substantial to eat. Perhaps a greasy fry-up would raise my spirits. I was reaching for my raincoat when the doorbell rang. Just my luck, I thought, as I saw the eggs and bacon disappearing from my morning's menu. If it was a client, I couldn't turn him or her away. Despite what other things were going on in my life, I still had bills to pay.

I opened the door and came face to face with Ralph Chapman. He was the last person on earth I wished to see this morning. It was as though the members of the Britannia Club were weaving a web around me.

'You keep very pleasant company, I see,' he said, pushing past me.

'Meaning?'

'I just saw our leader's daughter leaving here.'

I wanted to swear, but instead I said: 'Look, I was just on my way out. I have business to attend to.'

'She is a pretty little thing, I must admit. But dangerous goods, I would have thought. Toying with McLean's daughter is likely to get one's fingers burned … or worse.'

'I'd be very much obliged if you would go. I have neither the time nor the temperament for this conversation.'

Suddenly Chapman's demeanour changed. The smirking charm disappeared and his features took on an altogether more sinister look.

'That's a pity because I have things to say which I'm sure you'll find even less to your taste. Now, sit down and shut up.'

Before I could say or do anything, he had pulled a gun from his pocket and waved it in my direction. 'I have no desire to hurt you, Johnny, but if you don't do as I say, I might. I just might.'

I believed him. I did as he said. I sat down and didn't say a word. What the hell now, I thought.

'That's better. We have to talk. You've made things very tricky for us, you know.'

I shook my head. 'I don't know what you're talking about.'

'No, of course you don't. That's practically the only saving grace about your behaviour in this affair. You are a bumbling amateur innocent abroad.'

'And what does that make you?' I asked with a sneer.

'I'm a government agent – that's what it makes me. I've been spying on the bastards at the Britannia Club for ages, trying to collect sufficient evidence to send them down for eternity. You didn't think that we were going to let a gang of thugs like the Britannia Club operate without our surveillance?'

Could I believe my ears or was this some elaborate trick to flush me out into the open?

'A government agent who goes around threatening Jewish café owners, eh?' I said.

Chapman sighed theatrically. 'If you're supposed to be a fascist thug, you've got to act like one. I was just a stone's throw away from having enough evidence to bag the whole lot of them. As it is we're already picking off the lieutenants one by one, but it's the generals we're after, and the leader.'

'Sir Howard?'

Chapman shook his head. 'He's the puppet. We want the puppet-master.'

'Who is that?'

'Don't know yet, that's what has been holding us back. It's taken me over a year to worm my way into the organization and reach a position of trust. I was due to join the inner council where I would have discovered all I needed to know and then you come along with your heroics and queer my pitch. I've slipped down the greasy pole again in favour of you. It's the inner council that makes all the important decisions and the secrecy of its operation is guarded vigorously within the club itself. It's a dangerous privilege to be invited to join. We know you're no more a fascist sympathizer than … Winston Churchill.

We know your game, your bloody amateurish game. Noble but misguided. So instead of me, it'll be you at the inner council meeting tonight.'

'So why are you here?'

'I've just come to warn you. I know what you're up to but this isn't a job for bloody amateurs. You've got to watch your back. They are not stupid. They'll suss you out sooner or later – and it could be sooner. Watch yourself, Johnny. At the moment they like you and trust you but if they get one whiff that you're playing a game with them.... My people know about you but they'll not interfere – it might jeopardize my position. You're on your own, Johnny boy. Don't trust anyone ... they're all a bunch of two-faced bastards.'

'How do I know you're not the same?'

He smiled. 'You don't. You're just going to have to take me at my word.'

My instinct told me to trust him but my common sense advised me still to be wary.

Suddenly, he leaned forward and placed the gun on my desk. 'Here, I reckon you'll need this. I suspect that you and tight corners are going to become well-acquainted in the near future.'

'What are you after? What is so special about the inner council?'

'It is controlled by whoever is the real force behind the Britannia Club. Despite all our efforts we've not been able to put a finger on him. He has a direct link with Germany, possibly Hitler himself, and we suspect the club is forging links with other fascist groups throughout the country in readiness for the invasion.'

'The invasion?'

'France has already fallen to the Nazis. Britain is next in line. We need to nail the leader and get hold of the details of all the members of the club and its nationwide links.'

'Where do Sir Howard and Guy Cooper come into all this?'

'Misguided fools. The worse kind, of course. They are blinkered and malleable. Without such bigots, the fascists wouldn't have a hope in hell of getting a foothold in this country. Mosley was another one.'

'Why are you telling me all this?'

'To forewarn you. I tried to frighten you off, but you still scrambled up on to the diving board determined to plunge into shark-infested waters. This is not a game. Your life is at risk. One false move and you'll be occupying a cardboard coffin.'

'You paint a lovely picture.'

'I can't help you in case my cover is blown, so do not come staggering to me for help. However, if you do uncover any vital information …'

'I can come staggering to you then.'

'That's about it.'

'Where do I stagger?'

'Get a message to Captain Miles Stanhope at the Reform Club.'

'Who's he?'

'I am he.' He gave a mock salute. 'Goodbye, Mr Hawke. I wish you luck, although I don't think luck on its own will be enough to save you.'

With these pithy words he gave me another salute and left.

I sat where I was for some time, digesting the unsettling message that Chapman had delivered. It certainly did seem as though I had been some kind of naïve fool in getting myself mixed up with the Britannia Club but there was no retreating now. I'd waded so far into the treacherous waters it would be almost as dangerous to turn back as to carry on. I picked up the gun, felt its cold hard shape in the palm of my hand. 'It's carry on I must,' I said to myself, slipping the pistol into my coat pocket.

forty-one

Despite Chapman's revelations and the unsettling effect they had on me, added to all the other unsettling events that had invaded my corkscrew of a life in the last few days, I was still determined to fill my face at Benny's café. Then I would visit my brother at the hospital in the hope that he had rallied sufficiently for them to be able to operate. I wasn't a praying sort of fellow, but I sent a short message to the Big Man upstairs, asking that Paul be allowed to live.

'You heard the news?' were the first words spoken to me by Benny as I entered the café.

'You're bringing your prices down?'

Benny didn't even smile. Instead he held up a copy of the *Daily Mail* and pointed to the headlines. The Royal Navy had lost nine ships in the evacuation of Crete. More lives sacrificed for Hitler's mad dream.

'That's put me right off my breakfast,' I said.

'How do you think it makes a little Jewish fellow feel? It seems there's no stopping Adolf. I can feel him breathing down my neck. I expect the Hun to come marching up the street any day now.'

I shook my head. 'Hell will freeze over before the Germans goose-step into London.

'So you say, but just in case I'll get my thick overcoat out of mothballs, eh?'

Benny raised a weak smile, but the worry lines remained.

'In the meantime, you can get me a fry-up and pronto. I've decided I'm not going to let the Boches put me off my grub.'

'Coming up,' he said, with some of his old enthusiasm, and retreated into the kitchen.

If the truth were known, I was just as worried and concerned as Benny about the war effort. We just did not seem to be winning. The face of this handsome city was now battered and disfigured thanks to the German Air Force and their ferocious *blitzkrieg*. Everywhere you looked there was evidence of the Nazis' handiwork. At the same time Hitler's tentacles were spreading even further, planting the swastika in the new territories across Europe and beyond. We all knew that the Führer's ultimate goal was to see that accursed flag flying freely in London. And I felt so helpless in all this. Little Johnny One Eye, unfit to fight for his country, sidelined and emasculated, pretending to be a detective in this crumbling city. I really believed in what Churchill had said about every soldier making a difference, every soldier being important. But I reckoned a Cyclops didn't figure.

I had these internal conversations with myself every now and again when I was feeling sorry for myself. It was almost a routine I went through. It was good to get such gloomy thoughts expressed and then out of the way. I always ended up by castigating myself for being so negative and self-pitying. I gave myself a metaphorical kick up the backside and told myself to get on with life. And I usually did. Who needs a psychiatrist when you have the strange inner working of the Johnny Hawke mind?

By the time I had got through the mental resuscitation process Benny was plonking down a plate of sizzling goodies before me: egg, bacon, beans and a lone sausage.

'Enjoy, Johnny. Next time it may be liverwurst and sauerkraut,' he said ruefully.

It was good to have a full stomach. It gave me the energy and what Benny would call *chutzpah* to face the rigours of the day. After leaving a generous tip and another comforting word to the frowning Benny, I made my way once more to Charing Cross Hospital. My little message to the Man Upstairs must have gone astray because, yet again, there had been no change in Paul's condition. He still lay, zombie-like, under white sheets, the tubes still running from his body to various machines. All it needed was Colin Clive as Baron Frankenstein to come in and pull the switch to reanimate him.

As I stared at the ghost of my brother one of the doctors approached me.

'Mr Hawke isn't it, Paul's brother?'

I nodded. 'How is he … really?'

'Well, there has been little change in his condition since he was admitted which was fine in the early stages as it allowed the body to stabilize and come out of the shock it's had from the damage done; but by now with all the drugs we're pumping into him, we should be seeing some signs of him starting to rally, some improvement in his heart rate. But we're not.'

'Is he going to die?'

The doctor turned his weary face to me. He was a man of about forty, but his features were criss-crossed with worry lines and his dry, thinning hair was almost completely grey. I reckoned that looking after the sick ages you.

'I am asked that question several times a day by concerned relatives,' he said softly. 'It's a hard one. When I was just starting out in medicine it gave me constant dilemmas. Should I ease the pain for the moment by lying or should I just tell the truth. I found that choice difficult. Then one day, I realized that I just had to tell the truth – the truth as I saw it at least. I'm not infallible. I could be wrong. The outcome may not be the same as I predict, but I felt that as a doctor and a trusted professional it was my duty to be honest with people. That's how I work it these days. So, in reply to you … yes, I think there is a strong possibility that your brother will die, but I can't be sure. The next twenty-four hours are critical. If he doesn't show any signs of improving, it will not be long before he regresses, slips away from us. Literally there is nothing more we can do. It's up to Paul now.'

I nodded, my dry throat denying me speech. I appreciated the doctor's honesty but that didn't stop me feeling as though I'd been hit by a London omnibus smack in the ribs.

The doctor gave me a tight smile and left me alone. I pulled a chair up beside the bed. I would have liked to have held Paul's hand but it was hidden beneath the covers which had been strapped down. I leaned forward, scrutinizing that white mask.

There was no sign of movement at all. If it wasn't for the gentle rise and fall of his chest and the slight whooshing sound emanating from where the tube entered his mouth, I would have thought he was dead already.

'Come on, Paul,' I whispered, leaning as close to him as I could. 'Come on, you bugger. Shake a leg. It's time you were stirring your stumps now. You've had your lie-in. You can't stay here for ever. For a start, I need you. I've always needed you. My big brother. Right from the days of the orphanage. Don't you remember? 'Course you do. You were always sticking up for me then, especially against Mrs Groves. Who could forget her? You said she looked like a fat scarecrow in a dress. But she was more frightening. Her and that stick of hers. D'you remember how you sneaked into her room and stole that stick so she couldn't beat us any more? You buried it in the rose bushes.' I laughed. 'I bet it's still there. Pity was she soon replaced that stick with a new one, one that had more thrashing power. You said she made it from the stays of her corset. Paul, Paul, do you remember?'

My words floated away but Paul remained still trapped in his own silent prison. And then suddenly there was some eye movement. The lids rippled and for a brief moment, they flickered open, just enough for me to see the blue beneath before they closed again.

I gasped with joy and looked around frantically for the doctor. He was nowhere in sight, but I managed to attract the attention of a nurse and I beckoned her to the bedside.

'I've just been sitting with my brother, talking to him, trying to get through to him and… he opened his eyes. It was only for a second, but he actually opened his eyes.'

'Of course,' she said with some sympathy. 'He will from time to time. It is an automatic reaction. It's not prompted by any external stimulus, I'm afraid. He's been doing it on and off since he was brought in.' She laid a hand on my arm. 'I'm sorry.'

'I just thought …' I said, my words trailing off as I gave a dispirited shrug.

I sat for another half an hour or so chatting to Paul, talking about the bad old days we shared together, our common experience of growing up in several orphanages, hoping that some of it was filtering through into his brain, stirring something inside his head, tugging him towards consciousness. It seemed I was wasting my time. There was no visible change in Paul whatsoever.

As I got up to leave, a little spark of anger ignited within me. I leaned over as close as I could to his masklike face.

'Listen, pal,' I growled, 'the next time I come here you'd better be sitting up, stuffing your face with toast and chatting up the nurses – or else. Is that understood, you bastard? Good!'

I hadn't got more than a hundred yards from the hospital when I was approached by a well-built, red-faced man in a tweed overcoat. He asked if I had a light. I pulled out my lighter and obliged.

'That's very kind of you, Mr Hawke,' he said, blowing the smoke away.

'You know my name?'

'Certainly. More than that.' He gave me a knowing look.

'Who are you?'

'Just a messenger, no more.' So saying he slipped a small book into my hand.

'What's this?'

'A good read, I should say. Very instructive.'

With that he moved backwards at quite a pace, quickly losing himself in the crowd. After I had recovered from my surprise he had disappeared completely from view.

I examined the book. It was some dull philosophical tract, but written in ink on the fly leaf was a message: *The meeting tonight is at 12 Cheyne Walk, Chelsea. Tell no one and come alone.*

forty-two

I looked at the address written on the flyleaf of the book that the red-faced stranger had given me again and smiled. At first I found something comical, farcical even, in the method of its delivery. It was like something out of an Alfred Hitchcock movie. Very *Thirty Nine Steps*, very cloak-and-dagger. My second reaction, however, was one of less amusement. How, I wondered, had this 'messenger', this minion of the Britannia Club, known where I would be in order for him to pass the book over to me? It wasn't a coincidence that he saw me in the street. He had known where I was. There was only one answer to the question. I had been followed. I was under surveillance. They were checking me out. What else did they know?

Instinctively I gazed around at the throng of anonymous pedestrians flowing past me. Was one of them watching me, shadowing me? Had anyone slowed down, pretending to tie a shoe-lace or to light a cigarette, or stepped into a doorway, waiting in the shadows for me to make my next move? I could see no one, no one suspicious, but I suppose that's what you expect to see when you are being tracked by a professional. Suddenly I felt very vulnerable ... naked and exposed. I guessed my friend Ralph Chapman/Captain Miles Stanhope had been right: I was a naïve amateur where the Britannia Club was concerned.

With a sense of unease I slipped the book into my inside pocket and carried on walking, feeling now somewhat self-conscious about all my actions.

It was a bright, pleasantly warm day. I slipped off my rain-coat and carried it over my shoulder. The brittle spring was shifting towards summer. I glanced at my watch. It was just past noon. I wondered what to do with the rest of my day until the evening. I could go back to the office and wait, see if any rich client turned up offering me £1,000 to find their lost pussy-cat. Even if that were likely, the prospect of sitting in my dusty office all afternoon did not appeal to me, especially on such a lovely day as this. It would be quite nice to have a walk in the sunshine. Who knew for how many days I would be able to do this in the future – especially if hell was ready to freeze over and the Germans did arrive.

I pulled out the book once more and checked the address of this evening's meeting. It struck me that it would do me no harm to take a gentle stroll to Chelsea and check out the premises. After all, forewarned is forearmed. And so that was what I decided to do.

I made my way along Whitehall, down to the river and strolled along the Embankment in the direction of Chelsea. Occasionally I turned my head to look behind to see if I could spot some phantom shadow trailing me, but I saw no one who looked a likely candidate. Perhaps I was overreacting. The passing of the book was just to alert me to the fact that they had their beady eye on me, just in case. That point made, they'd leave me alone for the time being. That's what I hoped, anyway.

It was pleasant to walk along by the river, the sun glinting on its rippling surface, the trees hurriedly unfurling their leaves in the surprising warmth and the various vessels chugging past as though business was as usual and there was no war to contend with. And if I didn't raise my eyes high enough to take in the jagged outlines of the bomb damaged warehouses on the far bank, I could almost believe that too.

The comparative quiet of my route and the warmth of the sun on my face helped me relax and for some blessed fleeting moments I forgot the dark and dangerous business in which I was involved. Eventually I reached Chelsea and crossed over the road. This wasn't an area of town I was particularly familiar with. It was the home of the rich and privileged and as such not really part of my address book. I accosted a passer-by who looked like a native of this very smart jungle and enquired where Cheyne Walk was located. He was a tall, distinguished, elderly chap, dressed in flashy tweeds with a bright shiny monocle screwed into his right eye. He could have passed for Lord Peter Wimsey's dad. He gave me directions in a perfectly polite manner but I couldn't help feeling from his expression and tone of voice that he regarded me as some kind of lowly tradesman who had wandered beyond the confines of his designated patch.

Following his instructions, another ten minutes walk led me to Cheyne Walk which ran parallel to the river. It was a broad tree-lined street with a series of smart detached stone built houses. The war was merely a dream here. Rather as in Manchester Square, there was a quiet, protected, surreal quality to the place. The *Luftwaffe* wouldn't dare drop any bombs here. Even the birds sang softly.

I walked slowly, casually up the street, smoking a cigarette, checking off the numbers. Number 12 was a large, white-stuccoed property, three storeys high with a broad flight of steps leading up to an impressive front door. It was the sort of house one expected a government minister or a rich and discreet film star to own. I wondered who did own it. Probably Sir Howard McLean. As I was pondering this, a large black car purred round the corner and pulled up outside the house. I slipped out of sight behind a large beech tree and watched.

A liveried chauffeur emerged from the car and opened the rear door. Two men in dark suits got out. I hadn't seen either of them before. They were deep in animated conversation as they mounted the steps. The door of the house opened and Sir Howard appeared in the entrance. He stepped forward to greet the visitors and performed a Nazi salute. The two men responded in the same manner.

A chill ran through me. For such an exchange to take place in broad daylight in London on a fine, sunny afternoon was unreal, unthinkable. I had never seen the Nazi salute except at the cinema in movies or in newsreels, or when some joker was making fun of Hitler, but here it was blatantly performed in all seriousness. Chapman had been right. I had been naïve to think I was just dealing with a nasty group of misguided fanatics.

198

The three men disappeared inside the house and the door closed behind them. The chauffeur slipped inside the car and drove off.

And so another dilemma was served up hot and steaming on Johnny Hawke's plate. What was I to do now? Grab a cab and rush round to Scotland Yard and alert the coppers that I'd seen three men doing Adolf Hitler impersonations in a house in Chelsea? If they took me seriously they would probably send a few squad cars round and then what would happen? What evidence would they find? These Britannia Club people were far too clever not to have planned for such a contingency. Eels learned how to be slippery in their presence. These villains would wriggle out of such a situation with ease. However, even if the police were able to nab a few fascist ne'er-do-wells, they still wouldn't be able to nail the whole organization.

If I didn't go to the police what the hell could I do? I felt inside my jacket pocket, my hand curling comfortingly around the hard lines of the gun. Well, I knew the answer to that question but it did not make me feel particularly happy. However, the choice was clear. I had got myself into this mess, and I had to get myself out of it. Anyway I could do more damage inside the vipers' den than outside. Perhaps I would be able to do something for my country after all.

I made my way back to the Embankment and retraced my steps while the fragile timbers of a plan began to put themselves together in my mind. At Westminster Bridge I stepped into a telephone box and made a call.

forty-three

That evening I dressed myself in my best black double-breasted suit, white cotton shirt and red silk tie, with a flashy hanky peeking out of my top pocket, and I put an extra shine on my shoes. To complete the film-star appearance I doused myself liberally in some cheap cologne. I grinned at my own reflection staring at me from the cracked mirror over the wash-basin in the communal bathroom which I shared with the three other occupants of Priory Court. I may not possess the handsome features and *savoir-faire* of Cary Grant or Clark Gable, not even of Mickey Mouse, but I reckoned I didn't look too bad that evening. That was as it should be; after all it was to be a special occasion.

I knew a clear head was essential but so was some Dutch courage and that came in the form of neat whisky. I decided to treat myself to a couple of stiff ones at the Velvet Cage before I finally screwed up my courage to join the Nazi party!

It was a little before seven when I checked my hat and coat in at the Cage and wandered into the bar. It being early, the place was quiet. There were few customers, the musicians hadn't set up for the night and the thick veil of tobacco smoke which would mask most of the area later that evening was still in its infancy.

I sat at the bar and ordered a double whisky, no ice. The owner, the resistible George Cazmartis, wandered over to me and slapped me on the back.

'You're looking pretty smart this evening, Johnny boy. You out with a lady?'

Although I disliked Cazmartis, he always treated me as a bosom buddy. I tolerated this because I liked his club. It was my second home.

'Who knows? The night is yet young,' I replied, forcing myself to grin civilly at him.

The barman returned with my drink.

Cazmartis waved his hand in a cutting motion. 'On the house, Ray,' he said to the barman, before slapping me once more on the back. 'Have a good evening.'

I grimaced into my drink. 'Cheers,' I replied, taking a swig. It warmed and relaxed me and it also informed me that I should stop at this one. Another double would help me relax too much. I really needed all my wits about me once I got to 12 Cheyne Walk. I reckoned there were a few blue touch-papers going to be lit tonight and I needed to be on my toes. I drank slowly and thought about the evening ahead. I couldn't know exactly what to expect but I knew a lot would depend on my convincing portrayal of a Jew-hater.

I was just able to hear the first number by Tommy Parker and the boys before my watch told me it was time to go. I hailed a taxi outside the club and was soon on my way through the quiet streets of London to my appointment with the inner circle.

There were several cars parked in the quiet tree-lined avenue when I arrived. I waited for the taxi to depart before I made a move. I breathed in the cool night air, hoping it would calm the little kittens playing energetically in the pit of my stomach. The sky was now a dark, steely blue and the ghost of a full moon was gradually making its presence felt.

Casually I approached the door of number 12. It opened before I could ring the bell and I was admitted by some sort of flunkey, a tall thin man in a dinner suit.

'Good evening, Mr Hawke,' he said in a way that suggested that I was a regular visitor.

I nodded.

'Let me take your hat and coat and then you can go through to the drawing-room.' He indicated two large closed doors at the far end of the hallway.

'Thanks,' I said quietly, slipping him my coat and hat. I approached the doors.

'Don't bother to knock, Mr Hawke. Just go in. You are expected.'

Why did I find the words 'you are expected' so unsettling, I wondered as I opened the door?

From then on the evening took on the dimensions of an oddly remembered dream where all the angles are distorted and the faces are vague or exaggerated and rather frightening. The room was dimly lighted by two standard lamps, while a log fire in the grate sent flickering shadows leaping up to the ceiling. Heavy velvet curtains were drawn across two large windows at the rear which I assumed looked out on a back garden. At the centre was a large round table around which sat a group of shadowy figures who all turned in my direction as I entered. I suddenly felt naked.

One of the figures rose. 'At last, our new recruit, Mr John Hawke. Welcome,' he said moving through the shadows towards me. It was Sir Howard McLean. He shook my hand and directed me to take a seat at the table.

'Let me get you a drink. Whisky is your tipple, I think.'

'Yes, thank you.' He probably knew my inside-leg measurement and my collar size as well, I mused.

While Sir Howard busied himself at the drinks trolley, I gazed at the faces around the table. There was Guy Cooper, the two men I had seen entering the house earlier that afternoon and eight other men whom I didn't recognize but who scrutinized me with unwavering glances as though I were a specimen under a microscope. And there was Lady McLean. I must admit it was a shock to see her in this coven. In my naïvety I had not thought that she would be a member of the controlling force of the Britannia Club – had supposed that she was in fact just a dutiful wife with a misguided sense of loyalty. It seemed that I was wrong. I had been fooled by her surface charm and civilized behaviour.

Sir Howard handed me my drink and then resumed his seat. At this point I expected him to take charge of the meeting, but it was Lady McLean who spoke.

'Now we are all here, we can begin. Mr Hawke you join us

at a very crucial meeting. As we all know, there can be no doubt that a German victory in this war is guaranteed. One only needs to read the newspapers to learn of Hitler's successful strategies and victories. Remember how easy it was for him to occupy France. Now it's our turn. His air force has shattered this city and turned its inhabitants into frightened rabbits. The Germans' next move will be to cross the Channel. It is imperative that we are prepared for that eventuality. We must be ready to welcome them, to aid them in forging a peace with us. Our Government in their wilful stupidity have ignored the voice of the British fascists to their own disadvantage. Foolishly, they believed that by interning Mosley, Chesterton, Leese, the Duke of Bedford and the others, they could crush our movement. I can tell you, Mr Hawke, they have not crushed our movement, they have set it afire, they have driven it to strive all the harder. It is just that for the time being our actions are covert and secret. But we are stronger and more resolute than ever. And when the Germans arrive our voice will be heard all over this land and our anti-Jewish policies will be implemented.'

Lady McLean was not really addressing me now, but rather a rally in the Reichstag. Her voice rose with imperious passion and her expression changed. Her eyes flashed coldly with a touch of madness and her features hardened in the dim light. She was no longer the demure, civilized upper-class woman whom one pictured arranging flowers and opening garden fêtes. Here was a ferocious zealot with a determined, unnerving fervour and a steely heart. As she paused, all those sitting at the table drummed the top with their fists as a form of applause and approbation of her sentiments. The noise echoed around the room like the rumble of artillery fire.

With heart-stopping clarity I now realized that this apparently gentle and refined lady was in fact the driving force behind the Britannia Club. She was the leader the government had been after. While appearing to be the subservient partner to Sir Howard she had successfully hoodwinked my friend Chapman and his masters. Only those in the inner council knew of her real strength and power.

My mind was reeling as I listened to her words and yet I realized I had to respond in kind. I managed to mouth the word 'Excellent,' while joining in the table-drumming routine. At length Lady McLean held up her hand to silence us. Then she turned her attention in my direction again.

'First let me introduce you to two of our trusted lieutenants, Robert Mersey and the Honourable Tim DeVere.' She indicated each of the men in turn with a fluid hand-gesture and we exchanged polite greetings. 'We also have with us tonight six leaders of regional outposts of the British Union of Fascists, outposts which the authorities in their complacency believe no longer exist. We have Mr Brownlow from Bradford, Mr Carpenter from Birmingham, Mr Godfrey from Exeter, Mr Evans from Swansea, Mr Rayner from Newcastle and Mr Preen from Glasgow.'

At the mention of their names each of the six men in turn gave a sharp and surly nod in my direction. I reciprocated.

'It is wonderful to meet you, gentlemen', I enthused. 'I had no idea that the movement was so strong, so widespread and—'

'So clever.' Lady McLean finished my sentence for me with a grim smile. 'Now, I have saved the great treat until last. We are honoured to have with us this evening two officials of the Third Reich who have brought communications directly from Herr Hitler.'

At the mention of this name the butterflies which had been fluttering nervously within my tummy suddenly began rampaging around in hob-nailed boots.

The two men I had seen entering the house that afternoon swept the table with their steely grins. 'I have pleasure in introducing Colonel Hermann Kruger and Lieutenant Friedrich Reinhard, representatives of the Third Reich and emissaries of Herr Hitler himself.'

It was clear that the other men around the table were as surprised as I was by this announcement. Colonel Kruger rose to his feet and acknowledged us all with a curt bow. Apparently, it was time for his speech.

'Lady McLean, gentlemen, I bring you greetings from the

Führer and congratulations for the work you are doing here in your country. It is reassuring to know that while your misguided government still holds the belief that they can win this war against the might and power of the Third Reich, there is a body of men and women in your country who have the foresight and the courage to work for peace. You are well aware that the real bad apple in the barrel of Europe is the Jew. They have tainted our countries for too long. Now is the time for retribution.'

More table-drumming.

'With the blessing of our Führer we have come to forge links with you in preparation for that day, that day which will arrive quite soon when we shall march into London and assume power.'

I felt sick to my stomach. Not because of what this Nazi was saying. After all what should I expect of one Hitler's minions to spout but claptrap about his hatred of the Jews, the power and invincibility of the Fatherland and how they would soon defeat the British forces. It was the bloody nodding donkeys sitting around the table, nodding in acceptance of this nightmare scenario, nodding their freedom and their birthright away that infuriated me. British nodding donkeys not only ready but eager for a German invasion, a German occupation, a German government ruling Britain. I felt like standing up and shouting abuse at the lot of them, telling them that the day would never come when those bastards in grey uniforms would tramp through the streets of London, arms aloft in a Hitler salute. Never. But to do such a thing would be signing my own death-warrant. Here I was in a nest of vipers in a flimsy disguise as a junior viper. One slip of my disguise and I would become a viper *entrée*. I took a sip of whisky in the hope that it would quell the rising tide of my mixed emotions.

Colonel Kruger had resumed his seat to more table-drumming and Lady McLean was addressing us once again, or to be more precise she was addressing me.

'There will be time later for a more detailed discussion as how we can co-ordinate our resources for that much anticipated day when the German forces will arrive to relieve us of this blinkered government and expunge the presence of the Jews from our country. However, before that we must initiate you, Mr Hawke, into the inner council.'

Initiate? I did not like the sound of that word. No one had mentioned anything about an initiation the other evening. Little cold tendrils of fear began sprout. I said nothing but tried to look eager.

'I have already informed our friends here of your quick-thinking and courageous action the other evening and of your fervent desire to help our cause at the highest level....'

'I am anxious to do all I can,' I said with enthusiasm. A Hollywood contract was waiting; either that or a shallow grave.

'Good man,' piped up Sir Howard.

Lady McLean gave a sharp look which silenced him. It was clear who was the captain of this ship.

'However,' she continued, returning her gaze to me, 'it is important that we can be sure of your intentions and motives in wanting to join us in the inner council. You must prove yourself to us. This is a privileged role and a key one and we have to protect ourselves from ... how should I put this ... infiltration from the wrong type. A spy in other words. We have to be very careful. You understand?'

I certainly did. How could I not? I was a spy.

'Of course,' I said. 'I am prepared to do all I can for the cause, to prove my dedication.'

A smile touched her lips. It was brief, it was cold and it never reached her eyes. 'As they say, actions speak louder than words. Guy, I think you can bring in our special guest now.'

Without a word Guy Cooper sprang from his seat and left the room. His mistress's voice had spoken. I could see from the expressions on the faces of the other men, apart from Sir Howard, that they were equally puzzled as to what was happening. The two Germans exchanged questioning glances, but nothing was said and we waited in silence. A few minutes later Guy returned, dragging another man with him. The stranger shuffled into our presence, his hands bound and his mouth tightly gagged. His face was bruised and there was a livid cut on his forehead.

I recognized him and I saw from his eyes, wide with shock and horror, that he recognized me also.

It was Benny.

Instinctively I half-rose from my chair, but some inner sense of self-preservation prevented me from saying anything.

'Of course you know this man, Mr Hawke.' Lady McLean's imperious tones cut through anticipatory silence.

'Yes, yes, I know him,' I said, my voice querulous as I resumed my seat.

'The owner of the café which you frequent on a regular basis, Benny Slawinski.'

'Yes.'

'The *Jewish* café owner.'

'Yes.'

Lady McLean reached below the table and produced a small dark object which she held up to the light. It was a gun. A Luger pistol fitted with a silencer. She stroked it as one might a favourite pet, then she placed it on the table.

'There will be one less Jew in London tonight. One less obstacle to contend with when we have secured a peace for our fellow Britons. You, Mr Hawke, are going to carry out his execution. You are going to kill him.' Deftly she slid the gun along the table so that it stopped directly in front of me.

'You are going to prove yourself to us, demonstrate your hatred of the Jews by killing one of their kind. Pick up the gun and shoot the little swine.'

forty-four

Nurse Rutherford's job when she first came on duty was to go round the ward and check on the patients, note the latest emendations to the record charts hanging from the ends of the beds, and ask those patients who were still awake or conscious if they needed anything. Nurse Rutherford liked being on night-duty, there were fewer staff around, especially doctors, and she felt more in charge, more important than in the hustle and bustle of a day-shift. The ward was her domain and unless there was an emergency or an urgent admission she felt in total control. She prayed every night that there would be no air raids with the resultant casualties to disturb the tranquil waters of her night duty.

Nurse Rutherford did her tour of the patients briskly and efficiently. Only one old chap, a Mr Norris, who had lost an arm and a leg when his house was bombed was awake. He asked for a cup of tea, 'very strong with two sugars.' Nurse Rutherford said she would see what she could do. She gave him a sweet smile and stroked the old chap's forehead. He returned the smile stoically and closed his eyes. Bet he's in the Land of Nod when I bring him his tea, she mused as she reached the bed of her last patient. She looked down at the pale, immobile face just appearing above the sheets. Poor blighter, he'd been in about three days now and it looked as though there was still no change in his condition. She checked his record sheet. Just as she thought, no change. She reckoned he'd never recover now. He'd been away too long, away down that deep dark tunnel. He'd never scramble back.

From habit she adjusted the bedclothes and was about to go and get Mr Norris his cup of tea, when suddenly the patient opened his eyes. They didn't open gradually but snapped open as though he had been shocked out of his slumbers. Nurse Rutherford gave a little start. The patient's head turned in her direction and his blue eyes focused on her, the pale, thin lips fashioning themselves into a weak smile.

'Hello, I'd love a drink,' he said clearly. 'My mouth is awfully dry.'

forty-five

Time stood still.

Or so it seemed to me. Everything was locked in the moment when I had been presented with the Luger and the challenge to kill Benny. In the dimly lighted room everyone had become frozen shadows, staring at me with the eerie static features of a waxwork tableau, like an exhibit from Madame Tussaud's Chamber of Horrors, only these fellows were alive and dangerous.

I looked down at the Luger on the table before me, disbelief clouding my thoughts for a moment. I glanced over at Benny, his eyes wide with fear, his body rigid with apprehension. And then I returned my gaze to Lady McLean, whose hard, triumphant features taunted me. She knew that I couldn't do it. She knew I couldn't kill Benny. She thought she had trapped me. I was an exhibit for her tame German audience.

Damn her!

I couldn't afford to falter. Not now. Not after I had come so far. I reached for the gun. It was a slow deliberate action. I smiled back at Lady McLean as I took the Luger and held it firmly in my right hand. I wanted to surprise her, confuse her. I succeeded. The broader my smile grew the less confident she seemed. Her brow furrowed with uncertainty. All this time my brain was racing. Was the pistol really loaded, I wondered? If they really didn't trust me, would they allow me to take possession of a live weapon? It had to be loaded with blanks, surely? Otherwise I could just spray the assembled throng. Shoot at least one of their number. Maybe they just wanted to see if I would fire the thing at Benny. That would be proof enough of my hatred of Jews. But if it was loaded and I pulled the trigger ... I could not take such a chance. It was a form of Russian roulette and I wasn't going to play.

All these thoughts and actions took but a few seconds in reality, but as I experienced them they seemed be part of a long slow dream.

Then I broke the spell; I propelled things back into real time. Clumsily I dropped the Luger and it fell to the floor.

'You seem rather nervous, Mr Hawke,' observed Lady McLean.

'Not nervous, just a little accident-prone,' I replied, bending down apparently to pick up the weapon. As I did so, I slipped my own revolver out of my pocket instead. There was no doubt about it being loaded. Rising again I took aim at one of the standard lamps and fired. With a pleasing explosion the light went out and the room grew darker.

One of the Germans swore in his native tongue. The rest of the vipers grew agitated. Chairs were upturned, some of the men, all but silhouettes now, began to make their way to the door, to escape the madman with the gun. Meanwhile I moved swiftly over to Guy Cooper and Benny. Before he knew what was happening I had welted Cooper across the face with the butt of my gun. He gave a cry of pain and fell to the floor.

A shot rang out and I felt the bullet whiz past. I ducked down, pulling Benny to the floor with me.

'Get him. Get him!' screamed Lady McLean above the confusion.

I scrambled out of sight under the table. As I emerged from the other side I fired again, extinguishing the second standard lamp, thus plunging the room into total darkness. Further shots were fired. Flashes of red flame ignited the dark for a split second, revealing a fantastic shadow-play of disorientated figures. It was as though we were playing a surreal game of hide and seek.

Above the mêlée someone called out: 'Get the light-switch.'

Swiftly I crawled across the carpet towards one of the tall windows at the rear of the room. I was nearly there when someone trod on my arm.

'He's here,' the fellow cried. I shot the bastard in the kneecap and the informer toppled on top of me with a guttural scream.

I hoisted him up and, casting him to one side, continued towards the window. Thankfully the search for the light-switch had not borne fruit yet and the room was still in darkness.

More random shots were fired as I slipped behind the long curtains. Hurriedly raising the blackout blind, I smashed the glass with the butt of my revolver, making an aperture large enough for me to stick my head out. Then, retrieving the trusty police whistle so kindly loaned to me by my friend Detective Inspector David Llewellyn, I gave three sharp blasts on it, the shrill, urgent sound piercing the silence of the cool, dark night air.

Suddenly a hand grabbed the back of my collar and dragged me through the curtains into the room again. I stumbled backwards and as I did so someone's fist connected with my nose, but remarkably I managed to retain my balance.

'Get the lights,' cried my assailant and, as if by magic, the room was immediately bathed in bright electric illumination. For a moment everyone seemed dazed by the sudden change from total darkness to garish brightness and froze in mid-action. Gradually, all eyes turned to focus on me. If looks could kill, I'd have been dead in seconds. I saw that my assailant was none other than Colonel Kruger, doing his bit for the Fatherland. Taking advantage of the lull in activity, I returned the compliment for the Motherland, and smashed him in the face.

As he fell to the floor with some Germanic oath, there were sounds of a commotion in the hall and more shrill whistles.

'It's the police!' I cried. 'Time to surrender, I'm afraid.'

Lady McLean, who had been over by the door let out a guttural noise, not so much a deep scream, more of an atavistic roar of anger. She took two steps towards me, raised her pistol and fired. It happened so quickly I hadn't a chance to duck. I felt a red-hot searing pain as the bullet tore into my flesh. Immediately I felt bilious and was certain I was going to be sick. The bile rose in my throat and then, thankfully, retreated. So shocked was I that I wasn't even sure where I had been wounded; my whole body seemed ache. Gradually the light began to fade as though someone was inking in my eyeball and then sounds grew fainter. The last thing I remember is my legs melting rapidly and my body rushing to embrace the carpet. I have no memory of hitting the floor.

forty-six

I awoke with a start. Some horrible dream, forgotten immediately, had catapulted me into wakefulness. My body seemed to ache all over, but in particular my cheek throbbed and my shoulder felt as though it was on fire. I screwed up my eyes and shook my head, trying to shake my memory into place. It very quickly shifted into position: the house in Chelsea, the Luger, Lady McLean's challenge, Benny, the darkness, the mayhem, the thump in the face and the shot. Like some nasty newsreel footage, the whole ghastly scene came back to me in vivid Technicolor.

Well, I mused philosophically, I'm not sure what happened after I lost consciousness but it appears that I'm alive.

With some difficulty and a certain amount of pain I pulled myself up into a sitting position. I was in a hospital bed and it was dark. The small ward was only illuminated by the light from the corridor which spilled in through two porthole windows in the doors at the end of the room. It seemed that all my fellow patients were sleeping. There was a chorus of gentle snoring like the hum of bees in a summer meadow.

In the dim light I examined myself. My left arm was in a sling and there were dark splotches which I took to be blood decorating the dressing around my shoulder. That must have been where I had been hit. I gave my shoulder a gentle squeeze and winced. It was tender and painful. Yes, it was where I was hit. I was also aware that I had a dressing across my nose which, as I felt it, seemed have grown to the size and had the texture of a large uncooked sausage. I had Colonel Kruger to thank for that, I supposed.

I tried to get out of bed but in doing so I knocked a metal bowl from the bedside cabinet. It fell to the floor with an echoing clang which resounded through the ward. Remarkably it had no effect on my drugged fellow patients, who snoozed away unaffected by the din, but it did arouse the attention of a nurse, who suddenly appeared through the swing-doors and advanced towards me with unnerving speed, her shoes squeaking wildly on the tiled floor.

'And what in the name of Saint Patrick do you think you're doing?' she said in a fierce whisper.

'I was trying to get up,' I replied simply, my voice sounding a long way off.

'What on earth for? You've only been in the bed an hour.'

'Where am I?'

'You're in Charing Cross Hospital. Now get back into that bed immediately.' She brought her pretty, stern face close mine. 'Now do as you're told or you'll know what's what.'

I grinned in a rather dopey fashion and suddenly realized that I had been dosed with something, probably some drug to dull the pain and make me sleep. Something that was only just beginning to work.

'Will I live, Sister?' I said rather dramatically, flopping back into bed.

'Of course you will, you silly man. It was nothing but a mere scratch. The doctor had the bullet out of there in quicksticks. You'll be as good as new in no time.' She tucked in the sheets, almost strapping me into the bed, but now I didn't mind. All of a sudden I felt delightfully sleepy. My head seemed lighter and my shoulder didn't ache quite as much.

'Thank you, Sister.'

She chuckled. 'And thank you for the promotion. It's Nurse Grogan actually.'

'That's nice,' I said inconsequentially and drifted off into a deep and soothing sleep.

I was roused gently by voices: a man's and a woman's. They were close to me. Some instinct told me they were talking about me. I opened my eyes. Daylight streamed into the ward and standing over my bed was my nocturnal friend Nurse Grogan and Detective-Inspector David Llewellyn. They were both smiling.

'I suppose the hero is allowed a lie-in today,' said David.

'Just this once, eh?' replied Nurse Grogan. 'Would you care for a cup of tea, Inspector?'

'I'd love one. Two sugars please.'

'I'm sorry to interrupt your little tête-à-tête but I wouldn't say no to a cuppa myself,' I croaked from a very dry throat.

'Say please,' grinned Nurse Grogan, enjoying this charade.

'Two sugars … please.'

'That's a good boy.' With another smile thrown in my direction, she departed.

David pulled up a chair and sat down by the bed so that his face was on a level with mine.

'How are you feeling, boyo?'

'A bit groggy but rather better than I did last night.'

'Well, there's no lasting damage. You'll be out of here in a few days.'

'What about last night? Did you get 'em all?'

David's face split into a wide grin. 'We did, along with the two kraut officers. They were a nice surprise bonus. The lot of them are all in the chokey now and that's where they'll stay for the duration. We've had those regional lads in the interrogation room one by one. Not a backbone between them. They squealed like stuck pigs. We got all the gen we needed about the network of fascists nation-wide and we've already been in touch with police forces around the country. Within the next few days they'll be rounding up the rest of the bastards. Lots of arrests will be made, I can tell you. Naturally some will slip through the net but what is important is that we've effectively scuppered the organization. We've also got a list of the club's bully-boys who take pleasure in beating up Jews and setting fire to their property. Just wrong 'uns mainly, with no particular political leanings. Paid thugs. We'll have 'em all.'

'That's good,' I said, thinking of little Barbara Cogan and the burnt-out shell of her house.

'Mind you, that Lady McLean's a tough nut. She's not said a word since we clapped the handcuffs on her.'

'She's the Queen Bee,' I said. 'I reckon she's more Nazi than the Nazis.'

When the tea arrived and I'd gulped it down, I recounted in detail the events of the previous evening to David as he made notes, punctuating my narration from time to time with satisfied grunts and the occasional question.

'You're a bit of a hero on the quiet, aren't you?' he said, when I'd finished. 'It took real guts to do what you did.'

I shrugged. 'I don't know. I just wanted to do something for... for the war effort. They won't let me fight in the army ... so....' I found words of explanation deserting me.

'I understand,' said David quietly, looking at me over the rim of his tea cup.

'Oh, Benny!' I said suddenly remembering. 'Is he OK?'

David laughed. 'Is he OK? You must be joking. He's fighting fit! He wouldn't even be checked over by a doctor. He was determined to open up his café this morning as usual. "No bleedin' fascist is going to stop me running my business. I have my regulars to see to". David gave a terrible impression of Benny.

I grinned, glad that Benny was all right. I felt guilty about him. He'd become part of the ordeal because of me, because of my involvement with the Britannia Club. I just hoped that he didn't bear a grudge. And then another thought struck me. It was as though my brain was shrugging off the medication and starting to function properly again. 'Do you know what's happed to the McLeans' daughter, Eunice?'

'Ah, she's been brought in for questioning. I sent a squad-car around to her flat in Bayswater in the early hours of this morning to scoop her up.'

'I don't think she's directly involved with activities of the Britannia Club....'

'Maybe not, but her sympathies lie in that direction. Blood is thicker and all that.'

I felt sorry for the girl. I knew that she was a naïve innocent whose views had been cultivated and tainted by her monstrous parents. Of course, I couldn't be sure how much direct involvement she had with the operations of the Britannia Club, but I suspected none at all. In the time I had spent with her I had grown fond of Eunice and though I was not infallible in my judgement of people, I believed that she was essentially a decent person; she just had the misfortune to have Lady McLean for a mother. What, I wondered, would become of her now? My little reverie was interrupted by the reappearance of Nurse Grogan.

'You have a visitor,' she said, pushing a wheelchair up to the side of my bed. Its occupant, dressed in pyjamas and dressing-gown grinned at me. The face was still pale and gaunt but the eyes sparkled with life.

'Hello, Johnny, been in the wars again, I see.'

I gazed at my brother with disbelief and joy and then my vision blurred as my eye moistened with tears.

I had one other visitor later that day. I'd managed to eat some lunch and slept again. I had just roused myself from my slumbers when I saw a familiar figure shambling down the ward towards my bed. He was carrying a small packet and a limp bunch of daffodils.

It was Benny.

He plopped the daffs on the bedside cabinet, then leaned over and gave me a kiss on the forehead. 'You look dreadful,' he said.

'Thanks. You've come to cheer me up, have you?'

'To do my bit, yes. How you feeling?'

'A bit stiff in the shoulder, but I'll live. But how are you?'

He waved his hand in a dismissive manner. 'I'm tickety-boo. We Slawinskis are made of sterner stuff. It'll take more than a few fascist hoodlums to upset me.'

He meant it, too. He appeared totally unscathed by his experiences of the previous night. Even the cut on his forehead appeared to have healed. 'When they snatched me, bundled me into a car I was a little frightened, I grant you, but when I saw you there I knew I was going to be all right. I knew *you* wouldn't shoot me.'

I laughed. 'You liar. Your eyes were out on stalks when I picked that gun up.'

'I ... I was acting.'

I laughed again. 'Sure you were.'

Benny's eye's twinkled and he nodded, giving me a soft grin. 'You did well, my boy.'

'And you did, too.'

'So how are they feeding you here?'

'Not a patch on your food, I can tell you.'

'I thought so. That's why I brought you this.' He handed me a small packet wrapped in greaseproof paper. 'One of my best salt-beef sandwiches on rye bread with some of that pickle that you like. That'll help build up your strength.'

'Thank you, Benny.'

''S' nothing. When you get out, come into the café and I'll cook you one of my special breakfasts ... on the house.'

'Hey now, don't get too reckless in your old age.'

'You're right,' he grinned. 'For half-price. How's that?'

forty-seven

I stayed in hospital for a few days, but I was itching to leave. Worn out by my constant nagging they eventually let me go home, rather glad to be rid of me, I suspect. I wasn't exactly a new man yet but I was making a valiant effort to sprint down that rocky road to full recovery. My shoulder was still stiff and painful and I couldn't grip things firmly with my left hand but the doctor assured me that it was just matter of time before flexibility returned and I could function normally.

I visited Paul several times in hospital, sitting by his bed, talking, attempting to re-establish the connection that we once had. We had both been at fault in letting our relationship falter and fail. I knew that as orphans we had an innate drive to prove our own independence in the world and that inevitably had led to us drifting apart. As we chatted, gradually the barriers were dismantled and we were once more able to remind ourselves of who we were and what we really meant to each other. Of course, the war and circumstances would eventually part us but this time we resolved to keep in touch, not to sever that invisible bond again.

Paul's return to health was to be much slower than mine. He had several weeks of hospital food to look forward to before he would be able to leave, and then the army had to decide what to do with him. He was still classed as a deserter after all. However, he'd managed to scotch whatever demons had prompted him to behave as he did. I knew and he knew that he was not a coward. I sensed that he'd emerge from this experience a stronger man. With time and some sympathetic help he would be back with his unit. It was just a matter of time.

I stood on the steps of the hospital, glad to slough off the strange antiseptic miasma that permeated the place. I took a deep breath and inhaled a lungful of good old London air. That was better, if a little dusty. It was a lovely warm June day and I knew I was lucky to be alive but my spirits were low. Despite having put paid to the Britannia Club and their dangerous endeavours, the war was still going badly for us. My efforts hadn't altered that fact. And while the German threat hovered like a black cloud on the horizon, there was really nothing to feel good about.

I walked back to Hawke Towers in a foot-draggingly dismal mood. The old place looked the same, apart from more dust than usual. The small bottle of milk by the stove had solidified so I made myself a cup of black Camp coffee and then put a record on the gramophone in an attempt to cheer myself up. The music was lively and toe-tapping but it didn't raise my spirits. I felt empty. After all the drama of the last week, coming back to my silent home gave me an overwhelming sense of anticlimax.

And then the doorbell rang. Ah, a client. Please God let it be a client. Let it be a client with a juicy problem. Something to occupy this weary mind of mine.

It wasn't a client.

It was Eunice.

She looked terrible. He face was pale and drawn and her eyes were red and puffy from long bouts of crying. She was without make-up and looked like a bedraggled child.

'Hello, Johnny,' she said in a monotone. 'Can I come in?'

I ushered her inside without a word. We went through the office into my little sitting room.

'Can I get you a drink? A coffee. You'll have to take it black, I don't have milk. Or maybe something stronger?'

She shook her head. 'I'm OK.'

She looked far from OK but I didn't comment.

'The police let me go,' she said in the same dreary voice as though she was addressing the furniture rather than me.

'I'm glad.'

'Are you? Why is that, Johnny? Why are you glad?'

'Because I don't believe that you've done anything wrong.'

'Done anything wrong. You've elevated yourself a bit, haven't you? From two-bit private detective to moral judge. Johnny

Hawke pronounces. Let the girl go, she hasn't done anything wrong.'

I lit a cigarette and watched her. She was going through some kind of performance, maybe one that she had rehearsed several times while she was in custody. I wasn't going to interrupt. She needed to get it out of her system.

For the first time she looked me in the eye and I saw something of the old fire, the brittle spark in her glance. 'Don't offer a girl a cigarette,' she said in a mock sulk.

I reached in my pocket for a packet.

'Don't bother, I'll smoke my own,' she snapped petulantly, opening her handbag and withdrawing a long, sharp knife. The blade glistened in the gloom. 'Or maybe I'll use this instead,' she said, thrusting it towards me. 'I bought it this morning with the sole purpose of using it on you.'

'Why on earth would you want to do that?'

'You have to ask? You traitor. My parents are in gaol because of you.'

'They are in gaol because they're traitors, in league with the Nazis, our enemy who are the process of bombing this city to bits. Your parents were ready to sell this country down the river because of their mad beliefs.'

'They only wanted what was for the best.'

'And does that include murder and torture? Burning the houses of innocent people because of their race and religion? I'm afraid it's time to face the facts, Eunice. I don't believe you knew half of what your parents stood for or did in the name of patriotism. They may not have dirtied their own hands, but they are as steeped in blood as the thugs who carried out their orders.'

With a cry of anguish, she came at me with the knife. I stepped sideways and knocked the weapon from her hands. By the time she reached me all the fire and fury had gone out of her and she fell sobbing in my arms.

'You bastard,' she said, burying her head on my chest. My shoulder throbbed with pain but I gritted my teeth and tried to ignore it. I stroked her hair and held her. Neither of us spoke and I waited patiently for the sobbing to subside.

I knew her tears were part of her acceptance – her acceptance that what I had said was the truth. She had tried to channel her hurt and anguish towards me, but when it came to the moment, she couldn't do it.

Being an orphan who had never known my father or mother, I could not imagine what it must feel like to suddenly realize that your parents, the two people who brought you into the world and loved you, were not simply cranky zealots with a mission to purify our country, but were in reality monsters, traitorous monsters, prepared to sanction anything to achieve their inhuman goal. But I knew that I would cry too. Long and hard, I would cry.

Strangely, Eunice was like me now: an orphan – cast adrift on a very turbulent sea.

Eventually the tears stopped but she still clung to me. I held her, kissing her gently on the top of her head, but saying nothing. I just didn't have the words. After a time, I pushed her from me gently and sat her down on the sofa.

'Let's have that drink, now, eh?'

She nodded, dragging a handkerchief from her pocket and mopping her face. I poured us both a generous whisky and sat beside her. She took a gulp and coughed a little.

'I'm not used to spirits so early in the day,' she said, inconsequentially.

'What will you do now?' I asked.

She shrugged. 'I've got an old aunt in Scotland. I think I'll go there. I couldn't stay in London now. Not now ...' The tears started again but she fought against them. Suddenly, she put her hand on mine. 'I wasn't going to hurt you really. I just wanted to lash out. I feel cheated somehow and you were the only one I could get to.'

Despite myself, I grinned. 'Tell me about it. The story of my life.'

Eunice grinned too. 'I liked you, Johnny. I liked you a lot.'

'Past tense?'

'Well, it wouldn't work now, would it? Besides I've lots of mental sorting out to do and you would only complicate matters.'

I nodded in agreement. Again, the story of my life.

We sat in silence for some time drinking our whiskies, strangely at peace, thinking our own thoughts. At length, she rose and picked up her bag.

'I think it's time I went.'

'Are you sure? You could stay the night....'

'No. Fresh start. We both need a fresh start.'

I walked her to the door.

She kissed me tenderly on the lips. 'I really did like you,' she said again in a wistful whisper and then walked out of my life.

I felt numb and helpless. I swore, loudly and with passion, I swore. Then I poured myself another drink and slumped down in my chair.

Fresh start. The phrase slipped back into my mind. That's what we'd all like wasn't it? A new beginning. But that was something that me and millions of others would have to put on hold until the war was over. And one day, God willing, it would all be over. As the evening sunlight slanted into my room striping the floor with strange shadows, I raised my glass in a toast to that eventuality.